Advance Praise for *On the Edge of Now*:

"*I picked up a copy of this book out of genuine curiosity—put it down only after a marathon read. WOW! Exciting twists and turns with just the right dose of suspense and intrigue. So eager for the next book! A brilliant new author, and one you won't want to miss!*"

—FAITH WOOD, AUTHOR, the *Accidental Audience*

"*A great break from reality while still feeling real. The author has a true understanding for human emotion!*"
—*B. Hager*, freshman in high school

"*This book will be the death of me! In study hall, at one point I freaked out by what happened to a character—now my peers are convinced I'm crazy . . .*"
—*S. Mayer*, freshman in high school

"*A fun book, and a great read!*"
—*J. Cox*, freshman in high school

"*Brian McCullough is an exceptional author who paints vivid images of new worlds, cities, and characters. Perhaps best of all, it kept me intrigued and, each time I set his book down, I looked forward to picking it up again—I wanted more! I love how the characters learn to adjust to diversity and challenges of each new world, and how they grow through each new acquaintance they meet. I found myself wondering if they will ever see their world and families again. I want to know what happens next!*"
—Debbie Reid-Krahn

Kevin

Enjoy !

[signature]

ON THE EDGE OF NOW

BOOK I
THE DEPARTURE

ON THE EDGE OF NOW

BOOK I
THE DEPARTURE

BRIAN McCULLOUGH

McCullough Media,
Calgary, Alberta, Canada

DEDICATION

To Dad—my biggest fan

PROLOGUE

present day

The Section Commander and two Action Teams surveyed the situation from the only open-ended exit of the alleyway.

"If I understand the circumstances correctly, we have three teenagers—apparently unarmed—fleeing, and now they're trapped in a blind alleyway. And, you were afraid to move in on them because you saw a light? Is that correct?" The Commander laced his question with purposeful incredulity. "What's your name, Officer?"

"Grimes, Sir."

"Okay, Grimes, fill me in . . ."

"Sir, we don't know if they're unarmed. Look! That's one weird light source down there, and who knows what's going on? Check it out—it's pulsing! And, that's not all—the air has an odd feel to it." Grimes glanced at his superior, unsure if he were babbling. He was. The disgusted look on the Commander's face confirmed his suspicion.

"I don't have time for this bullshit." The Commander turned his back to the young officer, motioning his agents to gather 'round. "Move toward the light, and form two offset lines extending the width of the alley. Anything larger than a mouse doesn't get through. Flashlights, on. Let's move!"

As the trained teams stretched the breadth of the alleyway inching forward, a raised voice echoed toward the three young people huddled at the end. Chaotic footsteps. Then, a booming command.

"Move! I'll hold down the fort—I'm right behind you! Move! Now!"

There wasn't time to debate the issue. Her best friend grabbed her in a fierce hug, fearing the worst, while he placed his arm on her shoulder, his other hand to the side of her face. No words. Simply a smile, and a nod of acknowledgment. Without looking back, their bodies fueled the pulsating archway as they vanished into its core, creating a surge of brilliant white light.

Good! The remaining teen glanced around the corner of an overstuffed dumpster shielding her from the approaching agents, their flashlights sweeping the area as they speculated on what they just witnessed.

It was time.

She retreated to her position directly in front of the archway feeling the immense void of the light's source drawing her toward its opening, filling her with an almost physical compulsion to step inside.

The voices! Closer now!

With little time to think, her mind formed a picture of her mother looking back at her, smiling.

"Oh, what the hell!"

CHAPTER ONE

_____

a month previous

"Who the hell knows?" His expletive echoed off the vintage paned windows. "The playing field is massive—everybody's got a theory!" Kyle rubbed his eyes, attempting to focus his thoughts in a more productive, skillful direction. Quantum mechanics, wave theory, and string theory. Super string theory. M theory. If that's not enough, there are always the multi-verses concept. Ten or eleven dimensions. Hey—what about parallel dimension theory of not the same, but similar universes? Why not wormholes?

Wormholes would be cool.

He paused to savor that idea—however, Class II or III civilization technology is critical to harbor a hope of using one effectively. The incredible amount of energy required is absolutely beyond current capacity. Besides, only minuscule amounts of matter are likely to squeeze through such an opening.

Kyle bounced out of his chair, and headed to the fridge for a beer. He had been at it for months, trying to find the key energy element required to utilize a worm hole. That's if anybody could ever find one! And, therein lies the problem with being a theoretical physicist—it seems as if most of what they do is so . . . iffy. Then, there's the big question—the moving target. Successful development of a Unified Theory of the Universe. *I should've been a plumber,* he thought as he considered his job selection decision— clearly, it was a bit faulty. *But, success with a more radical approach moving past conventional thought would be worth it.* Wouldn't it? He wasn't sure.

By nature, Kyle is a solitary guy, spending most of his working hours at home. He's less than interested in wasting time at both ends of the day commuting back and forth— time he can never get back. Fortunately, his employer is a company recognizing its top employees need their own spaces and ways of doing things. They don't need anyone looking over their shoulders each day—and, perhaps most important, no dropping into offices unannounced for consultations or meetings—phone, video conferencing, or Internet suffice. His own, at-home space allows Kyle to work any hours he wants with minimal interruptions. Hell, he can delve into the mysteries of the universe while parading around in his skivvies if it suits him!

There's something to be said for freedom.

Some say Kyle is an incredibly brilliant scientist, although no one would ever guess it by looking at him. An upscale beach bum would probably be the first choice. Nor would anyone guess he enjoys keeping physically active when not solving the problems of the universe. At five foot ten and 165 pounds, he appears trim and wiry—sandy, slightly longish hair, and warm intelligent brown eyes enhance his facial features, creating an overall agreeable look. Yet, despite his questing scientific nature, Kyle is relaxed, funny, and down-to-earth. Dogs and kids love him—so do the ladies. Dates? Not a problem.

While overcoming his somewhat hermit-like attitudes toward work, he manges to enjoy a night or two out on the town whenever possible. It forces him to engage in what society has brewing, and developing relationships is easy enough—however, commitment issues are a whole different ballgame. The appealing combination of attraction and intelligence persistently eludes him.

Every man needs a quest, he thought, as he considered what to wear for his evening out. *Maybe tonight.* Recently, he met a likely candidate while browsing through a local art gallery—attractive, especially in all the right places, but it was her openness and interest that struck a chord with him. Usually, he took chance encounters with the proverbial grain of salt—but, this evening, there was more of a 'chemistry' anticipation. Far more so, in fact, than anything he felt for any other woman in quite some time. Lately, his dates and relationships seemed mundane, blurring together with little definition.

Somewhere in the middle of shaving and choosing a clean pair of khakis, his thoughts detoured to his younger brother. For years, it was the two of them—after their parents' passing in an automobile accident, he filled dual roles of parent and brother to his younger sibling who was quietly popular, politely aloof, and generally respectful. Not bad for a seventeen-year-old just graduating high school. One concern, however, was his brother's apparent lack of response to women—gals who appeared to show a real interest in him. Obviously, it was time for a chat with his little brother to sort out any difficulties or pitfalls that may steer him in the wrong direction. Yes, his brother had a social connection with a group of people—however, in Kyle's view, it never hurts to expand the social network to gain more experience and confidence. It's a fine balance between quality and quantity—a concept Kyle has to work on himself. *Fine teacher I'll be,* he thought, staring down the mirror. *I can't commit to a serious relationship myself.* He chuckled at the irony. He liked what he saw—a confident man in tan slacks, a light blue casual shirt, and dress leather jacket. *Good enough—take me or leave me!* Dinner reservations were for seven o'clock, and he needed to get moving to pick her up in time. He opted for one of the fine dining restaurants in town, convincing himself he wanted to go there only for the quality food. It had nothing to do with impressing his new date—well, maybe impressing gets in there somewhere, but he refused to acknowledge it.

By the time he was ready to leave, his brother still wasn't home—a note was in order. He scribbled the restaurant name on a notepad they kept on the library table by the front door, soon to be on his way following one last check in the hall mirror.

He looked the same as he did five minutes ago.

Money? Not an issue. His parents' financial affairs were in impeccable shape when they passed, bequeathing a small fortune to their boys. Their father owned a successful business and, when it sold, the brothers' financial concerns sailed out the window. Nonetheless, Kyle believed in making his own way, and that's the attitude he wanted to bestow on his brother. "Earn what you have in life," he lectured him, "and success will fall in your lap." He preached a fiscally conservative lifestyle despite his own weakness for nice wheels. In his driveway sat a new, brilliant white, kick butt, Porsche Cayman S two-seater sports car. When possible, why not arrive in style?

Before taking the driver's seat shortly after six-thirty, he walked slowly around the car brushing the palm of his hand lightly over the beautifully crafted hood. According to Kyle, there is always time to admire beauty. He loved the feel of driving, especially on the freeway when he had the luxury of amping it up to fifth and sixth gear. Still, in such a car, he struck an admirable figure—the envy of many no matter the speed.

As he backed out of the driveway, he couldn't help but think the evening was going to be special.

****

Things didn't go as planned. Half past midnight, Kyle arrived home with a bag of mixed feelings—his date was as expected, but also surprising. From his perspective, the evening went well, and both of them had a good time. But, there was something different about her—Kyle sensed an interesting undercurrent of connection throughout the evening, and he couldn't quite figure it out. *It's too early*, he thought, as he relaxed with his usual evening nightcap of hot chocolate. He swore it helped him sleep, but anyone in the know knew he was a chocoholic.

Rewind. She was bright and cheery. Conversation with her wasn't stilted, or difficult. That was a welcomed change—first dates often exhibit a shy, awkward situation. Or, the couple babbles senselessly about inconsequential drivel. Not that night. Once started, conversation was effortless, and they showed genuine interest in each other's jobs and points of view. Kyle found himself wanting—

needing—to know as much about her as possible. Somehow, she put him at ease, encouraging him to talk about his work, and he did so with pride. She seemed sincere, displaying a keen interest in all he said—interesting, since she might not have understood the complexities and nuances of theoretical physics. Nonetheless, her lack of understanding mattered little, and they were as comfortable together as old friends who simply picked up and carried on from their last conversation.

Though it was late, Kyle was bursting to tell his brother about his evening. Not that he would be interested, of course, but Kyle considered it brotherly duty to listen to him blather on about his date. He pressed his ear against his brother's bedroom door—nothing. Disappointed, his date report would have to keep until morning.

Sleep wasn't going to come easily.

CHAPTER TWO

Definition: *empty hand*

An ancient martial art encompassing the total body's functioning concurrently to effectively transform one's hands and feet into principal weapons.

Karate requires a combination of speed, reflexes, and strength that translates into power when blocking and striking. It embodies physical conditioning, self-awareness, mental strength, and alertness—and, when performed correctly, karate results in self-confidence, calmness, and inner peace.

That's why Tag took classes.

While not actually looking forward to thirty minutes of warm-ups and stretches, he knew they were a necessary evil—without them, the result was diminished performance. Injuries, too. So, he used this time to help his mental and physical beings meld, and as he completed the pre-bout preparations, the class worked through basic stances, blocks, punches, and kicks—fundamentals requiring a mastery of combining position, balance, coordination, and form. Throw in speed, power, reflexes, technique, and conditioning, and the result is increased spirit and endurance. The object is to deflect an opponent's attack while simultaneously marshaling one's own. Offense should combine strikes with hands and feet by using the smallest surface area to impart the highest impact on the equally small surface area of the opponent. The result? Less resistance to the power of the attack.

Sensei moved the class into Kata which is predetermined patterns of movement, blocks, and kicks, involving attack and defense. Then Kihons, which are more complex. Finally, they ran a series of Pinans—a combination of more complicated maneuvers. Each Pinan involved between fifteen to twenty-one separate moves in varying patterns and sequences. But, Tag's favorite was the Nifunchis series—rather than moving in all directions as most Pinans, he moved sideways along the wall alternating blocks and avoiding attackers' leg sweeps, initiating his own strikes against imaginary opponents. It never failed to invigorate him for what was to come for the remainder of the class.

They quickly moved to practicing sweeps, hooks, and takedowns followed by practice sessions of Kihon Kumite— prearranged sparring moves. Then, the final exercise— free sparring. Class members selected padded gloves for the bout, junior students first. The two senior students sitting together began their own mental preparations by clearing their minds as well as directing their thoughts to each other. One by one, sparring opponents fell, and Sensei finally nodded to his two remaining upper-level students. Moving to the center of the floor they faced each other, bowed, turned to Sensei, and bowed again. Then, fighting stance.

"Yoi! Hajime! " Sensei commanded his fighters to ready themselves and begin the competition.

Tag focused his breathing to settle himself—it was easy to get hyped up with an initial adrenaline rush at the open of a free sparring match. Although he was aware of class members seated on the floor surrounding him as well as Sensei's moving to a safe distance to control the match, Tag directed his attention to Jason, his opponent. Jason was two years older, smaller, Blitzkrieg quick, and experience was on his side. However, it wasn't the first time Tag went up against him—they were evenly matched, and both already achieved the coveted black belt. But, like all fighters, Jason had a weakness—a tendency to telegraph his offensive moves. Tag studied Jason closely especially when he was engaged in a match with other members of the class, or involved in the occasional outside tournament with other dojo fighters. Sensei taught both fighters to keep their eyes riveted on the opponent, displaying no emotion. Nothing.

The emotion thing proved difficult for Tag's opponent for he hadn't quite mastered the technique—his tendency was to tighten his eyes ever so slightly, and subtly change his body language preceding his attack. Tag wasn't sure whether the tell appeared obvious to Jason's other opponents, or whether it were something only he noticed. Either way, it provided an edge to balance Jason's advantage in speed and experience. Tag also exhibited an uncanny ability to determine his opponent's next move—he wasn't sure how he knew, but in millisecond flashes he moved seamlessly from attack to defense, going in for the deciding and final move, or deflecting his opponent's aggression.

They slowly circled each other in the center of the combat area, thirty class members watching silently—the only sound was of bare feet moving lightly on the wooden floor. Tag was satisfied to stay in a defensive mode, waiting for his opponent to initiate the first offensive sequence. Prior to the first move, the match was a balancing act between planning an attack and standing at defense. Hours of fruitful training allowed each man's body to react without apparent thought.

Jason struck first. Kicks. Reverse punches. A back-fist strike. However, the tell from his opponent allowed Tag to drift backwards, throwing a pattern of inside, outside, low, middle, and high blocks—just as Sensei taught him. Then, without warning, he thrust forward on the attack targeting the limited area of head and torso. Height and reach served him well, displaying a distinct advantage with leg and arm strikes. Tag's attack drove Jason backwards to the edge of the combat area, but his series of strikes were successfully averted by Jason's superior defense techniques.

No surprise.

They backed up so they had more room to maneuver. Offense. Defense. Strike. Retreat. Streaming sweat gave false impressions for neither were particularly tired or breathing heavily due to their superior training and conditioning. Jason attacked with several hand strikes followed by a right leg roundhouse kick directed at his opponent's left side, just under the floating rib. The tell. Tag anticipated the move, and Jason slowed just enough that his roundhouse kick arrived a tick too late. Tag juked to his left, repelling the kick with a right-armed, outside middle block, then feinted with a left-hand strike to the head. Another block by Jason, torso exposed, and Tag immediately threw a right-hand strike while shouting, "a Kiai" to startle his opponent.

"Yame!" Sensei ended the bout, awarding the match to Tag. Both men bowed as they had at the beginning of the bout, and the class formed a line—white belts on the left, higher belts on the right. They faced Sensei who stood with several of the black belt students to his left while facing the rest of the class. Ritual and protocol followed and, before Tag left, he spent several minutes speaking with various members of the class, receiving their congratulations—not only for his success, but for how the bout unfolded. Sensei joined them, nodding to Tag.

"Are you prepared?" He referenced the upcoming tournament with a dojo from Denver.

"Yes—I feel fresh and eager. However, I must admit to certain misgivings concerning my level of experience, having a newly minted black belt."

"As you should be. Concern yourself not with another's expertise—perform only within yourself, and matters will unfold as they should."

Teacher and student chatted for a few minutes until Tag headed to the locker room for a quick shower before heading home. It wasn't a long drive, but long enough for him to think about his years in the karate program. He remembered his first class with a brand-new gi and matching white belt, the ends sticking out stiffly. He recalled his initial disorientation and awkwardness. Simple exercises and patterns seemed complex and confusing—an ill-timed growth spurt caused the learning process of kicks, punches, turns, and spins to be cruelly hampered by an often and almost comical result. Now, he was a calm, highly capable, self-confident young man—mentally and physically. At a little over six feet and 195 pounds, Tag moved lightly on his feet with a grace unexpected of someone his size—or, his age. He liked the feeling after class or a karate workout—pushing physical limits cranked his mental acuity and awareness a few notches, making him feel more alive.

His thoughts shifted to his older brother as he rounded the corner to home. The evening before, he turned in early knowing he needed rest for his early-morning karate class, so he missed Kyle's return after spending the evening with his newest date. When they talked about it several days before the big event, Tag found it interesting that Kyle seemed a bit nervous—unusual for his brother who had quite a touch with the ladies. *Well, if Kyle pulled it off last night, I'll meet her soon enough!* He chuckled at the thought of his brother embroiled in a serious romance.

Within minutes, Tag was unlocking the front door, relishing the thought of being home. Since their parents' deaths, neither brother once hinted they should consider moving. Home was home—fond memories reinforced by living there.

Always a source of comfort.

Tag opened the door just as Kyle emerged from the kitchen, a fresh mug of coffee in hand.

"Do you want one of these?" He raised the mug in a welcoming salute.

"Yeah, that will be great!" Tag plopped his keys into a dish on the hallway table.

"How was the kick-ass class?"

"I wish you wouldn't refer to it in such a disrespectful manner."

"My pardon. I have no wish to offend."

"I trust there will be no further derogatory remarks in that regard." Tag struggled to keep a straight face at the standing joke.

"Yeah, whatever. On a more serious note, anything new on the karate front?"

"Not really—it was a standard class today. Although, we did have free sparring matches, and they don't happen often."

"How did you do?"

"Alright . . ."

"Come on, give." Kyle knew there was more to the sparring than his brother was willing to discuss.

"It was a pretty good match."

"You make me feel like a dentist sometimes."

"What does that mean?" Tag wasn't great at playing dumb.

"You know what I'm talking about—it's like pulling teeth to get anything out of you. I mean, I appreciate the modesty thing, but, please—give me an answer. So, starting again, how did you do in the match?"

"I won—but, it was tight."

Kyle looked at his brother with a combination of respect and amusement. At times, Tag displayed a surprising level of maturity for a young man still in his teens. However, it was becoming more of a chore to get him to talk about himself. He wasn't shy—just reluctant to boast. He had no problem talking about his friends and classmates, always mentioning the positive things in their lives. It was Tag's nature to put others first and support them, and seldom did anyone hear him dwell on one's shortcomings. But, talk about himself? A different story.

"There's a karate tournament in Denver in a couple of weeks, and our dojo is sending a team to compete. I think Sensei is selecting three in the class to go, but he hasn't officially picked the team."

"Are you in the running?"

"Not sure. Sensei did tell me to make sure my gi was clean, though."

Kyle smiled. "That sounds promising. If you go, will the team travel together, or do you need a ride up to Denver?"

"Let's find out if I'm going first—I think I'll know at the next class."

"How do you feel about the tournament, if you go?"

"Okay."

"Are you nervous about it?"

"Not particularly. It will be fun—I haven't been to Denver for a while."

"Hey, if you get picked to go, why don't we go up there together? I'd like to see you compete, and we could kick around Denver afterwards."

"Yeah, I'd like that." Tag decided it was time for Kyle to spill the beans.

"Your turn—how did it go?"

"How did what go?"

"Oh, c'mon—you know perfectly well what I'm talking about . . ."

"Oh, yeah—last night. The date."

"Exactly. The date."

"She was okay."

"Excuse me? The way you've been acting the last few days, and it ended up as just okay?"

Kyle concentrated on exhibiting a somewhat wistful, disappointed look. "Well, sometimes things aren't what they seem."

"Ah. Maybe the next one will be better." Tag eyed Kyle closely, noting a body language not quite matching what was coming from his brother's mouth. In fact, he looked like a cork ready to explode from a champagne bottle. *Okay*, he thought. *I can play the game, too.*

"Sorry, man—better luck next time. So, are you planning to work this weekend, or do you want to do something together?" It was a good strategy—Tag suspected that changing the topic was something his older brother couldn't handle right now.

True to form, Kyle ignored Tag's last comment. "Although expectations were high, I have to say she did have several redeeming qualities."

"Redeeming qualities?"

"Yes—well, she was nice and everything. Kind of pretty in a plebeian sort of way."

Plebeian? Man, was he milking this!

"Well, you know—kind of a girl next door look." Tag could see it happening—the unraveling.

"When did you ever date the girl next door?" Tag had the pleasure of seeing several of Kyle's recent dates and they were definitely lookers.

"We never had a girl next door of suitable age. So, I gather this one is crossed off your list?"

"Not yet—I believe in giving people a second chance."

The jig was up. "She was great! Funny, charming, intelligent and, oh, so beautiful!"

"Is that all?"

"Seriously, I really like her." Kyle paused, recalling how much he enjoyed the evening.

An insistent scraping at the back door interrupted their conversation. Since Kyle was closest, he opened the door and in bounded one hundred and forty-five pounds of furry exuberance. Tall and rangy with slightly wiry, light tawny hair and topaz-colored eyes, Lego was a mixed breed of Wolfhound and Great Pyrenees—long legs, and a trim body. He was almost three years old, but sometimes he bounced off the walls like a brainless puppy. Still, he was a lifesaver for the brothers—the two years following their parents' death was difficult and they grew closer, each trying in his own way to support the other. The addition of Lego as an eight-week-old pup helped them turn the corner—something fresh and alive that relied on them made them stop their inward focus. Oh, Lego was work— chasing him, training, and trying to put the house back together after he blew through like a tornado. And, of course, the cleanup after accidents—but, they both loved him, and wouldn't change any of it.

He completed the Three Amigos.

Kyle was still in his sweats, not wanting to take the time away from his research to get dressed. There was no point—he didn't have anything on his docket, so why not take the opportunity to lounge a bit?

"How's school going? You must just about be done with classes . . ." Kyle felt it his duty to monitor his brother's grades much like his parents would have done.

"Yesterday was the last day—exams start on Monday, and my first one is on Thursday."

"Are you ready? Studying?"

"Pretty much, I covered everything as we went along, and I have some review."

"Good—I'm sure you'll do fine." Kyle sounded just like his dad, and he was sure his little brother would perform well on the tests. Kyle surreptitiously hoped Tag would follow in his footsteps and pursue science—however, it was becoming apparent Tag leaned toward liberal arts. And, he was very good at it—non-linear thinking. He loved concepts. Philosophy. Creativity. Kyle appreciated his brother's interest in his scientific line of work knowing Tag genuinely tried to make sense of his convoluted descriptions of the research. But, it wasn't easy.

With their parents gone and Tag only twelve years old, Kyle rather successfully balanced the roles of mom, dad and big brother. Amazingly, he pulled it off while finishing his doctorate and streaming directly into some pretty heavy-duty research in a highly complex field. Still, he made time for the ladies.

Kyle decided to broach the subject again, "What about girls?" This was always a sticky one with Tag.

"What about them?" Amused by his sibling's overprotective concerns, Tag had no intention of making this easy for his older brother.

"Well . . . anyone of interest?"

"Define 'anyone of interest.'"

"Quit messing around—you know what I mean."

"No, I don't have a person of the female persuasion in whom I am overly interested." Tag considered stretching out the game, but Kyle was a little touchy on the subject of his love life. "I like girls. I just haven't found one that seems right for me yet."

"It's not a requirement, you know, to wait for the perfect girl. Just go on a date for crying out loud!"

Kyle saw the look in his brother's eye and held up his hands defensively, "Okay, subject closed."

"For now."

Time to change the subject. "So, what else do you have planned?" Kyle tried to be as unobtrusive as possible.

"I was thinking of getting together with a couple of the guys to see if they want to get a game going. After that, maybe a hike."

"War game, I take it?"

"Yep."

Tag was an inveterate gamer who subscribed to the *look them in the eye from across the board, and see them sweat* approach. He showed little interest in electronic shoot-em-ups that relied mainly on reflexes. With karate, there wasn't anything the matter with his reflexes.

"If you go for a hike, why don't you take Lego with you? He could use the exercise and keep you company. He loves snooping in the back country."

"Sounds like a plan. Maybe I'll try that ridge line you and I hiked last month."

"That's fine, but make sure to take a backpack with the usual goodies."

Tag eyed his brother. "Yes, Dad." He grinned, rolling his eyes at his brother.

The brothers discussed the possible trip to Denver over another cup of coffee. Drive or fly? Drive. After all, Kyle had the car to make such a trip and, by the time each brother had to get on with his day, plans were coming together. Kyle grabbed a donut as he headed into the study.

"Tomorrow is Sunday. We should do something together before your exams, and the trip to Denver."

"I'm in. Maybe, we should include your new lady friend?" Tag grinned at his brother, fully aware of the dig.

"That's a great idea! A good way for you to meet her—I'll ask!"

It pleased Tag to see his brother happy and upbeat at the prospect of time together, including his new gal. *Man, I hope she likes dogs—Lego could be her worst nightmare!*

The thought made him smile.

CHAPTER THREE

T ag contacted Jeremy to set a time for early afternoon to continue his favorite war game. The brothers ate a quick lunch together, then Kyle was off on another wheel mission, leaving Tag with extra time to kill before he had to head out. It sounded like the perfect time to plug into a few tunes and take a catnap.

It didn't take long for his thoughts to drift back to the previous day—the last day of classes. He walked down the hallway with mixed emotions, picking up the excited energy from the jumbled crowd of students noisily exchanging yearbook greetings while slowly gravitating toward their classrooms. Except for seeing a few of his classmates during upcoming exams, he realized he would never see most of them again. Some teachers would fade to memory—a fact he considered a blessing—yet, somehow, he felt an undefined sadness. He was usually a bit reserved, but his moods were always upbeat, and his morose feeling made him uncomfortable.

He ticked off his classes in his mind. First, math. A partial saving grace for Tag's least favorite class was the teacher and, apart from being favored in the looks department, she actually made the class as interesting as it could be. Although not his strongest subject, he was in the top five students and he continued to surprise himself, and his brother. Nope—nothing to worry about. Just review. Next, Chemistry and Spanish—same thing. So far, the high point of the day appeared to be lunch. At least it gave everyone another opportunity to visit, say goodbye, and pledge the usual promises to get together and stay in touch.

Tag spotted his group clustered at one end of the lunch room and, although seemingly impossible, they made more noise than usual. As he approached the table, several of his friends launched less than stellar comments in his direction, making Tag realize that not much changes with this group—and, it was a big part of why he enjoyed the mix of intelligence, goofy personalities, and offbeat ideas. Thankfully, none of them took themselves seriously and, for Tag, they were a constant source of amusement. Two girls managed to scoot over on the crowded bench creating just enough room for him.

"Hey! Have a seat!" Stevie invited her friend to slide in, but as he sat down she sensed a peculiar unease. Usually, he was calm and confident—nonetheless, something was bothering her good friend. Attractive with a line of eager young men awaiting her approval, Stevie always paid attention to Tag, drawn to him as if pulled in by a powerful magnet. He wasn't the most handsome boy in school. Not even in the top ten. And, it weren't as if he were the most celebrated jock—no, he certainly wasn't the most popular boy. Tag was friendly and sociable, but quiet and reserved at the same time. For Stevie, there was something more— intangible—and, she liked it.

As the group buzzed about the last day of school, Stevie

was aware of the girls who watched Tag, their mentally noting whom he talked to, as well as how long he lingered in conversation. She also noticed the large, tough, and more violent-prone crowd at school seemed to be aware of Tag and, although they coexisted with him, they didn't feel threatened and paid him a level of respect. Everyone knew of his karate skills, but, there was something else about him—something undefined, beyond physical.

Stevie jabbed Tag with her elbow, "You look like you just sucked on a lemon," she accused, arching her right eyebrow.

He laughed. "Nope. Just wondering whether our group will remain intact—after exams, what will keep us together?"

"Well, I'm not sure about the others, but I don't intend to make myself scarce." She hesitated. "I intend to see you after we finish school in a—more personal way." There. She said it. And, she was happy to get her confession out of the way.

"I think I'd like that. Let's make it through exams, and then get together." Tag knew where she was going with this, and he didn't mind the implication—after all, Stevie was bright and, as Kyle would say, 'definitely a looker.' He admitted there was an element of chemistry, but he had yet to take the next step. *Now? Why not?* It was a pleasant thought . . .

Then, there was Brooke. Strategically seated on Tag's other side, she was in a perfect position to hear everything.

"I'm not going anywhere after exams either, so what about you and me?" There was no denying her approach was direct.

Kyle would love this! Tag thought as he answered her question. "Yeah—that would be great." The rest of the group studied the exchange in a manner reminiscent of fans choosing up sides in a competition, so Tag quickly changed the subject to safer ground involving exam schedules, and future plans for work or college.

"What's your birthday, Tag?" Zoe sat directly across from him, and decided to come to his rescue.

"November 7th. Why?" *Thank you, Zoe!*

"I'm reading my horoscope, and I thought I'd check yours. Let's see . . . Scorpio. That's the most complex sign. It says today is a good day to learn and look forward to opportunities for developing new personal relationships." Zoe realized the significance of the prognostication given the Stevie-Tag-Brooke situation. "Tomorrow's horoscope," she continued quickly, "says to be watchful, and to be aware of trouble or danger. Use your instincts to avoid it." Normally, Zoe didn't take the daily horoscopes seriously, but something tingled her senses when she read the last one. Intuitive, often her feelings proved to come true.

"Who believes in that stuff anyway? It's just made up for entertainment value." Before Tag could respond, Cooper piped in from across the table, and Cale added his two cents, as well.

"Astrology is historically thousands of years old and it has some scientific aspects, as well as relationships between people and their environments."

Cooper turned to Tag. "Someone told me your brother is a cosmetologist . . ." Tag looked at him as though he just grew horns.

"Kyle doesn't do make-up, Cooper. He's a cosmologist,

developing theories of the universe. Cos-mol-o-gist."

"Cooper, you're a moron." Cale again tacked on his comments. Cooper, in his infinite wisdom, immediately assessed embarrassment was a better deal than listening to a lengthy diatribe by Cale about astrology. Just then the bell rang, signaling the beginning of the afternoon class sessions. Their final classes. The group members appeared reluctant to leave, each knowing it was the last time they would be together in school, at lunch, and it was something they took for granted all year.

They parted, each heading to his or her own class.

****

Geez! I need to get moving! Tag jerked back to the present as he glanced at his watch. Before bolting out the door, he checked on Lego in the backyard—the mighty beast was in attack position, lying on his back with legs pointing in four different directions, snoring softly. Everything was as it should be.

Tag climbed into his old truck, crossed his fingers, mumbled a prayer, and turned the key. The engine coughed to life, although not with a particularly rhythmic sound. Kyle offered several times to get Tag a better, newer vehicle, but Tag liked his old truck for its simplicity. It was something he could work on himself without the need for the expensive equipment required for today's newer, more complicated vehicles. Besides, he wasn't into having his ego stroked by owning prestigious wheels. Maybe his brother was, but he really didn't think so—Kyle simply loved driving an exciting car.

Saturday traffic was light, and it took only ten minutes to arrive at his friend's house. By the time Tag got there, Jeremy had already set up the game board, divided the game pieces according to each side, and was pondering the rules. The game was new to them, and each studied the rules for about a week—game play followed a familiar format, but the historical situation and its particular bells and whistles were different. This game was based on a Second World War, German vs. Russian scenario—a common theme in board games. The cool thing was it featured a hidden unit situation so an opponent had no idea of the type of unit encountered until combat occurred. Both players anticipated the feature's sparking surprises during game play—they preferred strategy war games with a more hands-on planning, control, and leadership aspect to determine if one player could out-general the opponent. It was like playing a form of chess, but with hundreds of playing pieces.

Despite the cerebral requirements of understanding fifty pages of complex rules, Tag and Jeremy enjoyed the social connection. It was an opportunity to combine discussion of historical perspective with any current topic. Tag enjoyed the planning aspect of the game, but he excelled at reading his opponent and anticipating his moves. Sometimes, Tag thought he experienced a flicker of recognition of what his opponent was actually thinking. Bizarre, he knew—yet real.

Getting used to the new rules, they played until Tag had to head out for his hike. Each had successes and failures, both enjoying the engagement, but by the time they ended their session, it was clear the game required months of playing time—especially since they could get together only once a week. They considered halting the game during exams, but they opted for using a bit of game play as a welcomed break from studying. The next game was slated for Tuesday.

By the time he got home, Kyle was already gone on his date with the new girl, so Tag organized and packed his gear, changed into a suitable shirt and hiking pants, and grabbed a jacket as he and Lego were off on their adventure. Even though it was summer, evenings were cool—he figured he'd be at the trail head by five o'clock which left plenty of time for a leisurely hike. As long as he came off the mountain by nine, he'd beat the plunging temperatures of a high-altitude night. He scratched a note to his brother, and slapped it on the fridge while Lego patiently waited for his master, knowing he was going for a ride. Soon, they were traveling down the road, his head firmly extended out the passenger's side window.

Not far from their destination, Tag felt the unsettled feeling again—as if something occurred recently, but he couldn't quite place it. *Maybe it's the end of the school year, and exams*, he thought—but they never affected him like that before. No, it was something else—something strange—bizarre—was happening lately. Initially, he considered it coincidence, but, its repetition convinced him otherwise. While driving at night during past weeks, streetlights popped on and off with increasing frequency, and it was so noticeable that Tag anticipated the occurrences by actively seeking the next one. The weird thing was they stopped the previous day. He wasn't sure what to think, but rejected the idea of telling anyone about the events because people would laugh at him or think he was nuts. But, with the strange feelings ramping up again, he wondered if the streetlight scenario were some kind of heads up or warning. If so, he didn't have a clue about what they meant.

These feelings, however, were different. They warned

something unusual was going to happen—to whom, and when remained unclear. He weren't sure if something were to affect him, Kyle or their friends, and it was like waiting for the proverbial shoe to drop. Frustrating, because it seemed the answer was just beyond his grasp and understanding.

"Whatever it is, Lego, I'm sure it's not going to happen to you, Buddy!" Lego cocked his head to the side with a quizzical look, and Tag could've sworn his dog was trying to solve the puzzle for him.

It was another fifteen minutes before they turned onto a gravel road leading to the back country, and the ridge line he and Kyle hiked several weeks earlier. He maneuvered the truck into an empty trail head pullout and parked, barely managing to move out of the way as Lego exploded out the driver's door, already on the hunt for something to chase. Tag locked the truck, and headed in the direction of the tail end of his companion disappearing around the bend of the switchback. He checked his watch—a few minutes before five o'clock. Right on time.

Burning off nervous energy in the backcountry always improved his state of mind, and Tag felt better physically and mentally after his body was moving about—especially if it involved the outdoors and included his now out-of-sight associate. As he traversed the slope and rounded the bend, he spotted Lego rooting through bushes, hunting real or imaginary foe. Both trekked along the ridge line at a steady pace following a game trail to the top, his dog on the hunt.

Tag fell into a comfortable rhythm as he hiked further into the backcountry. Lego took turns leapfrogging ahead or lagging behind, effortlessly covering double the territory. Normally, Tag's routine was to select a different area to hike, so, it was a bit unusual for him to return to the ridge line location soon after his last hike with Kyle. It were as if he were drawn there—not a conscious selection. But, why?

As the sun dipped below the highest peaks, its shading effect changed, diffusing color yet enhancing definition and outline, making Tag's surroundings appear more intense. When he arrived at strategically placed rocks forming a natural chair-like structure, he decided it was time for a break and whistled for Lego. They'd have to head back soon.

Each munched, and Tag wished Kyle were home before he left—some good-natured ribbing and a pep talk for his upcoming second encounter with the new damsel was in order. Undoubtedly, Kyle would have discussed the issue enthusiastically as he usually did when excited about something. However, when it came down to it, Tag considered his older brother to be an old-fashioned romantic by nature—not bad for a heavy duty egghead—and, he knew Kyle's new gal must be something extraordinary for Kyle never displayed such excitement and new heights of kinetic energy. *Good for him! Kyle could use a good dose of settling down with one lady for a while, rather than the feminine parade of the last few years.* Tag was glad he left his brother a note advising of the hike with Lego, letting him know about what time he would be home.

"Time to go, Lego! Let's head back . . ." Lego sprinted in front of his owner, instinctively heading toward the truck. Opaque light dimmed as they trekked down the far side of the ridge into a shallow valley spotted with trees, bushes, and strewn boulders. Light faded completely as they reached the valley floor, the surrounding ridge lines effectively blocking any remaining remnants of day.

Lego shortened the perimeter of the distance he traveled from Tag as darkness progressed, and a few yards ahead he appeared to be more alert than usual. Tag, too, sensed something different—it were as if the air were electrically charged. Suddenly, Lego stopped, his attention riveted directly ahead as Tag drew even with him.

"Wait!" Lego stopped abruptly, waiting for his master's next command. "What on earth is *that*?"

In the distance, a faint light emanated from the ground, its size difficult to calculate from their vantage point. Certainly, there were no homes or structures to account for its source, and it appeared to be steady. Not a flashlight. Not a campfire. Tag carefully crept forward, his footsteps well placed and quiet. Lego stealthily moved past him, head down, trying to sense what lay ahead, taking the lead. Within minutes they were close enough to distinguish the source—hovering a foot off the ground, its proportions were roughly that of an oval doorway with a sense of depth to it. Tag and Lego paused, listening intently, studying the area for the presence of someone—or, something.

They were alone.

Undefined colors swirled and shimmered within its perimeter, a pulsating essence of light and energy. Tag didn't know what it was, but it was unlike anything he had ever seen or imagined—nothing remotely prepared him for this. In his gut, he knew there was a reason to be there. At this place. At this time. In this situation.

Primeval instincts of fight or flight battled with his overpowering curiosity to proceed forward and engage the entity—if it were an entity. While outwardly aware of the event and inwardly focused on his decision, Tag stood, rooted in place. He lost track of time, almost as if he were a casual observer. Lego made the decision for him by slowly moving forward, a deep growl rumbling from his chest, hackles up. Tag focused on his dog, calling him back, commanding him to stay. He knew then he must do something. He moved closer, the pulsating light compelling him, but he sensed no danger.

It beckoned.

CHAPTER FOUR

While driving to pick up his date, Kyle categorized the litany of his failed relationships with women. They usually started out well—upbeat and friendly—but, invariably descended into disinterest, detachment, and discontent. All accompanied by a sense of restlessness. He suspected it was largely his fault due to his inattention and lack of available time. He also realized the lack of intellectual stimulus as well as a genuine spark were the most likely culprits for his flawed relationships. Although the relationships ended, it wasn't Kyle's nature to finish badly. Most often, the lady getting the boot appreciated his gentle kindness expressing his wish to change the relationship from romantic to friendship only. Quite a number of them remained just that—friends—periodically getting together with Kyle to talk, visit, and catch up. He enjoyed those times while systematically widening his range of female acquaintances.

Actually, they outnumbered his male friends.

Kyle arrived in style, performed a last-systems check at the door, knocked, and waited—he was determined not to screw up his chance of having a relationship with someone with whom he was smitten. Moments later, Jackie opened the door, and his nervous energy melted away as he looked at her—she was something! Beautiful, really. Her smile was wide with a natural charm, her shoulder-length hair a lovely, medium brown with a hint of auburn. The first time they met, he noticed her lively, hazel eyes changed color depending upon her mood or what she wore.

She stepped back gracefully, opening the door wider as she motioned him to enter—at 5'7", she didn't have far to look up to meet his gaze as he moved past her. Once inside, he turned, arms open, inviting her to an embrace. She accepted without hesitation, seeking a more intimate connection with him. Of course, he was in no hurry to end the physical connection given that at 120 pounds, medium build, and a generously curvy figure, Jackie presented a delightful package to either hold, or behold.

"Are you combating sensory deprivation? Or, finding it difficult to articulate your thoughts?" She giggled, realizing Kyle stretched his greeting beyond the usual social norm.

"Neither, I just live for the moment."

"It was more than a moment . . ."

"Geez, Woman, don't rush me!" Both enjoyed the playful banter, and Kyle particularly appreciated her ability to be witty and fun.

"Did you plan anything else for the evening? Because, eventually, you'll have to let me go for a bathroom break."

"We'll deal with that issue when it arises."

Laughing, Jackie stepped a safe distance away, motioning to follow her into the kitchen. No problem—he had a delightful view from the back—shapely legs attached to a delightful undercarriage. As if reading his thoughts, those lovely hips started swaying in a more pronounced fashion. Suddenly, she pirouetted, flaring her coral and white sundress, her bare feet and legs reminiscent of a sultry Spanish dancer. Kyle stopped, mouth open as she finished with arms extending gracefully overhead. It was obvious she had quite an effect on him.

"Are you having trouble breathing?" Jackie loved to tease.

"Yes. No. I mean, I'm okay."

"For an overly educated man, you seem to be having extraordinary difficulties with your diction."

"What? Really? How do you mean?"

"Would you like something to drink?" Realizing continuing in this vein would be too easy, she let him off the hook.

"Sure—beer?"

"I have Corona, Heineken, or Sam Adams."

"Any of those will do—thanks." He was still in recovery mode as she grabbed two bottles from the fridge.

"Bottle, or glass?"

"Bottle is fine."

They clinked their bottles in salute, each taking a good pull as they silently eyed one another, private thoughts racing about how to proceed from here.

"Would you like to go out, or stay in?"

"You took me out to dinner last night, so why don't we stay here and order something in."

"Works for me." Kyle took advantage of his skill for dramatic pause. "Last night, I rambled on about myself, ad nauseum. Now, it's your turn. I want to know a lot more about you—what you think, where you've been, your plans, and how you're going to get there."

"Whoa! One at a time!"

She was delighted he showed a genuine interest in her, the real her, and not just the attractive external package. With a healthy self-respect, Jackie accepted her outward appearance described by many as beautiful. It took some doing to not let that kind of praise turn her personality into something less desirable—eventually, she conquered any negative effects upon her ego.

"Where to begin? Well, you know I work in an art gallery, since you first met me there—however, I haven't told anyone I have plans to open my own gallery."

"When? Where?"

"Not sure—I'm still working on that. My college background is in the arts, and I've been lucky enough to be blessed with a creative nature. So, opening my own show is a logical extension, and my present job is perfect for learning the business side. Right now, I'm trying to save enough to be in a good position to approach the bank for financing. Eventually, I'll get there."

"Well, perhaps I can assist you on the financial end, if that's the only thing standing in your way."

"Please! I didn't intend . . . I mean . . . I didn't intend to suggest I need help from you! Don't misunderstand!"

"Relax—I know you didn't mean anything of that nature. I just want to help you move forward."

"Sorry—I appreciate the generous offer but I can't accept. You just met me a few days ago—you don't even know me!"

"I know enough."

Jackie teared up and before the flood started, he felt compelled to rescue her with a hug.

"Hey, we're supposed to be having fun, right?"

She nodded and smiled. "You're most correct, Sir. Tell me more about your brother."

"In a lot of ways, Tag's not like me at all—he's much younger, taller, and muscularly built. He's in exceptional physical condition because of long-term Karate training, and he loves the outdoors—in fact, his athletic activities are more individual rather than team oriented. He's smart, but where my interests are scientific his are more arts based, including a real love for music. T.V.? Not so much."

"Music and the arts. Hmm . . . I think I like him better than you, already!"

"Hey, he's only seventeen!"

"I can wait." Another tease.

"Yeah, right. Well, until then, you have me."

"Tell me more . . ."

"Well, I have lighter hair and dark eyes, and Tag has black hair with quite exceptional green eyes—it's an interesting combination. He has a good sense of humor, somewhat on the dry side, and he has a decent circle of friends. Although, I have to admit I have some concerns regarding his lack of interest in dating."

"I take it he's shy?"

"Shy? I guess, although I don't think of him that way. More . . . reserved."

"Well, there you go. He's just being thoughtful in choosing someone interesting to him. He'll be fine, just let him go at his own speed."

"How can you be beautiful and wise at the same time?"

Jackie laughed. "As the saying goes, *you ain't seen nothin', yet!*"

"Really, I can't wait."

"You do realize that having to work for something makes you appreciate it that much more . . ."

"How much work are we talking about?"

"I'll keep you posted . . ."

****

Tag dropped his backpack on the ground and inched nearer, his focus directed at the extraordinary sight. At ten feet he cautiously circled the object, observing it from every direction, his visual senses on overload as the stationary, slightly concave, hovering phenomenon exploded brilliant, pure colors. No matter the direction, he faced an apparent opening—no back, nor sides. He moved closer, leaning forward to see the center—a shimmering filament led away from the opening, pulsating slightly with a sense of profound power. And, tranquility. He peered into the center's veiled archway—into another place. At another person. Another being. The indescribable presence compelled him forward as though someone or something was drawing him into the light.

He entered the aperture, Lego's howl echoing as he felt himself morphing into an ever-changing shape—like a rubber band when pulled. Gravity had little effect on him, but it wasn't a floating weightlessness—rather an energetic forward movement without a sense of drag or friction. Energy cocooned him, but without effects of extreme heat or radiation. He was warm despite his awareness that outside of his enclosure there was extreme cold—a vast space. He was moving with unfathomable speed.

What have I done? Exhilaration raced through him, sensations vacillating and shifting between reality and unreality. Tag knew what it was like to meditate, and this wasn't it. He was acutely aware of the events, but wondering if it were happening only in his mind. *But,* he thought, *my body feels this experience—it must be real!*

Suddenly, it stopped as the light spewed Tag from its grip. On the ground, he found himself lying face down, gasping for breath. Cold sweat and nausea coursed through him, amplifying a distinct feeling of unease. He rolled over, allowing his mind, spirit, and soul to return to his body—the knowledge of how to do so a gift from Sensei. He concentrated on the reintegration of his complete being as he felt himself floating directly above, looking down at his form still in a prone position.

As he felt himself become whole, movement in his body returned and he managed to sit up, his awareness of his surroundings returning. He slowly stood, and surveyed the area—the archway, gone. His backpack, gone. Lego, gone.

Tag honed in on his surroundings—from what he could see, everything seemed the same. But with his backpack nowhere in sight, he didn't have a flashlight, and the mountain valley was as black as ink, the only light from radiating stars. He placed his position by the constellations—his knowledge of the stars a gift from Kyle. They were exactly where they should be. Still . . . the sense of unease. He should be in the same place.

But, was he?

CHAPTER FIVE

DURANGO CITY
FEDERATED STATE OF COLORADO

R ose loved having her bedroom window wide open—
there was nothing quite like a soft, late spring evening
breeze blessed with the fragrance of blooming
peonies. There was also nothing quite like having the
house to herself—the family left that morning for a short
vacation on the West Coast since her younger siblings
finished school for the term. So, her parents herded the
three of them into the car, and off they went. For how long,
she wasn't sure—they'd return whenever they were ready.
In the meantime, she had every intention of making the
most of the peace and quiet, and it would come in handy
while studying for the battery of exams beginning in two
weeks. Promotion to an Advanced Placement Institution
required achieving an exceptionally high standing, and
scoring superior marks was imperative for acceptance to
her school of choice. *I'll worry about that later,* she thought,
pushing her books aside for the rest of the night. Truth
was she relished the interlude, allowing her to kick back
and relax for the next several days prior to zeroing in on

her most difficult subjects. She sat at her desk, staring out the window at the spring green of aspen leaves, her mind wandering back to the previous twenty-four hours—being late for school the previous morning put her in a testy mood . . .

As usual, the hallways teemed with students, but she managed to snake her way through them without too much difficulty. Because it was the last day of school, she wanted to have enough time to hang out with her friends, but being late squirreled that idea. She was late to History, darting through the door just as it closed. Rose couldn't recall a time when she was the last to arrive—neither could her instructor, Mr. Leonard, who scowled as she took her seat. But she wasn't about to take any grief from him—she glared back, daring him to make a comment. Wisely, he chose to turn his attention elsewhere.

It wasn't until the end of the period when the crusty instructor made his patented move—in every class this year, he culled one student as his target. That day, his unlucky choice was Abbie—a diminutive, awkward girl completely unable to defend herself. He initiated his assault with a series of rapid fire questions, not pausing long enough for an answer, then continuing with a torrent of sharply-barbed remarks depicting her inability to answer the simplest question. Abbie shrank into her seat, recoiling from the onslaught, incapable of responding. Despite witnessing similar episodes for most of the school year, Rose was appalled by the ferocity of his vicious attack. Somehow, she managed to contain her surging anger, focusing her displeasure in a laser-like stare. Unnoticed. He riveted his attention on Abbie, his mental evisceration method like an entomologist routinely dissecting the latest insect discovery.

Enough was enough. "I believe Abbie, unfortunately,

suffers from laryngitis. Therefore, I'm happy to answer for her." Rose stood, confronting her adversary with confidence. Her tactic worked—she answered the instructor's questions, successfully diverting his attention from his original objective. He studied Rose, attempting to determine her real purpose, then returned his attention to Abbie. Nobody's fool, Abbie immediately spewed out a series of alternating coughs and throat clearings, exhibiting all of the signs of someone desperately in need of a glass of water.

Rose's long, red ponytail snapped as she quickly glanced from Abbie to Mr. Leonard, meeting his gaze and holding eye contact. Silence lingered in the classroom as Mr. Leonard recognized the direct challenge, his class eagerly awaiting the outcome of the contest—he seemed unsure of how to respond. All eyes were on him, some reflecting triumphant indignation. He looked again at Rose, debating whether or not to push the issue.

"Will there be anything else?" Rose pressed her instructor to take the bait—her ability to size up and read people allowed her to determine Mr. Leonard, although tyrannical, was a coward. He paused, realizing his pursuit of the competition was a minefield ready to explode. Not one to normally back down, he also realized if he continued his assault, things could turn out badly. They would turn out badly. Choice made. He moved on to outline further subject review as students exchanged knowing glances, thrilled with Rose's victory. From there, students moved from class to class, none as eventful as first hour.

That evening was for family, everyone gathering for a home-cooked dinner. Chaos ruled as her parents and siblings attempted to organize themselves while packing for their trip the following morning. Rose took turns helping, thwarting her siblings' attempt to take all of their worldly possessions. Although they delighted in testing her patience, she knew once they were gone she would miss them.

Lori, her mom, was an energetic, striking, petite redhead, and Rose admired her sociable, witty personality combined with inner strength and a sense of duty. Her dad, Nathan, was the opposite—tall and rugged with a wiry athletic build. Where Lori was strong and in command, Nathan was peaceful, modest, and happy to be in a supportive role behind the scenes. As a child, Rose learned he had a strong dose of common sense coupled with a friendly nature that always drew people to seek his advice. There was something calming about him, for Nathan possessed a natural connection with the rhythm of the land and universe. Rose loved her parents dearly, but, like most families, the impending separation was a healthy break for everyone. After dinner, they chatted about her upcoming final exams, as well as reviewing what she needed to keep an eye on while they were away. Soon after, everyone made their ways to bed, anticipating an early morning start.

As often happens, the departure Saturday morning was delayed by last minute details, but, eventually, the safari was on its way and Rose spent the balance of the day organizing her study schedule as well as running errands. She decided to begin the study schedule on Monday which left that evening and all of Sunday to do whatever she pleased. Cleaning out her closet seemed a good idea—after all, what better time to try on everything she owned? First, music. She cranked up her stereo before pulling a bright, summer sundress. She slipped it on, pirouetting in front of the antique floor-length mirror, the hem flaring with each twirl. Its colors complemented her complexion and figure—or, so she was told.

She focused on her reflection—assessing. Scrutinizing. She was tall—almost six feet—with a lean, athletic build. At 135 pounds, she was slender yet feminine. Long crimson hair accentuated her large expressive blue eyes as well as her cheekbones—high and defined, but not gaunt. Her chin was strong and proportional, lending a rather regal appearance. But, Rose was more like her father—unlike many redheads, her completion was darker and not the typical porcelain associated with most gingers.

Two good things about Rose—she had common sense, and she was honest. Exaggeration and conceit were not part of her repertoire, and such a bent toward objective truth allowed for objective opinion—she liked how she looked! Yet, as she waded through countless clothes, enjoying the music, she couldn't shake the feeling that an exceptional event was about to unfold. An undercurrent of uneasiness bubbled up earlier that day, but she couldn't pinpoint what or why—details unknown. All she knew was she felt unsettled and apprehensive.

Unsure.

****

His throat raw and hoarse, Tag took a break from calling Lego—strange, because his faithful dog always responded to a hail, and he wasn't prone to wandering off unexpectedly. Lego's mournful howl echoed in his mind as he recalled his last connection with him. *Maybe he went back to the truck*, he thought as he unsuccessfully searched for his backpack. He didn't like the idea of combing through the meadow in the dark, but concern for Lego forced the issue and starlight illuminated the backcountry, providing enough light for Tag to make his way back to the truck. Except—there was no truck. No dog. *Did I follow the wrong trail?* Tag thought he knew exactly where he parked. Now? He wasn't sure. Worry nibbled away at his self-confidence and, after weighing the options of whether to go or stay, he opted to take action rather than await unknown events. He backtracked along the dirt road to the highway, heading in the direction of Durango—and, home.

The long trek home gave him plenty of time to think, and the clock ticked as he considered his dilemma. The road was more visible now with soft moonlight reflecting from its surface. It was odd, though—there weren't any cars traveling the highway. Sure, it was the middle of the night—still, someone other than he should have been traveling the black-ribbon road. He silently complimented his foresight to grab his jacket and hiking gear—the night brought a chill, and the way was long. Finally, after hours of a steady mile-eating pace, the plume of city lights softened the darkness. Durango!

He closed the gap between nothingness and the rising town on the horizon, recognizing the grid work of streets and buildings outlined by their lights. Durango wasn't a big city—or, town. To some, it was quaint. Rustic. Relief rushed through him as he quickened his pace, but something—unfamiliar—made him stop. The view! The view was all wrong! Some things were as expected, others were not. No, something was weird—new buildings were where they didn't belong.

He trudged on, finally reaching the town's limits, welcomed by a what he thought would be a familiar sign— DURANGO CITY.

Tag's complete disorientation began.

CHAPTER SIX

DURANGO, STATE OF COLORADO

By the time Kyle arrived at his front door, he knew what he was going to say. Somehow, though, his preplanned words fell short, cheating his true condition. So, he decided to let the words tumble out and Tag, sharp individual he was, would figure it out—his evening with Jackie was a colossal success! Yep. Tag would figure it out. Kyle, quite by surprise, moved beyond enthrallment with Jackie to something more—concrete.

"Tag! I'm home!" Nothing. "Hey! Tag! You here?"

Kyle checked each room in the house for his brother and the beast—again, nothing. Then he remembered—the hike! He headed for the fridge for it had long served as the family message center. There it was stuck smack dab in the middle as an obvious reminder to his brother that he and Lego were hiking at the discussed location. Kyle couldn't help feeling let down—he couldn't wait to tell him about his evening with Jackie.

He checked his watch. *They should be home by now,*

he thought as he glanced at the clock on the microwave to make sure his watch was correct. *They're probably on their way back* . . . a thought mingling with the fleeting idea that Tag's old truck may be broken down. Too wound up to even think of going to bed, Kyle figured he'd catch up on his backlog of emails while he waited for his brother. After that, he immersed himself in working on his latest theory. His progress in the last few months was steady, but the concepts he was dealing with were incredibly complex. His advancements seemed microscopic compared to the bottomless pit of questions about the Universe.

Kyle surfaced for air sometime around two in the morning—still no Tag. No Lego. At first he thought he was so engrossed in his work that he didn't hear them come home. He checked Tag's bedroom, then the rest of the house. Then outside for Lego. Not a trace. He called his brother's cell—it patched immediately into voice mail.

He began to think the worst.

Time to call Tag's friends. He didn't care if it were in the middle of the night—this was about his little brother! Unfortunately, the majority of Tag's friends weren't in their address book by the land line—their contact info was in Tag's phone. Even so, he began a series of calls, each one becoming slightly more desperate. No one had seen his brother.

After the last call, Kyle collected himself, confirming his belief that Tag was solid, responsible, and capable of looking after himself. His dual role of older sibling, quasi-parent, usually didn't weigh on Kyle to any great extent, but, at this moment, the load was getting a lot heavier. Whatever gene controlled the trait relating to protective instincts was functioning in overdrive.

Next, the police. Then ambulance services and hospitals. With each call, Kyle wasn't certain which was worse—hoping the police or hospital had Tag, or getting a negative response from each. If that happened, Tag would still be missing. With the former, Tag would be in trouble or hurt, but at least Kyle would know where he was.

By three-thirty, the glimmer of a possible answer began to surface, something Kyle never would have considered before—maybe Tag was with a girl! That was it! Kyle clung to this idea, reveling in the simplicity of such a safe, happy answer. Sadly, he discarded the idea when he objectively considered it. Possible? Yes. Likely? No. As shy as Tag was he would have let on he was seeing a girl. Besides, his brother was one of the most considerate and responsible individuals on the planet, and it was implausible he wouldn't leave a note, or contact him. The final nail in the girlfriend coffin was Lego was with his brother.

As brilliant as he was, Kyle passed worry hightailing it straight to panic. Uncontrollable, random thoughts accompanied by graphic visualizations of nasty things happening to Tag bombarded him, some sequences starting before another one completed. Finally, he drew upon his ability to focus his mind, halting the barrage of negativity. As he calmed his nerves and relaxed his muscles, one thought permeated everything—*this bullshit isn't working.*

The obvious choice was to physically search for his brother. He knew the rough location based upon the note because they hiked the area recently, and he was familiar with it. Once outside the city limits, the terrain turned rough, and hiking could be a challenge. Right now, the foremost difficulty was the lack of visibility—it was the middle of the night. That would only work if Tag had a mechanical breakdown, and he was either still with the truck, or walking to the highway. If that happened, Tag should encounter passing traffic even at such a late hour. The thing that really bothered him was if Tag had mechanical trouble, he would have called his brother. Cell coverage wasn't an issue, and the bottom line was Tag hadn't called nor responded to Kyle's myriad messages. Knowing sleep was impossible, Kyle quickly changed into hiking gear, retrieving his backpack which he always left in a prepared condition, ready to grab and go. He grabbed the keys to the Subaru parked in the garage, and followed the most obvious roadways in the off chance Tag was on his way home. That unlikely event didn't manifest itself, so, he continued onto the highway, proceeding at a modest pace, carefully scanning the sides of the road.

No sign of Tag.

He turned onto the gravel road leading to the trail head, headlights on high beam, illuminating the narrow roadway and side ditches. Each time he eased the Subie over a rise in the road, his hope soared only to be quelled when he realized Tag wasn't there. Over the last rise, the road ended in a pullout where hikers could park their vehicles. He stopped, got out, leaving his headlights directly shining on an absolutely gorgeous sight—Tags's old truck! *Thank God!* Finally, something positive! He snatched his flashlight from his backpack, and began searching the immediate area without luck. Kyle alternated calling for them with blowing a whistle, hoping either sound would elicit a response. Nothing but silence.

First light was still a couple of hours away, and as much as he wanted to, heading off in the darkness armed only with a flashlight was ill-advised. He reluctantly climbed back in the car, reclined the seat, and eventually drifted off into an unsettled, disturbed sleep.

Tag knows how to look after himself. At least Kyle's last thought before drifting off offered some sense of promise.

****

It were as if mental synapses which were previously hardwired suddenly short-circuited and tore apart, rendering themselves useless. It could have been seconds, minutes, or hours—he had no concept of how long he stood planted by the road desperately seeking understanding. As he examined the periphery of the city just up the road, the combination of the familiar juxtaposed to the missing and unrecognizable catapulted Tag to a place beyond perplexed. Just ahead, he noticed what looked like an observation area with a bench seat beside the road, and the simple act of focusing on moving toward it gave him the needed impetus to reboot his mind. His energy drained, he settled onto the hard bench taking deep breaths to calm himself just as Sensei taught him.

He reviewed the possibilities. *Okay*, he thought, *I know I'm not dreaming. Am I having a paranormal experience? Possibly. Not likely.* Although the unfamiliar situation was disorienting, everything appeared clear and real in the physical environment, and there was nothing mystical nor magical happening—simply something different. Altered perceptions. He still had a few hours before dawn, and he needed sleep—all he had to do was stretch out on the bench, quickly surrendering to exhaustion.

****

"Get that damned light out of my eyes!" The piercing, blinding light was so intense Kyle couldn't look directly ahead at its source. "Cut it out!" Now completely awake, he sat up straight in his car seat changing the angles so the intense beam of light wasn't causing retina damage. It didn't move. As the cobwebs cleared, he was slightly embarrassed about getting pissed off at an inanimate object—the sun—shining directly on him. His neck had a crook in it, and his mouth had that stale, sour, early-morning taste. *Now what do I do?* he wondered, noticing Tag's truck. Reality and a clearer mind forced him to remember and relive every concern, worry, and panic-stricken thought. He grabbed his backpack from the rear seat and scanned the area, pausing only long enough to draw a sip from his canteen as well as visit a suitable tree.

The unmarked trail he and Tag followed a few weeks earlier traversed the mountain up to the ridge line making for a less taxing hike. Excellent views and bright morning light confirmed there were no other hikers in the area yet and, as he neared the top of the ridge, shouts for his brother and Lego echoed loudly enough for anyone to hear. No response. He continued to follow the trail, this time signaling Tag with a high-pitched whistle.

Nothing.

Kyle sat on a boulder flanking the trail, uncertain of where he and Tag dropped into the valley the last time they were there. *C'mon Kyle—think! Did Tag retrace our previous path, or did he take a different route?* He didn't know, so he dropped over the ridge zigzagging across the hillside, following the natural line of descent. As he approached the valley floor, lodgepole pines merged with ponderosas indicating declining altitude. A seasonal stream trickled its last water as Kyle moved onto the valley floor alternating between calling out, whistling, and listening. A response! He whistled again, listening for what he thought was the distinct sound of a dog, and he called Lego's name, moving in the direction of the sound. He stopped. Nothing. A series of sharp, short whistles. Then, the unmistakable, beautiful sound of a dog barking not far away!

Kyle sprinted through the trees, their branches whacking him in the face as he serpentined through the woods. He burst into a large clearing dotted with rock formations that looked like benches—in the middle was Lego! As soon as he recognized his master, Lego launched himself like a torpedo, target acquired, on a direct intercept course. Kyle stopped abruptly, scanning the area for evidence of Tag, then quickly refocused on the considerable canine mass hurtling toward him for an exuberant greeting. Kyle wasn't sure who was more glad to see the other!

"Where's Tag?" Lego immediately recognized the name, and ran ahead of Kyle to a large flat space between two adjoining rock formations. As he drew closer to his target, the dog's behavior switched from joyful to frantic. Kyle moved steadily toward him noting the abrupt alteration in Lego's mood and posture, frantically moving from Kyle to the rock formations several times as if trying to show Kyle where he last saw Tag.

As he approached within a few yards of where the dog centered his attention, Lego let loose with a mournful howl, his tail tucked fearfully between his legs. Close examination of the ground revealed some sort of disturbance occurred here—low foliage was flattened in a uniform circular manner and, in its center, the soil appeared to be melded together forming a series of increasingly smaller, concentric circles.

He scanned the area where Lego was standing beside

a familiar object—Tag's backpack! Judging by the flattened grass, it was clear Lego stayed beside it until he heard his owner's whistle. Kyle methodically opened the pack, noting its contents—as far as he could tell, everything was still there. His brother appeared to have dropped the pack and disappeared without much in hand.

Hopeful Tag was nearby, Kyle called out for his brother. Nothing. The whistle. Same result. Searching the surrounding area, Kyle called Lego to him, taking advantage of Lego's ability to cover more territory, perhaps catching a scent of his brother. Tag had to be there—somewhere!

****

The roar of a large truck passing by snapped Tag out of a surprisingly restful sleep, considering a park bench wasn't an ideal choice for comfortable accommodations. Immediately, his mind went to work—everything that happened to him the night before painted in vivid detail.

If I'm ever going to figure this out, I need to get into town and see what's going on, he thought as he trudged toward the outline of the city, absorbing the situation while trying to make sense of changed landmarks—or, in some cases, missing landmarks. Cars were different, too—some drastically, others subtly.

Other than the occasional car or truck, Tag was alone. There were few signs of urban or rural life until he spied a newspaper box twenty yards up and on the opposite side of the road. *Finally! Maybe now I can figure out where I am!* No traffic in sight, he jogged to the other side, a bit more tentative than he anticipated. *Do I really want to see this?* He hesitated, debating, then squared himself directly in front of the newspaper's front page prominently displayed behind the glass enclosure. Day—check. It was Sunday. Year—check. Yet, the name of the newspaper was unfamiliar—The Durango City Herald.

Tag never heard of it.

He sought explanations that would not come, and it wasn't until sometime later he suddenly became aware of his immediate surroundings. Akin to a homing pigeon and without conscious thought or plan, he arrived on the street directly across from his house. There was just one little problem—it wasn't there.

****

Rose awakened surprisingly early for a Sunday morning, considering it was her self-directed day off from studying. After the usual morning chores, she stood in front of her closet considering what to wear, finally deciding on something casual. Pouring over clothes trying to decide what to wear was unusual for her—most of the time, she grabbed whatever was handy. Today, however, intuition told her she had to look good that day. She selected a brightly colored summer dress in blues and greens which accentuated her red hair, her only makeup a bit of mascara to enhance her eyes. Once her hair was up in a ponytail, she was satisfied with her reflection.

She ventured out early with no definite plans for the remainder of the day. The morning was clear with a delightful breeze stirring the bottom of her knee length summer dress as she completed everything on her list of things to do. As she plowed through the items, she found herself thinking of the good things in her life—family, friends, and what she planned to do after graduation. Her lifestyle was okay—no big complaints, but no real excitement either. Her future? Strive to get to the next education level—then what? She wasn't sure, but she was conscious something was missing in her life, like a pot sitting in a drawer patiently waiting for someone to put it to intended use.

Oh well! I'll figure it out! As she rounded the corner to home, she noticed a young man standing on the opposite side of the street, staring at her house. He didn't move—just stared. He was unaware of her and she stood for a moment, watching him carefully. Finally, she stepped into his line of vision—he was oblivious.

Really? Rose crossed the street and approached him, her attitude changing as she observed a stunned, bewildered young man completely unaware of her presence. He was slightly taller than her, obviously in good physical shape, black haired, and a strong chin—attractive in a rugged sort of way. Although he focused his eyes across the street, she was acutely aware of their intense green, giving him an extraordinary aspect to his overall appearance.

"Are you okay?" she asked softly. He didn't hear her. Close up, he exhibited a commanding presence—however, her intuition regarding people told her this young man wasn't a threat. She moved directly in front of him and joked, "Hey, is anybody in there? Anybody home?"

Finally, his gaze moved from across the street and fixed directly on her, studying her intently. Her previous self-assurance immediately dissolved, and she experienced a sudden desire to fuss with her hair and rearrange her dress, both of which she struggled not to do.

"Is everything okay?" Perhaps a failed attempt to not look so awkward . . .

"I think I'm alright—just a little confused." With the sound of her voice, the haunted look on his face began to dissipate. His voice was deeper than expected, and Rose enjoyed the way he focused intently on her. Only her. The young man radiated a harnessed intensity as well as the promise of power, speed, and fluidity of motion. All contained and available if needed. None of this frightened her in the least.

"I'm Rose, by the way."

He smiled. "By which way?" She noticed the tension in him diminishing as they spoke.

"By any which way!" She laughed at her own joke.

"Witch or which?"

"Enough already! And, you are . . ."

"Tag is my name, lost is my game."

"Pardon me?"

"To be honest, I'm not entirely sure where I am!"

CHAPTER SEVEN

Worry mounting, Kyle observed Lego's stress and confusion even though he was with one of his owners. *No way he would voluntarily leave Lego out here,* he thought as he scanned the nearby area. Kyle knew his brother well enough to know abandoning Lego to fend for himself was out of the question—unless something were beyond his control.

The two of them unsuccessfully searched the surrounding area, Lego constantly returning to Tag's backpack as if he expected his owner to return at any moment. Kyle examined the location where he first observed the disturbed ground—the whole thing didn't make any sense. There wasn't obvious evidence of wild animal activity, or signs of a struggle of any sort. The only thing he had to go on was the strange patterns etched in the vegetation, and he couldn't make heads nor tails of them. To an untrained eye, there were few signs of anything— foul play or otherwise.

It didn't take Kyle long to determine why Tag didn't answer his phone—it was in his backpack, turned off. *Well,*

I guess I can't do anything here, he thought as he hoisted the pack onto the opposite shoulder from his own backpack, calling Lego to him. Reluctantly, they started the hike back to the trail head, Kyle calling and whistling the entire way. He left a note for his brother on the truck's windshield, indicating Lego was with him, and that he was searching for Tag. The only choice now was to contact everyone he could think of—it was time for a marathon of calls. Again.

By the time he arrived home, Kyle decided one of two things would happen—Tag would show up, or he would be located that day. He immediately checked for any emails—nothing. Next, land line messages. Same. He sat, methodically plotting his next move, and soon began calling emergency services seeking any information concerning his brother—all were sympathetic, but none could help. He made sure to leave his name and contact info with each in case anything turned up, receiving their polite assurances they would get in touch with him.

Next, Tag's friends. Of course, they were concerned, promising to get in touch with Kyle if they heard from him. Several offered to conduct their own searches, a response he appreciated. The more bodies looking for Tag, the better—still, it was little consolation, and the time arrived to face the one primeval emotion taking a staunch stand within him.

Fear.

Kyle quickly discovered what it felt like to feel alone, and he considered calling Jackie, but wasn't sure if he should involve her. Yes, she seemed to be a person whom he could trust and rely upon, and he was sure she would be willing to help. Nonetheless, he recently met her—truth was he didn't know much about her at all, and he wasn't sure if it were the time to find out.

Emotion won. He dialed her number, second-guessing his decision, but when he heard her voice he knew calling her was the right thing to do.

"Hi, it's Kyle."

"What's wrong?" Jackie instantly recognized the sound of tension in his voice.

"Tag is gone!" Kyle's voice caught as he blurted raw emotion into the phone.

"Do you think something happened to him?"

"I don't know . . ."

"Where are you now?"

"Home—I'm calling everyone I can think of, and I can't find him."

"I'm on my way—don't go anywhere!"

It was a good feeling knowing Jackie was there for him at a time when he really needed her, and it was a scant fifteen minutes before she was knocking at his door. He hugged her tightly, a feeling of optimism returning as he held her. She let him be the first one to break the physical connection, closely observing him as they moved apart. He led her into the kitchen as she prompted him to fill in the details, which he did in a concise, orderly, scientific manner.

Jackie remained silent as he took her through every step of his investigation, finally determining Kyle needed someone to take charge.

"This is what we're going to do . . ."

****

Rose examined the stranger standing before her with a skeptical eye, mulling over what he said, weighing the options. Was he simply lost? Drunk? He appeared to be neither. Drugs? Maybe. Who knows? Maybe he was all of the above . . .

Finally, Tag realized a delightfully attractive young woman was talking to him. He put his immediate concerns aside, and began the ritualistic task performed by many other hormonal driven young men in similar circumstances—checking out her inventory. Nearly as tall as he, the structure of her face was exquisite—high cheekbones, and sensuous full lips without being pouty. Her eyes were an intoxicating blue, and although her hair was in a ponytail, it was easy for him to imagine her striking red hair framing her stunning features. She was trim, and obviously athletic—not to mention the curves in the right places. *What a classic beauty!* he thought as he watched her figure out the next step in their conversation.

Rose found his awkward manner endearing, complete with an unexpected bonus—the delicate arousal of her senses. "Well, you're here—in Durango City, of course. Are you looking for somewhere in particular, and can't find it?"

Oh, God—how am I going to explain this without sounding like a total nutball? Tag toyed with several approaches, rejecting each as Rose patiently awaited his reply.

"I understand this should be Durango, but, the buildings are a different size and shape, and some I don't recognize at all—other things are missing. However, the surrounding countryside is the same." As soon as the words left his mouth, he was appalled at how ridiculous he sounded.

Is he joking? She wasn't sure, but, her finely tuned intuition screamed he spoke with sincerity. "Where do you live?"

Tag pointed to her home across the street.

"I know you're confused, but you have to understand—that's where I live."

"But, mine is supposed to be right where yours is!"

"Tag—why don't you come with me, and we'll go inside. You look as if you could use something to eat." Her voice was soothing to the agitation he could feel building again.

"I'd like that—I didn't realize how hungry I am!"

****

Jackie wedged herself into a cozy corner of the sofa, turning sideways for a direct view of her companion. Kyle sat lost in thought allowing her the opportunity to study him closely without engaging in conversation. *He's handsome,* she thought, *but, he's so much more than that—strong and open minded. For an egghead, he's surprisingly witty and charming!* She considered all admirable qualities, and spending time with him certainly wasn't a chore!

She reviewed everything Kyle told her about the situation, as well as their previous discussions about his brother. Something about the whole thing simply didn't add up—although she never met Tag, she knew from

Kyle's descriptions that his younger brother was sensible, resourceful, and considerate. Would he strike off on his own? Doubtful.

"Please don't take this the wrong way—but, from your descriptions of Tag, he sounds like a clean-living kid with no obvious alcohol, drug, or party issues." She smiled before continuing. "And, he certainly doesn't sound like a skirt chaser."

Kyle shrugged his shoulders.

"I'm thinking Tag is responsible enough to not leave you in suspense as to what's up."

"He never has before, so why start now?"

"So, for now, we can discard the possibilities of his being off with a friend or some gal pal without his telling you?"

"Agreed."

"Contacting emergency services yielded no result, and ditto for his closest friends?"

"Yes." Kyle merely answered her questions, showing little emotion as if he were in shock.

"Well, that leaves us with several remaining possibilities. Since you found his truck parked at the trail head, he may be lost. Or, hurt. Both would explain his inability to get back to his truck—however, he had the dog with him at some point, but they got separated. Somehow." Jackie hesitated before continuing, choosing her words carefully to soften the effect.

"There is no way Lego would willingly leave Tag!"

"I understand. Well, then, he left the area by some means, the how and why undetermined. I think we need to focus on the first possibility, and look for Tag at his last known location with or without the help of the authorities. If we contact the police, maybe they'll issue a statewide bulletin . . ."

Kyle considered her observations. "Sounds good—it's driving me nuts just sitting here, not knowing or doing anything!" He thought about Jackie's suggestion for a few seconds. "I'll get Lego to help with the search." He jumped up, and grabbed the leash from a coat hook by the back door. "I'll be right back!"

Jackie waited, surveying the room with particular interest in pictures displayed on the fireplace mantel, each one set in a freestanding frame. Obviously, all related to Kyle's family—several were of his parents in various settings, two including the boys when they were young, and another just of the brothers. Large and handsomely framed, the two boys were in the foreground, arms over each other's shoulders, in a countryside setting. The picture appeared recent, and it was clear Tag was taller and broader than his older sibling. Still, despite the differences in complexion and body shape, there was no question of the family resemblance. The photograph confirmed the picture she visualized in her mind—Tag's face and body language radiated a self-confidence and a sense of authority unusual for a young man. There was something about his eyes . . *he looks like a leader*, she thought as she studied the photo, plucking it from the mantelpiece, intently focusing on Tag.

"Where are you?" she wondered aloud.

****

The design and construction of Rose's home piqued Tag's interest as he stood in front of her house mentally comparing similarities.

"Well? Shall we?" Rose led the way, unlocking the door with Tag close behind. The exterior of her home was painted a light honey color, its walls smooth and without creases. As they crossed the threshold, Tag noticed the interior walls were all one with a thickness of over two feet. *It's a pleasing effect*, he thought as Rose realized he wasn't following.

"I've never seen anything quite like this—what's it made of?" He touched the wall lightly as if to corroborate his question.

"I'm not entirely sure—it's some combination of soil, natural mineral additives, and a substance that binds it all together, hardening it into what you see now." She was happy to see his attention focused away from his apparent dilemma.

"Comfortable?"

"Great—cool in summer, and warm in winter!"

He looked down, noticing the floor was made of a similar stone-like substance, only darker. "Don't your floors get cold?"

"Nope, the house is heated and cooled by an in-floor geothermal system." Rose gave him a moment to digest what she told him. "Come on," she coaxed. "I'm starving, too."

On the way to the kitchen, Tag noted furniture and fixtures appeared to be made of familiar natural materials, such as wood and leather—nothing plastic. The design of the home was an open concept with little separating the kitchen from the other common living areas. Oversized windows and strategically placed skylights bathed the space in natural light, offering a feel of comfort. The kitchen, too, was comfortable, but, the appliances an unusual manufacture and design.

Rose touched a symbol on the wall, cueing a hidden door to swing open, revealing a small walk-in refrigerator.

"What do you like to eat?" She surveyed everything the refrigerator had to offer.

"Anything—anything is fine."

"Something from the garden?"

"Sounds good." Tag wasn't sure if he should continue standing, or sit down on one of the stools surrounding an island—sitting might seem a bit too familiar.

"Take a load off . . ." Rose gestured to one of the stools as she pulled fruits and vegetables from the storage bins, piled them into a colander, taking them to the sink for cleaning. She placed two, white square salad plates in front of her, then continued to prep their meals. Tag noted her graceful style and, in obvious fashion, sized up her appealing attributes.

She looked up, catching him in the act. "What?"

"Nothing . . ." Awkwardness oozed from every pore.

She stared at him for several seconds before concluding he was incapable of a reasoned response, and returned to her task. She smiled, glowing with the knowledge of the effect she had on him. Soon, they ate in silence at the kitchen table, their thoughts spinning. Interestingly, it didn't register with either of them their silence in each other's company was a comfortable and soothing experience.

"I need to call my brother, but, I left my cell in my backpack. May I use your phone?" Tag leaned back in his chair, his eyes trained on Rose.

"Cell?" She didn't understand.

It took a minute for it to register with him that she was unfamiliar with the term. "It's a hand-held phone— a telephone to call somebody." He mimicked the action of holding an imaginary cell phone in one hand.

She nodded. "That's not an expression I've heard before regarding a communicator. There is a small com-link device usually worn on the wrist, or the front of someone's shirt or jacket—it's called a COM."

"Do you have a phone—a communicator—I can use?"

"Of course! Come with me . . ." Tag followed her to the living room where she pointed to a device resting on a tabletop. "Just give it a direction of what you want it to do."

Tag felt like an idiot as he commanded the device. "Call Kyle Townsend." There was a momentary pause before the machine responded, "The communication cannot be completed." He turned to Rose. "Is there a directory—a listing of people's names, and phone numbers?"

Rose nodded. "Just ask it to search for a name."

He tried again. "Do you have a listing for Kyle Townsend in this city?" The machine immediately responded—no listing. A sudden weight descended upon him as though his last hope escaped his grip, and walked out the door. Startled by the pale, stricken look on his face, Rose took both of his hands in hers and, after a few moments, he responded to her touch, focusing directly on her.

He didn't know what to do.

"Let's sit down," he said. "I have something pretty heavy duty to tell you." Tag knew he had to be honest with Rose if he were to get any answers about what happened in his life within the last twenty-four hours.

"I know something strange happened to you." She hesitated. "But, I want you to know you can trust me with whatever it is that you want to tell me!" Another pause. "The more you tell me, the better I can help you."

Trust her, he did.

Tag told her everything.

CHAPTER EIGHT

H e leaned toward Rose, intent on explaining the events leading up to his appearance in front of her house. Tag continued to observe her closely, looking for a reaction, inwardly knowing she would probably think he was a nut. But, instead of diagnosing him as needing a mental health professional, Rose met his gaze, listening intently. It suddenly occurred to him she wasn't at all surprised by his tale. *Why am I sensing she was expecting something like this?* he wondered.

"Yesterday," she began, "I experienced some . . . odd feelings—not frightening, but they were definitely strange and unsettling. I never felt that way before." She studied him for a few moments, smiling knowingly, "I guess you were it!"

What does that mean? He wasn't sure whether she meant that in a good way or bad way. *Well, at least she's still smiling at me!* he thought as he observed her reaction, presuming he wound up on her good side. He returned the smile.

She glanced at her watch. "I have a fencing class in less than an hour—you're welcome to stay here, if you like. I'll be back in a couple of hours."

"Do you mind if I 'tag' along?"

"Funny—that's fine. Get your stuff and let's go!"

Truth was Tag was reluctant to be separated from her. He looked around the room in a mock search, patting himself down. "Apparently, I don't have any stuff!"

"Right—sorry. I'll get mine, and we can leave."

They lit out on foot, and twenty minutes of walking had them at the main door of a three-story building containing a number of businesses on the first and second floors, a substantial gymnasium encompassing most of the third floor. Rose greeted several classmates, briefly introducing Tag as a friend as he took careful note of how the guys interacted with her—their eyes lingering a bit too long on her retreating figure as she headed toward the locker room.

"Wait here," she ordered Tag. "I have to change."

He found a convenient spot with a good view of the class floor, enjoying the extra time he had to absorb the feeling of the place. It was similar to the dojo where Sensei taught his karate class—large windows admitting a healthy amount of sunlight, yet shaded to keep harsh light away from the eyes of combatants. The outer edge was finished in a neutral wood design, and a large central area with a darker surface was most likely designed for better traction. The high ceiling made for a pleasant effect, and racks containing several swords of various sizes and designs hung on the wall, lending a feeling of impending battle.

He was the only one in the room until Rose appeared

from the locker room accompanied by several classmates, all engaged in before-class banter. The fencing outfits were similar styles, padded in exposed areas, light colored, and designed to allow freedom of movement. Class participants began their own warm-up exercises, loosening and stretching out muscles, when a forty-something, medium built, lithe gentleman dressed in fencing attire entered the room, taking his mark on the center of the floor. Class members immediately surrounded him at a respectful distance. The instructor had arrived! He addressed a dozen students in a surprisingly deep voice, lightly flavored with a European accent—then, with preliminaries concluded, the students moved to the racks of swords, each selecting a weapon.

Tag wasn't familiar with the terminology of the instructor—the blades the students used were classically described as foils. Each weighed approximately fourteen ounces and measured forty-two inches in total length, three feet of which was the actual blade abutting the bell guard, and pommel. The foil allowed the user the ability to achieve the greatest speed of all fencing weapons— however, the penalty paid is the higher degree of difficulty required to master it.

Students paired off in evenly spaced locations around the central area of the floor. In turn, they donned protective masks and faced their opponents four yards away, blades moving in a salute and finally coming to rest in the guard position. Their blades extended forward, feet in line at right angles to each other, weight evenly distributed with their trailing arms arched upwards and bent at the elbows and wrists. Their bodies rested in a relaxed position, yet coiled for instant, powerful movement for attack and defense.

The instructor's command unleashed an urgent

outburst of movement from the adversaries as they fluidly moved into combinations of advance, retreat, jump-forward, and lunge. Parries. Attacks. Recoveries and counterattacks. To the average observer, it was like watching bees swarming in a hive.

Tag's martial arts experience allowed him to disregard the chaos, and focus directly on Rose and her opponent. Their dedication to achieve strength, stamina, technique, and speed was inspiring as he watched Rose's controlled movements without the energy-draining flourishes of her opponent. She alternated between attack and defense with silky motion, a suppleness amounting to an unexpected graceful continuity—incongruous for such a violent activity. By the end of the hour, Tag knew he could trust Rose completely.

Mask off, she joined him after the intense action, her face beaded with perspiration.

"Bravo, Mistress of the Blade! Your retinue salutes you!" Tag bowed dramatically.

"Park your retinue right here, while I shower and change. Then, let's go somewhere and eat, I'm starving again!" Rose laughed as she headed for the locker room.

Twenty minutes and a short walk later, they landed at a hybrid restaurant—part restaurant, part cafeteria. Nothing unusual about that other than the menu descriptions weren't particularly familiar. Tag decided on something sounding suspiciously like a hamburger, and Rose seconded his motion by tapping an illuminated strip on the edge of the table, verbally placing their orders. A green light on the strip flashed three times confirming their selections.

They silently eyed each other, neither needing to fill

the void with conversation. *I can't recall feeling so naturally at ease with someone as I do with Rose— except Kyle,* Tag thought as he looked at her. She felt the same, thinking even though she didn't know where he came from she was glad he made the trip!

"Was there a hellishly good joke told, or are you two having some sort of contest?" Two young women approached their table, and Rose stood to greet them with an embrace, each in turn. Tag also stood, watching the mutual greetings. Both girls sized up Tag, registering their approval with a nod to Rose.

"Ladies, this is my friend, Tag—he stopped by to visit me, and catch up on how things are going. Tag, these are my friends, Belinda and Glory."

"The pleasure is, indeed, all mine. How may I be of service to such gentle creatures?" Anticipating a satisfactory response to his wit, Tag looked at the three girls, instantly recognizing the 'what the hell are you doing look' from Rose. Belinda then exploded in laughter and appreciation! Glory contemplated his remark, tilting her head, a small smile playing on her lips.

"It's nice to meet each of you—do you go to school with Rose?"

"Friends from school—that's us!" Belinda quipped. She thought Tag was cute in a quirky way, but Glory thought differently recognizing there was something unusual going on. She focused her attention on Tag—intuition told her Tag was resourceful and strong. Currently, however, something was disturbing his usual sense of confidence and self-worth.

Thankfully, the conversation between the girls

continued, excluding anything directed at him. That was okay—he was content to stay on the periphery of the situation, watching the interaction between Rose and her friends. Eventually, their conversation wound down and the two interlopers bade farewell to both of them.

"Next time," Rose suggested, "perhaps it would be best if you pretended to be a mute."

"I am now, Mr. Low Profile," he assured her.

When it was time to leave, Tag felt an obligation to pay. "I'd like to pay for lunch—when do we get the bill?" he asked, drawing twenty dollar bills from his wallet.

"These aren't going to work, so don't worry about it—my treat."She placed her right thumb on the illuminated strip on the table, and Tag watched as a small green light blinked three times.

"Done!"

Tag still wasn't sure what to make of everything that happened over the course of the last twenty-four hours and, on the walk back to her house, they discussed his situation as well as what to do next. Both agreed it seemed prudent to return to the exact location where he arrived, but Tag was a bit uncertain. He described where the previous evening's event occurred and because Rose hiked through the area many times, she had a rough idea of the location. Before long, they collected the necessary water bottles, backpacks, and other necessities needed for their hike, and Rose plucked a set of keys from the rack by the back door leading to the garage.

Her car looked similar to cars he was used to, but as she backed out onto the street, Tag realized its motion was exceptionally smooth and quiet.

"I'm not familiar with this type of vehicle—how does it work?"

"Electro-magnetic."

"How the heck does that work?"

"I don't know—I just get in and turn the key. It's magic!"

The rest of the trip unfolded in silence, each of them focused on their own thoughts.

"Turn here." Tag indicated to a gravel road and, within a few minutes, they reached the parking area at the end of the roadway. Empty!

"I don't get it—this is where I left my truck yesterday evening. It wasn't there this morning, either."

"Let's hike to the spot where everything happened, and where you lost your dog." Rose could hear the stress in his voice as he realized something was terribly wrong.

"Lego."

"Pardon me?"

"My dog's name is Lego."

As they began their hike, Rose sensed Tag's apprehension. "Lego is an interesting choice for a dog's name—did you get the idea from the children's building blocks?"

"No, not after the children's toy. We named him after Legolas."

"Who?"

"You know, a Prince of the Elves." A blank look. "Lord of the Rings!"

Rose shook her head. "Never heard of it."

"Really? It's a great trilogy of books—even better as a series of movies."

She sensed his frustration as they trudged up the mountain, approaching the ridgeline. Tag stopped for a few minutes, examining the 360° panoramic view of several valley systems—no movement anywhere. Rose, in the meantime, divided her attention between the scenery and watching him.

"No one in sight," he commented, pointing to the west. "That's the valley Lego and I went down yesterday. Let's head that way . . ." Rose nodded, and soon they picked their way down the mountain to the valley floor, Tag calling to Lego without response. He recognized the terrain from yesterday evening, but it appeared different in the mid-afternoon sun compared to the failing light of the previous evening. Eventually, they came upon a configuration of large rocks in between two gentle swales in the valley floor. Tag stopped suddenly, his full attention zeroed in on the center of the rock formation.

"This is the spot, I'm sure of it!" He inched forward, checking the ground in front of him before taking a step. Rose mimicked his careful approach, following directly behind.

Boot prints were evident in the loose soil, and Tag carefully placed his left foot beside a well defined print. It matched. The trail of boot prints led to a large patch of disturbed ground—it looked as if something, or someone, laid down. Adjacent to that spot was physical evidence of some sort of occurrence—it appeared as if a source of intense energy crystallized the soil in a series of raised, concentric circles spanning a diameter of several yards, a nearby bush flattened. Tag quietly observed the scene for several minutes, and Rose wasn't sure what to say—silence was working pretty well, so she stuck with that. But, an uncomfortable awareness surged within her—a sensation of another presence, possibly two. She glanced at Tag, who stood looking at her with an odd look on his face.

"Do you feel it?" Rose's voice was barely a whisper.

"Yes."

"What do you think it is?"

"I'm not sure. It's as though we're not alone, here." He scanned the area to confirm their suspicions. "I can't see anyone—but, there is definitely a presence."

"It's kind of creepy—but, not scary. Weird."

Impulsively, Tag looked at his watch." What time is it?"

"Three-fifteen. Why?"

"Not sure—I just need to mark the time."

They widened their search taking turns calling for Lego. Without luck, they finally abandoned the area and headed back to town realizing something was out of whack.

Something they didn't understand.

It was pushing six o'clock by the time they arrived home. Rose suggested Tag help himself to anything in the kitchen while she hung out in her room for a bit. From the jumble of thoughts and images, it took her a while to assimilate and sequence their experience into some semblance of order. *Fantastic as it seems*, she thought, *Tag appears to have come to my world from somewhere else. Or, he's a raving lunatic, spinning a web of deceit.* The more she tuned in, the more her bullshit radar didn't ping—she felt comfortable discounting the latter. It occurred to her Tag was downstairs, undoubtedly processing the same information, concluding he was screwed. *Not on my watch, you're not!*

She headed to the kitchen.

Rose was right—Tag was brooding. His internal debate was just about petered out when she entered the room and, for reasons he wasn't sure he should understand, things seemed to be brighter simply due to her presence.

"How are you doing?"

"Better—now."

"I didn't mean to abandon you, but I had to distance myself to get an accurate feel for what's going on. It took a little work, but I finally came to the conclusion you came from a different place."

"Great, huh?"

"Tag, you can get through this—I'll help you . . ."

He studied her for a moment. "I know, and I appreciate it."

The doorbell rang just as they were delving into the possibilities of how they could determine what happened. They glanced at the front door, then back at each other, neither relishing the thought of company.

"Oh, no! I forgot! It's Claire—she's my best friend, and I invited her over for dinner tonight."

Tag didn't say anything. He wasn't sure he was ready to meet another of Rose's friends—he had much more important things on his mind, and there was a part of him that wanted Rose to himself. Especially since they were in this together . . .

"It's okay. Claire's a rock—I trust her completely."

"Hey—it's your house!" He paused. "But, let's not advertise what's going on."

"All right—but, just so you know, she's pretty sharp."

Rose greeted her friend as she did the two girls at the restaurant, and Tag steeled himself against not knowing what to expect. After giving Rose a hug, Claire's gaze locked on him as he stood to the side when Rose opened the door. *The energy level just went up a notch,* he thought as Claire walked directly to him.

"And—you are?" She was eleven inches shorter than Tag, packing 130 pounds into a strongly built, solid frame.

"Me. Who are you?"

"Who would've known there's another me in town," she teased with only a hint of a smile.

"Alright people, let's break it up!" Rose laughed, leading them into the kitchen, directing them to sit anywhere. She was the perfect hostess, making sure each had a drink of choice before beginning the dinner prep.

Claire's bed-head, dark blonde wavy hair framed her face—a face that wasn't particularly attractive. From the way she greeted Tag, he knew she was independent and energetic, but he sensed an underlying current of practicality and peacefulness, as well. But, it was her eyes that caught his attention—deep brown and intelligent, yet softened by compassion. No, she wasn't the most attractive girl, but she was interesting!

Claire's first impression of Tag was equally favorable, but she couldn't figure out what seemed different. She kept her eye on Rose noting her posture, behavior, and quietness were uncharacteristic, but she decided to wait until they were ready to eat. At Rose's command, they took their seats.

"Okay—what's, going on?"

CHAPTER NINE

Kyle was uncharacteristically quiet as he and Jackie headed for the backcountry where Tag went missing. They briefly stopped at her house so she could change into something more suitable for a rigorous hike, and Lego made sure everything was okay in the backseat by claiming his rightful place by the door, head hanging out the window.

Kyle thought of his university days—friends. Colleagues. Few kept in touch—but, right then, none of that mattered. Of course, he appreciated recognition by the university, his peers, and employer, but they held little importance compared to the hollow, draining loss of Tag. He realized he didn't need recognition from others—Kyle needed to satisfy only himself in his work as well as follow his compulsion to find what's out there. He glanced at Jackie, marveling at the fact she was willing to drop everything to help him even though she knew him for less than a week. She returned his look with a tight, determined smile.

There was a knot in Kyle's stomach as he turned onto the gravel road leading to the trail head. If his brother's truck were still there, it meant nothing changed—Tag was still missing. If it weren't there, well—that could mean several different things.

It was there.

"If we don't find Tag, I brought his extra set of keys for the truck—we can take it back to town." His voice faltered, not unnoticed by Jackie.

"That's fine—but, here's hoping Tag can drive it home, himself!"

"Amen to that!" It felt good to have someone with him, lifting some of the pain from his shoulders, and knowing what to do with it.

They retraced the route from the previous day, taking forty minutes to arrive where Kyle found Lego and his brother's backpack. As they approached the location, the dog recognized the rock formation and he bounded ahead, shifting into search mode. By the time Kyle and Jackie caught up with him, Lego was circling the spot with the strange markings. They stood still, observing the panoramic scene.

"I see what you mean about the strange markings in the soil, and the pattern of flattened plants." She paused, considering her next statement. "It does seem an event of some sort occurred here." She turned to Kyle as he stood riveted in place, expressionless. *He needs some space*, she thought as she surveyed the area. There was no sound—no birds, squirrels, or any other critter on the valley floor. Slowly, an odd sensation enveloped her, as if something—undefinable—were close, yet distant. Real.

Then it was gone.

"It's three-fifteen . . ."

"Is the time significant?" Jackie didn't quite have a handle on the time frame of Tag's disappearance because Kyle didn't know about it until Tag failed to return home.

"I'm not sure." He studied her carefully, and asked, "Did you feel it?"

"Yes. Something was here—it felt . . . unearthly. What do you think happened?"

"I have no logical, scientific explanation. I just know I felt something—somehow—in our presence."

"I think we better get the authorities out here to search this entire area . . ." Both realized Tag's disappearance was over their heads.

They needed help.

***

Tag and Rose each exchanged a nervous glance as Claire sat patiently, expecting an answer to her question.

"If I had to pick one person to get in on this, she's the one!" Tag looked at his accomplice, thinking she was nuts—but, once he thought about it, he realized one more person meant another brain on the case.

"I knew it! Get in on what?" Claire leaned forward, anticipating Tag didn't know what, but he was sure it wasn't time or space travel. Or, whatever it was . . .

Rose's endorsement was good enough for Tag.

"In the beginning . . ." He told her everything.

The end of his story brought no resolution. Claire sat quietly for a few minutes, contemplating Tag's bizarre tale. *She's going to tell me I'm full of crap*, he thought. *Or, she'll think I'm insane, drunk, or on drugs—maybe all of the above.* All would be better than her running away shrieking, calling for the authorities to lock him up. There was that possibility . . .

"Tag, I'm sorry to hear what happened to you—are you okay?"

"All things considered, I'm not doing badly. Physically, I'm all right. Mentally, well—it messed me up for a bit. The feeling of being lost is overwhelming." He paused for a moment, glancing at Rose. "But, the act of being found does wonders for the soul." She blushed, savoring the feeling.

"Really? Mush? Tag, if you don't mind, I'd like to hear more about where you're from." Claire wanted to know everything.

"Sure, as long as I get to hear about your world." It seemed a fair exchange.

Both girls recognized the effect of his statement, and they concentrated on eating while he wrestled with his new reality. Suddenly, he burst into laughter.

"I know I shouldn't laugh, but I always thought explaining my world to an extraterrestrial would be by my greeting little green men on my planet. Instead, I *am* the extraterrestrial—I'm in your world. Who knew?"

"I get the irony, but, never having met any little green men, I'm not sure how you stack up!" Claire enjoyed challenging him, and she had no doubt he was the real deal—not trying to get something for nothing.

"Well, he's not particularly little, but he does have lovely green eyes, if that's any consolation . . ."

"Back to the story . . ." Claire wasn't going to let Tag off the hook so easy!

"Where would you like me to begin? There's a lot to tell . . ."

"Why don't you start with where you live?"

"Okay—although much of what I've seen so far was in the dark, it appears to me the countryside is similar if not identical. The rural roadways have slight differences, but they follow the same contours. The biggest difference is the city itself—we call it Durango in the State of Colorado. The location is the same, but the layout and buildings are different, including Rose's house." He looked at Rose, then Claire. "The house my brother and I live in sits right here!"

"I know that makes it more personal, if that's possible— but, there are some similarities. For instance, we call this place Durango City in the Federated State of Colorado."

"I know. I saw the sign outside the city."

"The various states in our country are organized into the Federated States of North America."

"Ours form the United States of America."

"Okay, okay! Enough of the civics class! I'm more interested in music and science!" Rose grinned as she admonished them, enjoying their obvious like and respect for each other.

"I very much like the former, and not so much the

latter," Tag teased. "Let's see—different countries have their own folk music, but there is a broad range from orchestra, opera, country, pop, rock, new age, and a bunch more. Each has a distinctive sound, and they're worldwide. Rock 'n' roll started in the late 1950's and morphed into all sorts of offshoots." It suddenly occurred to him that influential artists in his world would not necessarily have appeared and made a mark in their world.

"Have you heard of Frank Sinatra?" No. "How about Elvis?" Yes. "The Beatles?" No, again. He shook his head. "Man, that sucks!" Yes, to Springsteen and Elton. No to Madonna, U2, and Coldplay. Tag wondered why they knew the names of some of the bands and singers, but not all of them. If some of them also existed here, what about him? *Do I have a doppelgänger in this world*? Perhaps he shouldn't ask.

Tag told of the loss of his parents, and how his brother, Kyle, had to fill every role—parent, brother, and friend. With genuine affection, he spoke about Lego . . . the girls could tell Lego was a sore spot, and not knowing what happened to his dog was shredding his guts. They remained silent, allowing him his moment to reflect.

"What kind of name is Tag?"

It took a bit for Claire's question to register.

"As a little kid, I tried to follow and hang out with my older brother and his friends all the time. Eventually, they began to call me 'Tag Along,' soon shortened to 'Tag.' I guess it finally stuck!"

"What's your real name?"

"Townsend. Gabriel Townsend."

"Gabriel." Rose unconsciously repeated his first name aloud. "Gabriel—I like that name!"

"When is your birthday?" Claire wouldn't let up.

"November seventh."

"Scorpio!" They looked at each other with mutual understanding.

"Why is that important?"

Rose and Claire glanced at each other, incredulous at Tag's question.

***

They spent another few hours sorting through the comparisons and differences between their worlds, making the sheer amount of information exchanged difficult to absorb. Each needed time, and Claire departed for home with a promise they would reconvene the following morning.

It was clear Tag would have to stay at Rose's. "You're too big to fit in my siblings' beds—your feet would hang over the end—so I think I'll put you in my parents' bed. You'll be more comfortable, and you'll have more room. Okay, with you?"

"No complaints, I'm just happy to have a roof, and a bed!"

"Good. Come on upstairs, and I'll get you set up."

Rose showed him the bedroom as well as the attached bathroom. Tag's clothes were in a disheveled condition, and he couldn't keep washing the same clothes each day—if he were there that long. She eyed him carefully, gauging his height and weight. "You're about the same height as my father—he's a bit thinner, perhaps. Still, I think his stuff should still fit. Have a look, and pick what you like." She opened her father's closet knowing he wouldn't mind. Her parents taught her to be kind to those who have less than they and, in this circumstance, Tag had much less.

"Thanks, I really appreciate this and everything else you've done for me." Rose thought she detected a wistfulness in his voice, imagining how he must feel.

"You look as if you can use a good night's sleep—I'll see you in the morning. Fair warning—I get up early!" After extending their obligatory goodnights, Rose retreated to her room hoping her guest would get much needed rest.

But, it wasn't to be. Tag lay awake, contemplating his day—his body was exhausted, but his mind whirled through the collection of images of recent events. Finally, he took advantage of the years of karate training and focused solely on his breathing, his body and mind harmonizing and relaxing. His thoughts sequenced in specific directions that made sense, allowing him to process events in a meaningful way. *I'm the same*, he thought, *but my thought processes are changing—everything I took for granted on Earth I'm comparing to this new world. In a lot of ways, Earth comes up short . . .*

He lay on the bed, reviewing what he learned so far—*life is different here. Efficient. Little waste and repetition. Education operates on a merit basis for students and teachers. Construction is meant to last for thousands of years, energy efficient. Did they solve the problem of using fossil fuels?*

And, what about the astrology thing? Finding out he was a Scorpio was a big thing to Rose and Claire, and apparently it was a big thing in their world. Tag recalled they were adamant when explaining individuals and the government supported astrological practices thereby influencing behaviors and directions to be followed. He tried to explain that on Earth, astrology had proponents—however, the majority of people didn't take it seriously. Most of the time, astrology was synonymous with entertainment value.

The girls were appalled!

Rose showed Tag their version of 'online,' and he spent considerable time comparing maps and projections. As it turned out, most of the landforms, rivers, oceans, and continents were physically identical to Earth—it was the political map that was an entirely different matter. He recalled explaining a bit of Earth's recent history, especially concerning World Wars I and II, the Vietnam War, Desert Storm, Iraq, and Afghanistan.

"We had a World War in the early 1900s—I guess you could call it World War I. However, we never had a Hitler or Stalin attain any power. After the World War, the countries of our world finally decided to put an end to wars by forming an overall, worldwide Council, made up of representatives from major regions of the planet." Claire's understanding of the current political landscape was pretty darned good, and it was clear she operated on a high intelligence level.

At first blush, Tag considered their achievements and political system laudable until Claire offered further explanation.

"Now, they have no wars and few conflicts. When something flares up, they ruthlessly suppress it. Crime is extremely limited—anyone caught is rehabilitated. Sometimes. Second time around? They're gone! One strike, you're out. Never to be heard from again . . ."

"Apparently, lawyering up isn't a big thing here . . ." Compared to the often chaotic aspects of Earth, the level of control by a governing body over global and individual actions was a shocking revelation to him.

"It seems logical that certain efficiencies developed here. Take money, for instance—there isn't any! Not having a currency means everything is paid electronically under strict security measures—which also means the authorities know where you are, when you were there, and what you're up to. Very convenient! So . . . following that line of thought, I'm not linked to the system. What happens if it becomes known I'm an outsider? I get the vibe the system does not tolerate anomalies well."

The girls listened intently. "With this kind of setup," he continued, "if they became aware I'm from another world, how will they react? Will I be accepted and integrated? Do I want that? Or, is it more likely they will treat me as some sort of freak or, worse, a threat? If they knew how I got here, will they visualize more of us are coming? It's not like I had control over the event, but, they might not accept my story."

Thinking of myriad possibilities, Tag finally drifted into a disturbed sleep, dreaming of questions asked to faceless people, providing no answers.

****

Rose propped her pillows against the headboard for

a better view of the moonlight flowing through the large windows, her mind cataloging the last twenty-hours. *About this time yesterday,* she recalled, *I was relishing the situation—freedom and solitude waiting to be unwrapped. Now? I don't have any idea of what will happen!* She, too, considered the possibilities. *Is Tag really from another world? Is it possible?* Despite wanting it to be true, Rose's thoughts betrayed her. *He's probably playing some elaborate practical joke at my expense—but, why? To get his jollies? To ingratiate himself, and take advantage of me somehow?*

Moonlight streamed through the window, casting a soft shadow on her bedroom door. Rose considered herself pretty good at reading people, and her gut told her there was nothing false about Tag. If there were, she would know it in short order. No, he was sincere, and she accepted his situation. Then, a new line of thought surfaced, one more faithful to her true nature—*I sense no trickery or falseness. This is very real to him, and I accept that.*

Countless questions swirled in her brain, yet she knew there weren't easy answers. She tried to put herself in Tag's place—how would she handle suddenly finding herself in a different world?

Sometime shortly after midnight, Rose yielded to a peaceful sleep, her last conscious expression a small, secret smile.

CHAPTER TEN

Rose was right—she was up early, refreshed after a solid night's sleep, eager to start the day. She stood in front of her closet, studying her choices more than usual, finally deciding on a white accented, medium blue summer dress that barely skimmed her knees, highlighting her willowy figure and stunning red hair. With no make up and only a few minor hair adjustments, she was ready to meet her overnight guest for breakfast.

She listened at her parents' bedroom door, then gingerly cracked it open—Tag lay sprawled on the bed, his tangled black hair a striking contrast to the pillow, one large foot dangling over the side. *You look like an overgrown kid*, she thought as she studied him. As if on cue, he awoke, his eyes riveted directly on her.

"Good morning . . ." Tag paused for a moment, then continued. "I don't usually start my day with a beautiful woman standing over me. But I'm not complaining!" Rose flushed with awkwardness and embarrassment.

"Okay if I grab a shower?" He theatrically peeked

under the covers. "Goodness, I'm not wearing anything!" It took a three count for a response, then hasty retreat.

"I'll see you downstairs!" Rose disappeared, leaving Tag to his own devices. Soon after, he arrived in the kitchen with towel-dried hair, wearing a pair of her father's slightly too long tan casual pants paired with a snug long-sleeved, plum-colored shirt—he didn't look too ridiculous.

"Not exactly a custom fit . . ." She eyed him from head to toe.

"They'll do. It's not as though I arrived with my own wardrobe!"

"Come—have something to eat." She motioned to the chair at the head of the table. "I have to go out—I belong to a singing group, and we practice every Sunday."

"I love music and I listen to it as much as I can—what genre do you sing?"

"I love just about everything, but I particularly enjoy singing jazz, laid back, and pop. Sometimes musicals."

"Most of those sound familiar—but, what's 'laid-back?'"

Rose paused, considering an appropriate description. "It's mellow, and makes good background music for social occasions."

He nodded. "We call that 'easy listening.'" Tag paused, wondering if his next question would be inappropriate. "Do you mind if I come along? I'd love to hear you."

"Only if you're a good boy, and finish all of your breakfast!" she teased.

"I promise I'll be good—I won't embarrass you in any way!" Rose acknowledged his promise as she pushed away from the table, piling their dishes in the kitchen sink, promising to do them the second they returned. Soon, they were on their way to the rehearsal place several miles away, walking instead of driving. *Just as well*, he thought. *It's better exercise.* It was an interesting perspective considering he hoofed it from God knows wherever it was when he landed in their world.

As they approached the next corner, three males about the same age as Rose and Tag stepped from the shadows of two buildings, blocking the sidewalk.

"Damn! I know one of these creeps!" Rose looked directly at Tag. "Listen to me—stay back, and let me handle this. I don't want them to focus on you." She held his gaze until he reluctantly nodded agreement. They approached the young men strung across the sidewalk, stopping ten feet from them. Tag stayed put while Rose advanced another several feet. The guy in the middle was tall and lean, sporting long, thick, curly hair. His wingmen were slightly shorter, each more stout than their obvious leader. He approached Rose, stopping directly in front of her.

"Rose—it's good to see you again. I've missed you." Leon tinged his greeting with a sneer.

Rose stood her ground. "As I told you before, the feeling is definitely not mutual."

"C'mon—why be like that? You and I are great together."

"There is no together, Leon—never has been, never will be."

Leon looked past her, fixing his sights on the young man pointedly studying the sidewalk, his body language indicating an unwillingness to engage in confrontation. He drew closer to Rose, signaling his companions—neither of whom had any concern for the faint-hearted individual standing behind her—to partially encircle her.

"Come on, Rose—try me. You'll like me!" They menacingly moved closer in an effort to intimidate Leon's target of affection. Rose knew he was baiting her, and smart money was on ignoring him—however, his irritating demeanor was beginning to piss her off. She stood straight, bristling with contempt while struggling to hold it together.

"There you go—don't hold back. You know you want me . . ." Leon reached to stroke her hair. Disgusted and determined not to flinch, she allowed the touch, meeting his challenge with a look of dismissal—doing so would annoy him the most.

She was right. A momentary flash of anger ignited on his neck, rising to a florid red as it reached his cheeks. Rose felt only mildly rewarded, however, for Leon adroitly recovered, refusing to let her best him.

"See? That wasn't so bad." He pushed further, extending his reach to touch her shoulder, his two sidekicks snickering while focusing on their leader's next move. "Who is your shy friend over there?" he asked, caressing her shoulder. "Is he antisocial? Perhaps, we need to meet him." For the first time, she was unsure of how to deflect them away from him. Tag was none of their business, and she didn't want Leon or any of his thug minions meddling in his situation.

Tag had every intention of heeding Rose's admonition and direction to stay put—until Leon took advantage of Rose's indecision by fondling her neck. Tag silently acknowledged it made sense to lay low and keep the lowlifes out of his business—but, as matters progressed, it was difficult to remain logical. Still standing several feet behind Rose, Tag manifested the image of a timid individual by adopting a body language of stooped shoulders and head down, his eyes never directly meeting theirs. Using his peripheral vision, however, he was acutely aware of every move they made. His frustration blossomed into seething anger as he listened to the verbal exchange between Rose and Leon. *Obviously*, he thought, *she wants nothing to do with this moron and his henchmen. Apparently, Leon refuses to take no for an answer . . .*

Tag's anger simmered as Leon slid his hand over Rose's shoulder, stroking the back of her neck. She stiffened her stance, transforming it from controlled defiance to hesitation and uncertainty as Leon glanced at Tag, a triumphant sneer contorting his lips. But, before Leon could register any motion, the unwilling stranger stood at his right side, staring intently at him.

"Move it, or lose it," Tag instructed.

Leon glanced quickly at his two subordinates, their annoyed expressions confirming his own thoughts that the upstart interfered. He noted the largest of his supporters was directly behind the stranger, offering an opportunity to confidently counter the stranger's command.

"It's time for you to pay the price for meddling— the odds don't look too good for you, asshole!" But, the interloper merely smiled, continuing to stand casually in front of his new nemesis.

"Tag, don't!" Rose sensed the calm before the storm, but it was too late—everything happened at once. The behemoth behind him launched a haymaker—a right cross punch—aimed at the back of Tag's head.

It never landed.

Before sidestepping away, Tag executed a strike to Leon's exposed right armpit causing him to release Rose, the momentum of the missed punch resulting in the attacker behind Tag to shift off balance with his right arm fully extended. Before he could recover, Tag moved in from the side delivering two blows to the torso, one of which was particularly effective landing just under the floating rib.

Then a spinning sidekick to the right knee.

The punk's leg collapsed, and Tag quickly assessed his next threat. Luckily, Rose stepped out of the way allowing Tag to concentrate on the gang's leader. Leon stood back holding his dangling right arm, its nerve endings sufficiently disrupted for a time.

The third gang member standing on the far side of Leon and out of the immediate action advanced on Tag, brandishing a large knife.

"Don't, man—this will end badly for you." Tag always believed in fair warning, but his opponent continued his advance, crouching in a well-balanced position, knife tip poised for battle.

Tag moved into Niko Ashi Dachi, a form of cat stance, whereby most of his bodyweight distributed on the back foot, his front foot drawn back with the ball of the foot resting lightly on the ground. At the forward thrust of the knife, he countered with a front kick, thwarting the attack but failing to dislodge the weapon. A second swipe lunged at Tag's chest, missing its mark as Tag swiftly moved to the left, his right hand gripping his assailant's extended wrist as the heel of his left hand struck the attacker's locked elbow. The knife struck pavement and bone shattered as

Tag stepped back, checking for casual observers as his opponent sagged to the ground. No one in sight except Rose.

"It's over—no one else is around. Let's go," he ordered, gently guiding her away from the point of battle. Although Rose experienced confrontation in a controlled, fencing environment, it didn't compare to what she just witnessed— raw, brutal action playing out on the street.

When they were blocks away, she exploded. "I told you to stay back! I had everything under control! In fact, none of that would've happened if you listened to me!"

"You can't be serious! I couldn't just stand there, and let him maul you!"

"I can damned well let anyone I like touch me— and, I didn't need to be rescued by you!" She turned and stomped off down the street, knowing it was unreasonable to castigate him—but, her control was low on the dial.

"You're welcome, by the way . . ." Tag watched her advance up the street, trying to understand what just happened.

He kept his distance, allowing Rose a chance to cool off. Finally, he noticed her taut, vigorous body motions beginning to relax as she changed her stride to a more normal walking gait. *At least we're making progress*, he thought as he slowly closed the gap, leaving a buffer zone of safety. *Oh, shit! Here we go again . . .* Rose abruptly pivoted, and marched directly at him.

He awaited the onslaught.

She stopped, a hard look on her face as she studied him. *Maybe, I should close my eyes, so I don't see it coming,* he thought as her eyes bored into his soul. But, she suddenly stepped forward, tears in her eyes, and hugged him tightly. He wrapped his arms around her as she quietly sobbed, her body gently shaking against him.

"I'm sorry," she murmured into his shoulder. "But, I was so scared—it's not right to take it out on you. I know you were just trying to help me . . ."

"Yeah, I was scared, too." Tag was torn between the physical contact between them, and what she was saying. "It's okay . . ."

Still clutching onto him, Rose pulled back to arm's-length to look him in the eye. "You were like a demolition machine back there!"

"Come with me, if you want to live!" He gave her his best Arnold Schwarzenegger impersonation. The blank look on her face told him what he needed to know—either his accent were really crappy, or she had no idea what he was talking about.

"You know, Arnold—the Terminator." A prompt was in order. Not a flicker of recognition. "Please—tell me Schwarzenegger was a big star in the movies here!" Rose shook her head.

Tag thought about that for a second, finding the idea of an Arnie-less society abhorrent. It was not only disheartening, it was wrong-headed, as well.

"I think, you can let go of me now."

He snapped back to the present. "Yeah—of course. Sorry." Reluctantly and with a bit of awkwardness, they moved away from each other.

"Come on! You haven't had the pleasure of hearing me sing yet!"

****

As he made his way home, the feeling and control slowly returned to Leon's right arm. Embarrassed, frustrated, and pissed, he targeted his anger on the stranger. *There's something not right about him,* he thought. *It's as if he doesn't fit in here—that asshole needs to go!* He remembered Rose called the stranger Tag—maybe this was enough information, along with a physical description . . .

He needed to find a COM-link.

****

They were finishing lunch when Claire arrived, and the girls immediately headed to Rose's room leaving Tag to entertain himself. He made himself comfortable in the living room, the morning's events foremost in his mind— he wasn't sure what he expected, but what he witnessed at the singing club wasn't it.

The outside of the building was nondescript and utilitarian, yet it was a more permanent type of construction that was quite prevalent in their world. The inside, however, was another story. Not fancy. Not even beautiful. But, the acoustic design was created with live music in mind—even without mics, the timbre of singing voices could be heard anywhere in the hall with amazing clarity.

Rose introduced him to the other members, exhibiting no ill effects from the violent encounter on the street. She moved about the group, conversing and joking with ease, while Tag took a seat as an audience member. The ensemble consisted of seven backup musicians—strings, percussion, keyboards, and wind instruments—who provided a tight, professional sound. Nine singers ranging from age nine to mid-fifties rounded out the group. After a quick tuning, the musicians and singers launched into a series of songs, covering musical styles, their performance very good.

Then, a highlight. The singers formed an arcing line, center stage, and Rose stepped forward as the musicians began an up-tempo song reminiscent of Celine Dion, or Whitney Houston. As lead singer, Rose's voice was pure and strong with an impressive range—but, what impressed Tag the most was the obvious joy radiating from her as she sang, creating an enchantress effect on stage. *Where's a recording studio, when you need it?* He was completely transfixed, and Rose was nothing less than amazing—he told her so several times on the way home.

After arriving home, tucked away in her room, Rose and Claire sat cross-legged on the bed with Rose recounting the events of the street confrontation in exquisite detail. Claire listened, reserving judgment—after all, she didn't really know Tag, and the truth was Rose didn't know him well either.

"It's fantastic—the way in which Tag arrived in our world, I mean. But—how is he going to fit in?" Claire's keen sense of sizing up the human condition kicked in, and she knew there was much more to the situation.

"Look, we know there are things about how our society runs that we try not to think about—and, we certainly avoid sharing with others." Claire's tone dipped into the serious range as she considered the logistics of Tag's situation.

"There is an underlying duality in people's thoughts," Rose agreed. "The government fosters a balanced, healthy and, in general terms, desirable lifestyle. But, we know it tracks everyone—it controls." Rose paused, thinking about the possibilities if Tag's story became public knowledge.

"The truth is we only have a choice about the small things, but when it comes to important issues—we don't count. Both of us know it's our job to conform—be too much of an individual, and see what it gets you." The girls sat, silent, as they thought about consequences stemming from unaccepted individuality. "I'll tell you," Claire continued, "unwanted attention leads to severe ramifications."

"So . . . in that context, where does that leave Tag? One, he's from an alternate world—if that were known to the authorities, what will they think? Somehow, I doubt it will meet with much enthusiasm."

"No kidding!"

Rose continued. "Two, he just kicked the crap out of three jerks—they deserved it, but, if the authorities find out, will it make a difference?"

"Do you think anyone witnessed the fight?"

"Jeez, I hope not! We left quickly, and Tag said he didn't see anyone else."

"What about Leon and his band of idiots? Do you think they'll tell anyone?"

Rose shrugged. "I don't think so, but you've met Leon—he's not exactly the guy you want to bring home to your parents. Vindictive and petty? Yes. Stupid? No. That kind of move would create more problems than it would be worth—especially for him."

"Well, maybe . . . Rose, this situation with Tag—are you sure you should continue to be involved with it? You can wash your hands of the whole thing. Maybe you could ask him to leave . . ."

"I'd be lying if I said I didn't grapple with the idea—but, I can't sit back and do nothing. It would be like abandoning him!"

"This could come back and bite you in the butt, you know—if the authorities get wind of it, things could get ugly. You know that . . ." Rose always counted on Claire to provide clarity to any situation, and she particularly appreciated her logical reasoning in such a volatile situation.

"I know. I know . . ." For the first time, Rose fully comprehended the seriousness of what was happening, and it wasn't fair to drag Claire into it. "You can get out of this right now! Tag and I won't say a thing to anyone about your knowing anything—I think it's for the best, don't you?"

"Hell no! Why would I want to do that?" Rose smiled at Claire's usual sass.

"Well, then, what were all of your dire warnings about?"

"I just wanted to make sure you carefully consider all of the ramifications of staying involved in this thing." Smiling, she teased, "I didn't want you thinking only with your hormones on this one!"

"Yes, there is that," Rose confessed. "He is a rather attractive package."

"That's an understatement! Well, since it seems that neither of us is prepared to abandon the quest, it seems prudent to determine how best to save Tag's butt. Ours, too!"

****

COM-link in hand, Leon struggled with an internal debate. He would love nothing better than to get even—better yet, it would be more satisfying to get one up on that son of a bitch who was with Rose. Contacting the authorities was always a risky proposition, but if he could make an anonymous call, he could minimize the risk. After considerable thought, it came down to one thing—his personal motto of 'cover thine own ass.'

Revenge won.

CHAPTER ELEVEN

After a detour to the police station, Kyle and Jackie arrived home, Jackie driving the Subaru and Kyle at the wheel of Tag's truck. As expected, the authorities were cooperative, promising to conduct a search of the backcountry area if Tag were still missing by Monday morning. It didn't thrill the officer that they moved Tag's vehicle from where it was abandoned—he was, however, kind enough to carefully examine the truck in the precinct parking lot. Agreeing to be in touch on Monday, Kyle and Jackie left, stress mounting. True, it was less than forty eight hours since Tag vanished, but it felt a whole lot longer. There was little to go on and, in a meager attempt to fend off the worst part of desperation, Kyle took minimal comfort from the knowledge his brother was sensible and capable of taking care of himself.

Even though they hadn't been gone for the day, it felt good to be home. Kyle dropped into his spot on the couch, lost in thought about how such a thing could have happened, while Jackie tucked her legs beneath her and scootched beside him.

"Hey, it's going to get better with the authorities starting the search tomorrow. They have the resources to organize the manpower needed, and they can check out things we can't." She tried to present a positive side, but feared she missed her mark.

"I know—we have to let them do their thing. It's tough, though—and, we have no choice but to wait. And, we still don't have any idea of how Tag went missing . . ." Kyle fell silent, wondering if he should tell Jackie what he really thought. If he said anything, she could think he was a nutball. If he didn't, she may get pissed because he kept his idea to himself. Either way . . .

"Okay, give!" Jackie's voice snapped him back to reality—apparently, she picked up on his quandary.

Decision made.

"Please try to keep an open mind about this . . ." It was a lame opening, he knew, but he had to continue. "My sense is that Tag is physically alright. I believe . . . I believe something extraordinary happened to him." Jackie took his right hand in both of hers, completely focused on what he was saying.

Encouraged, Kyle continued. "This is a little out there—well, maybe a lot. But I believe Tag . . ."

****

The girls paraded downstairs causing Tag to shelve a final decision regarding his situation as he turned his attention to them.

"We've been talking," Claire announced as she plopped down on the couch beside her friend. "I know— it's a shock, girls talking." He commented silently with an emphatic shrug of the shoulders.

"If I may continue without interruption . . ." Claire glanced at Tag, a glint in her eye. He enjoyed Claire's sense of humor and direct approach, but he silently confessed a sense of fear when he realized they had a plan.

"Have I finally been voted off the island?" The girls met his comment with synchronous blank stares.

He tried again. "Look—my staying here isn't a good thing."

Hurt flared on Rose's face, feeling the weight of his statement. *Crap! She took that the wrong way, and thinks I don't want to be here!* He leaned forward in his chair, speaking directly to Rose. "Please, forgive me—I said that badly. What I mean is that it is likely risky, perhaps even dangerous, for me to stay. As I understand it, the authorities here are not very tolerant and, considering where I came from, this is an abnormal situation. They may not react well to something outside of their direct control."

Rose's body language softened, encouraging Tag to continue. "On top of that, we have the little skirmish that happened today—it likely won't endear me to the powers that be." Tag allowed his words to sink in and, with a smile, assured Rose, "Understand this—I like it here. With you. You are most kind to me—I am a stranger, and you took me in. You certainly didn't have to do that. In fact, most people wouldn't have . . ."

Claire noticed Rose's lip quivering, her eyes brimming with tears. Having known Rose since they were seven years old, she never knew her friend—who was usually a tough-minded, controlled individual—to go all soft and mushy.

"Okay, let's talk about choices before anyone gets maudlin here!" She'd talk to Rose later.

"I don't want to get either of you into any trouble," Tag continued, "so, I should keep moving. Maybe, I can find a way back." He paused, half-hoping they would tell him he couldn't leave. All he got was the girls, nodding in agreement.

"There is no way we're going to put up with your simply walking off into the sunset!" The determination in Claire's voice was impressive. "All of this is speculation right now—nothing has happened to require any drastic action."

"True," Rose and Tag answered in unison.

"Now, that's not to say we shouldn't plan for various contingencies that may occur . . ."

"Makes sense."

"So—you're staying here, for now?" Rose wanted to make sure she understood Tag's comments correctly.

"Unless I have a don't-pass-go ticket home, there's nowhere else I'd rather be." Tag thought he saw relief pass through Rose's body as she sat back.

"Besides, how can I not be available for two, potentially distressed damsels?" How could he resist? Rose and Claire exchanged an 'oh, brother' look, followed by a 'what have we gotten ourselves into' glance.

The mood was definitely lighter.

The trio spend the next several hours hashing through

strategies for Tag's keeping a low profile, as well as options to deal with certain unwanted events occurring. They decided not to involve the girls' families—at least for now—in the details of Tag's situation. Ditto for all of their friends.

As they put the finishing touches on their plan, the COM-link on Claire's belt began to chirp. Claire and Rose continued their uninterrupted dialogue despite the insistent noise from the device. Finally, it stopped.

"Shouldn't you have answered that?"

"It's just someone sending me a data stream." Claire could see her explanation didn't make sense to Tag. "You know, a message of printed information."

He nodded. "We have the same sort of thing—it's called a text. But, why didn't you answer it?" Both girls eyed him with distaste.

"What?"

"Shall I educate the Bohemian?" Rose nodded. "Interrupting a conversation with someone else to answer a data stream is equivalent to . . . picking one's nose in public!"

"Wow! That goes on all the time with us!"

"What? Nose picking?"

Tag chuckled. "No—texting. You'd think most people were in a quick draw gunfight contest given the speed with which they respond—even in mid-sentence!" He thought about that. "What we do is downright rude! And, stranger still, it's taken for granted. I have to admit, your way is better."

Claire arched an eyebrow, proclaiming, "See, there's

always hope for the uninitiated!"

For their remaining time together, the girls educated Tag about astrology, expounding on its influence on individuals and society. Their government condoned and, in fact, encouraged astrological themes in life. Tag confirmed his observations of the landscape and heavens matching the physical surroundings and constellations in his world and, relying upon his confirmations, the girls used the time, place, and date of his birth to construct a detailed birth chart for him with the aid of a computer.

Claire reviewed the synopsis at the end of his chart, and handed it to Rose. She read it several times before joining Claire in staring at Tag.

"Does it say I'm going to win the lottery, or something?" His attempt at levity didn't work. Rose silently handed him the last page.

Your career is about a grand concept that can expand people's minds, opening them to a broader view. You may find your true calling in education, the law, politics, international work, or the humanities; but, whatever you do has the quality of lifting others to a higher level. You have versatile talents and the courage to use them and, as a leader, your upbeat attitude is an inspiration. Your work is never influenced by petty opinions.

"Coincidence, right? Seriously—I just stumbled into this! It's not like there was a plan, or anything!" Tag didn't know what to think, his words ringing hollow even to him.

****

Alone in his own room, Leon's thoughts punished him for what he'd done. All he ever wanted from her was for her to like him—but, somehow, he managed to screw it up every time. He tried, but he couldn't help himself—Rose was his addictive drug.

This time, though, was different, and he hoped his latest scheme wouldn't be detrimental to her.

Or, him.

CHAPTER TWELVE

The end of Floyd's shift was in sight. Not exactly bored, he filled his time with the usual activities and protocols, but, on occasion, it would be nice to have a little more excitement to liven things up.

As he moved through his duties, he recalled the start of his twelve years of service—three of them based in Durango City. Straight out of tech school, he was recruited and sent directly to the main training center located in Denver. After eighteen months, he relocated to Division One, the Spotter Division, as a roving agent covering an area of countryside and small towns in the eastern part of the state. Yes, that period of his life was a mixed cocktail of excitement, especially in the beginning—travel and identity changes allowing him to infiltrate each community undetected. After a while, he felt like the director in a stage performance, sorting through the characters, their motivations, and interactions with others. *Maybe I should have created a program of my different characters so I could keep track of all my personas. And, some people thought juggling was hard!*

His job wasn't without sacrifice—he could forget being involved in a meaningful relationship. He had few friends, and the prospect of a wife and family? Not happening. But, it weren't as if he didn't know what he was getting into— they warned him early on of the negative aspects of the job, and if it didn't work out for him, he had the opportunity to opt out and train in another division. Even so, he was young and eager without much concern for the future, and truth was most candidates stayed in the program. Lately, though, Floyd often reflected on his decision, unclear if he would make the same decision if he had it to do over again. *Probably*, he thought, *although, certainly not Division Seven!* He knew he was too squeamish to ever consider doing that job. Choosing a career path was one of the perks of the job, and he appreciated the SCF's allowing him to select his own area of training.

The Security Control Force, well-known to citizens as the SCF, was a global organization located in every country, its sole mandate to protect and preserve the World Ruling Council, including its local representatives. To further its objective, the SCF operated by rigorously enforcing directives issued by that controlling body. In the mid-1900s, it replaced the requirement for each nation to have its own armed forces, national security organizations, as well as local, state, or municipal police forces. With the advent of the SCF, previously overlapping, inefficient, and repetitive institutions were streamlined into one, global, integrated entity charged with maintaining worldwide stability and safety. As a result, major wars ceased, thereby eliminating nationalistic aims.

There was no need for an arms race, the development of nuclear weapons, or other such silly notions. Initially, the vast savings in the world's resources, energy use, and economy were hard to grasp—the new lifestyle initiated worldwide advancements in health, living conditions, efficient resource management, and pollution control. Impressive? Certainly. But, there entered a universal truth—everything has a cost, and the cost for citizens under the thumb of the SCF was the loss of enfranchisement and limited personal freedoms. No vote. No say about how things operated in society. And, it was wise to be cautious in actions and personal choices.

The Table of Organization on page 569 of the Security Control Force Training Manual offered the following:

DIVISION ONE—SPOTTERS' ECHELON

Individuals who circulate within the population, infiltrate undercover, watch for unacceptable behaviors and actions, receive and process data relating to informant tips, and coordinate with Scouts

DIVISION TWO—SCOUTS

Individuals who respond to data from tips and reports, investigate, and coordinate with Spotters and Sentinels

DIVISION THREE—SENTINELS

Individuals who comprise a paramilitary force, react to incidents, place persons of interest in custody, and coordinate with Scouts and Keepers

DIVISION FOUR—GUARDIANS

Individuals who act as protectors for key administration officials of the World Ruling Council

DIVISION FIVE—DEFENDERS

Individuals who compose a powerful, heavily armored force capable of protecting strategic locations and assets

DIVISION SIX—KEEPERS

Individuals who process persons of interest, confine them, await directives concerning them, and coordinate with Sentinels and Eliminators

DIVISION SEVEN—ELIMINATORS

Individuals who dispose of persons of interest as per directives, and coordinate with Keepers.

NOTATION: All Divisions will be supplied and integrated with key provisions, equipment and support personnel, as required to perform their service.

Floyd had to admit that for a huge, worldwide bureaucracy, the SCF was largely successful in controlling things for the leadership—not many people were crazy enough to take it on.

The sudden chirping signal on his COM-link yanked him from his reverie, and he answered with his usual neutral response.

"What is this regarding?" The call came from a public device.

"Uh, yeah—you should know a crime was committed by a stranger." A male voice. He pushed a button on his COM-link as the caller spoke, the display indicating a high level of stress in the voice. He knew from training and experience a friendly, conversational demeanor throughout the call worked best in order to encourage the informant to continue talking. Besides, the sophisticated SCF voice-recognition system was more efficient in identifying the caller if conversation were prolonged. Of course, everything was being recorded.

"Thank you for that information. Will you clarify some things for me?"

The man on the other end hesitated. "Sure—what do you want to know?"

"You spoke about a crime—did you hear about this from someone else, or did you actually see this yourself?" Floyd knew to never use the word 'witness' when speaking to an informant—the connotation of the word often persuaded the informant to reconsider disclosing further information, usually resulting in the termination of the call.

"I was there. Two friends and I were walking along, and this big guy with a girl came at us on the street—he jumped us, and started a fight!"

"Did you or your friends do anything to provoke this person?"

"Hell, no! He just started it for no reason—well, maybe to impress the girl."

Floyd's interest grew. "Do you know who the girl was?" Potentially, she was another witness to the event.

Silence. Floyd realized the informant likely knew who the girl was and, for some reason, didn't want to disclose her identity.

"Look—if the girl didn't participate, there's nothing for you to worry about. We just want to talk to her about what she saw." He used a soft, coaxing tone with one final nudge. "She won't be in any sort of trouble. It's just helping us get the guy who started this." He knew enough to not oversell, allowing the informant to draw his own conclusions.

More silence. Just as he was about to try another approach, the informant muttered, "I'm familiar with her—Rose. Her name is Rose."

"That's great. What's Rose's last name?" Gotcha! Floyd knew he had the voice on the other end. The following silence was brief, the voice finally whispering, 'Talbot.'"

"This guy who started the fight—do you know him?"

"No, I've never seen him before." The caller paused. "There was something different about him—I'm not quite sure what it was." Floyd had the informant talking—now to keep him that way.

"This is really helpful! I just need some details about your friends, any injuries, and a description of the guy who started it." The call lasted another five minutes before the informant ran dry. Floyd chuckled when he recalled his last question, which usually terminated the call, concerning the caller's identity. Sure enough, when he asked the caller's name, no answer—the call ended. No matter. Floyd's bullshit radar was reasonably sophisticated enough to determine something with the informant's story was a little off the mark. However, figuring it out was someone else's job.

He processed the information into the system along with his comments, and went about his usual routine to finish out his shift. Because the SCF system was so compartmentalized, Floyd knew he would never know the outcome of the investigation he just initialized. And, he was okay with that.

Within the hour of receiving Floyd's report, a Coordinator in the Division One—Spotters Echelon, contacted his counterpart in the Division Two—Scouts, who, in turn, dispatched a team of two individuals to investigate the matter. They began their inquiry by visiting Leon's two associates in the incident.

The first was a large, robust, young man who apparently was unable to get out of the chair due to his ever-present slouch. He elevated his right leg on a low stool, knee immobilized with a large coolant pack wrapped around it, and he was obviously in considerable pain. Unfortunately for him, the SCF team cared little about his physical condition—but, after a round of questioning, the team learned little more than the details outlined in the original report. This guy was either not too bright, or loath to talk—perhaps both. One thing he let slip, however, was Leon's name—no last name mentioned. By the way the sloth explained it, the Scouts assumed Leon was the informant and they decided to return later, if needed, for a follow-up interview.

The SCF located the second young man who was in the hospital undergoing surgery for multiple fractures to his right arm—clearly unavailable to speak with them.

Next? Rose Talbot. As the Scout team pulled up in their vehicle in front of her residence, they contacted their Coordinator requesting a background check on the Talbot family.

Within moments, they learned there were no reported incidents, concerns, or previous investigations regarding the family. As such, there was no reason to harbor any preconceived notions about the young lady they were about to meet.

Luckily, Rose, Claire, and Tag were seated in the living room, Claire positioned to have a clear view from the window facing the street. Suddenly, her gaze fixed on movement outside as a sedan-style vehicle pulled to a stop in front of the house. She immediately recognized the vehicle used exclusively by the authorities.

"It's pucker time!" A sickening feeling raced through her as Tag and Rose stopped talking, and stared at Claire. Now that she had their full attention, Claire gestured toward the front street. "It's the SCF! They just pulled up outside!"

Rose jumped up and looked out the window to confirm, then quickly faced the others. Her face blanched as she realized what was happening.

"Tag, you need to hide—now!"

Uncertain of who—or, what—the SCF was, Tag latched on to the girls' sense of urgency.

"What is it?"

"It's the authorities! Quickly—get out of sight!" She looked at Claire, adding, "You, too!"

Glancing out the window, Rose noted there were two individuals seated in the vehicle.

"There's no way I'm going to allow you to do this on your own! Look—this will work much better if we both respond to them, playing off each other." Claire always had an idea, and a weak smile came and went. "After all, we can play the silly, young girl card."

Rose's mouth tweaked in a brief, acknowledging smile as she focused on Tag who was finally getting the hell out of there. He stopped in the doorway and turned, assuming the worst. "How did they find out about me?"

Inspiration struck the girls at the same time. "Leon!"

"This is just great—I leave, and let the girls take the heat," Tag muttered as he turned to hide. He couldn't remember a time when he felt so inadequate.

Claire and Rose quickly exchanged brief ideas and suggested verbal cues, preparing for the impending investigation when the doorbell rang. Despite waiting for it, the sound startled them both. As the door opened, the team of Scouts faced two, late teenage girls—a tall, lanky redhead, and a shorter, sturdy, wavy haired, dirty blonde.

"We're with the Security Control Force." No I.D. None requested. "We're looking for Rose Talbot."

"I'm Rose Talbot. How can I help you?" Rose's voice was cool. Detached. They didn't answer her question immediately, and both Scouts focused on the companion girl in the doorway, expecting her to offer a name without prompting. Claire observed the senior member's friendly expression, as well as the younger investigator's pronounced glare. Neither fooled her, and she was more than willing to play the game.

"Hi, I'm Claire Booth—you know, from the southern Virginia Booths? At least they were—on my father's side going way back to my many times great-grandfather, John Booth. Now, he was apparently related to . . ."

Without even thinking about it, the senior team

member held up his hand, hoping to suppress the onslaught of drivel. The younger SCF member stared straight ahead. *Mission one—accomplished. Now, mission two!* Claire rejoiced in their obvious mutual aversion to her historical diatribe.

"We were advised that, earlier today, you saw an incident on the street. Is that correct?" Both men refocused on Rose.

"Yeah." Rose played the perfect airhead. Anticipating something more, the team members waited for more details, but from the blank look on her face, it was obvious her one-word response was, perhaps, a stretch for her.

"Well, what did you see?"

"Not much. Some guys on the street started to fight— it was scary, so I didn't look any more."

"Did you know any of them?"

Rose knew to tread carefully. "One guy kind of looked familiar—maybe." She hesitated, then added, "I'm not sure."

"We heard you were walking with a young man at the time."

Deciding that playing stupid actually took some doing, Rose asked, "Is that supposed to be a question?"

A sliver of exasperation escaped. "Yes, that was a question. Do you know the man who was walking with you?"

She gave him a confused look. "But, that's a different question."

Looking for something to punch, the previously calm

investigator struggled to hold it together. "Yes, it's another damned question! Just answer it!"

"Jeez, you don't have to yell at me! I did meet him on the street—and, he and I were walking together for a short distance."

"Sorry about that—do you know the man's name?"

Rose made a bit of a performance out of scanning her memory, at last triumphant in her search. "I think he said his name was Tag." She paused for effect. "Kind of a silly name, don't you think?"

He ignored her question. "Do you know where he's from?"

"Not really." The truth will overcome.

"Thank you for your help." Feeling as if he needed to distance himself from these young ladies before he possibly contracted their obvious mental disabilities, the senior member concluded the interview. He caught the eye of his junior partner as they proceeded down the walkway to the street.

"I hope those two never contribute to the gene pool," the younger one commented as he opened the car door.

"I hope you're right—and, I'm not joking!"

On the other side of the door, the girls embraced, laughing from a combination of joy in success and nervous relief that it was over. But, they knew—both understood it was far from over.

"We need to keep ahead of those guys . . ." Claire's sense of urgency would be instrumental in their keeping one step ahead in the game—and, a game it was. Both girls knew it and, in short order, their worldly visitor would know it, as well.

Rose nodded as they set off to find Tag.

CHAPTER THIRTEEN

Upon arrival at the Security Control Force command center, the Scout Team proceeded directly to the technical support area, initiating a threefold, broad-spectrum search. Targets: unknown male, first name, Tag, Rose Talbot, and Claire Booth—the last added simply due to her association with the other female person. Simultaneous inquiries over the last forty-eight hours concerned the whereabouts and movements of all three. Wide search parameters sourced all methods of tracking including GPS on motor vehicles, security cameras, inside buildings and exterior street views, as well as electronically controlled credit histories of all financial transactions. The final ingredient added to the mix—readouts from an implant surreptitiously inserted into each individual at the time of their scheduled inoculations at age five. This tiny device emitted a weak signal, and was useful for locating an individual over a short distance if their general whereabouts were known. The public, of course, was blissfully unaware.

A sophisticated computer configuration examined all of the sources, and only a few minutes passed before results poured in—nothing unusual regarding the activities of Claire Booth. The same for Rose Talbot. No positive identification nor a history of movement or activities for an individual named Tag. They did have one thing, however—based on a physical description of the unknown male and information provided in the initial source call from the informant, the system produced security camera pictures of three different male individuals moving about in public places—each roughly matched the description of their person of interest. Facial recognition software indicated two of the individuals were identified, name and personal data revealed. Neither had a name registered as Tag, although the use of a nickname was possible. The third male remained unidentified—no record of previous financial activity, nor a history of receiving a tracker implant.

Electronically, he was a ghost.

Next, cross-indexing the three males with the activities of Rose Talbot and Claire Booth—only one of them showed a connection with the females. Security footage revealed an unidentified male eating in a café, seated at the same table with Rose Talbot. The system confirmed the time and amount of the financial transaction for which Rose Talbot paid.

"She led us to believe she encountered this guy on the street just before the incident—a chance encounter. She left out the little detail of their lunch together the day before." The senior Scout Team member recalled the conversation with Rose, an incurable airhead. "It was an act! It was a damned act!"

"Another visit to Ms. Talbot?" The junior Scout Team member knew the answer to his question, but, due to protocol, he wasn't allowed to make decisions on his own.

"Absolutely!"

Things were about to change—in a big way.

****

While the girls dealt with the SCF Scouts, Tag positioned himself so he could overhear their conversation. Rose and Claire answered their questions, but as soon as the door closed, Claire verbalized what the other was thinking. "Those drones are going to run us through their system, looking for anomalies—Rose and I will register. Tag won't, and they'll come looking . . ."

"That means they're likely to return—soon. We need to get Tag out of here, but where can he go?" Out of the corner of her eye, Rose caught Tag coming out of hiding.

"Geez—I'm sorry I got you into this mess!"

Claire ignored him, thinking about every possible hiding place. "It's got to be somewhere where it will be difficult to find him . . ."

"A place free from cameras, and other electronic tracking devices . . ."

"Sparsely populated to reduce the chances of personal contact."

"And, it would be best to have a location where he has at least several choices to make an exit should they get closed in—more than one escape route."

Tag listened to their conversation as if it were a lively rally in a tennis match, finally chiming in. "Hey, I'm right here, you know." Rose and Claire gave him 'the look,' then returned to their brainstorming.

"Look," he continued, "I need to get away—break contact completely with both of you. Which means I should leave the area—that way, you should be in the clear, and I'm not your problem anymore."

"We've been down this road already—there's no way we're going to walk out on you!" Claire faced Tag, silently daring him to argue.

"Technically, it would be my walking out on you . . . " He watched her carefully, determining it was probable Mount Vesuvius's erupting would exhibit less kinetic energy than that about to explode from Claire.

"Okay! I get it! You're here to help, and, I need it. What do you want me to do now?"

"Good. I trust that's the last time we'll have that discussion!" Tag nodded as Claire continued. "I'm thinking a logical spot meeting all of our criteria is the location where you first arrived—plus, you're an experienced outdoorsman capable of surviving in the backcountry. Another bonus is you're already familiar with the area—in both worlds!" Claire's eyes twinkled, teasing Tag as if he were her own brother.

"I agree," he confirmed. "It will be a good spot—for now. And, you're right—no problem with camping out."

Rose shot Claire an appreciative glance. "Look, we need to get moving quickly before those goons come back. Tag, go into the kitchen and get something to eat. Meanwhile, Claire and I will organize some outdoor gear—when you're done, go upstairs and pick out some of my dad's stuff to wear."

"Roger that . . ." Tag beelined it to the kitchen.

Safely out of earshot, Clair and Rose voiced their mutual concerns. "This is the turning point—right now." Claire whispered just to make sure Tag couldn't hear. "Once we go down this road, there's no turning back. We will be a part of it—however it plays out."

"I know. But I already feel as if I'm into this up to my neck! Oh, I know this will come back on me—but, you said it yourself—we can't walk out on him!"

"No, we certainly can't do that!" Despite Claire's attempt to lighten the mood, both girls were clear on the severity of their situation. "Let's get busy . . ."

****

Before interviewing Rose Talbot a second time, the Scout Team Leader thought it prudent to render a verbal report to the Commander of the SCF, Durango City Detachment.

" . . . and, that's what we know, so far. We're about to interview one of the females for a second time." The Commander listened intently as his subordinate recounted how he learned of the stranger, as well as the team's initial visit to the Talbot home.

"I don't like this—not one bit. Don't do anything until you hear from me . . ." In situations such as this, the Commander had enough experience to know it was always wise to kick the matter upstairs, reporting it to his superior at the SCF Regional Office in Denver.

"I'll await your orders."

****

As the Security Control Force data system catalogued the report and forwarded it to the higher-ups, Rose and Tag arrived at the drop off parking area where he would head into the backcountry. As one last check, they confirmed his primary and secondary choices for setting up camp in the event she had to locate him.

"This is it—are you going to be okay?" Even though he was skilled in survival, she worried.

"Yep—I'll be fine." Tag hoisted his borrowed pack onto his shoulder, and faced Rose. Neither moved. Finally, Rose walked into his arms which seemed to magically open on their own. Enfolding her, he felt a sense of calm and reassurance, not wanting to let go. She leaned in, and softly kissed his cheek. "Keep well—I will see you soon."

"I will—and, you better!" He smiled and turned toward the trail, waving as she watched him climb up the ridge. Only when he neared the top did he turn to watch her car disappear down the road.

****

The Deputy Commander of the SCF, Denver Regional Office, was alone in her office when the preliminary report arrived from the Commander of the Durango City Detachment, ready for download. Like him, she was concerned about the anomaly concerning the unknown male being a total ghost to their system. It was bad enough someone reported a rare, vicious assault. What was worse, though, was the apparent deficiency in the system that allowed an unknown target to run amok in their city. It simply couldn't be tolerated—not on her watch.

Her directive back to her subordinate in the Durango City Detachment was blunt and concise—find the unknown target by any means required, including a broad sweep, and interrogate anyone associated with the incident. She further directed they detain individuals, as necessary, pending further directives. Within moments, the Commander tapped an illuminated silver strip on her desk, delivering her instructions to the Scout Team's Supervisor. Upon receipt, he immediately dispatched the original team of Scouts, together with several three-man Sentinel squads to effect the search for and detainment of those individuals targeted in the investigation. In a classic cover his own butt maneuver, the Commander fired off a reply to his superior in Denver, categorizing the diligent efforts he initiated to thwart this affront to their way of life.

It was about this time, three things happened simultaneously—one, Rose, pulled her car over to the side of the road, turned off the motor, and sat—lost in thought over what to do next. Two—Claire arrived home and, as she walked through the front door, waved a greeting to her mother who was in the process of answering the ringing demands of the front room COM-link. Three—a Security Control Force Technologist, charged with the duty of reviewing all electronic traffic sent and received by the Durango City Detachment, reviewed the original report as well as the Denver based directive concerning individuals named Tag, Rose Talbot, and Claire Booth. The last, coincidentally, had a different last name, yet had a familial relationship with the Technologist.

Time for a heads up, he thought as he engaged a specially shielded COM-link he secretly modified, placing a call to his cousin's residence.

CHAPTER FOURTEEN

The two original Scouts and two three-man Sentinel teams descended upon Rose's home in unmarked vehicles, no sirens, during the early evening—a time when the majority of residents were taking advantage of the delightful weather by sitting outside, or strolling up and down the street visiting with neighbors. Their unobtrusive arrival triggered the citizens' efficient return to their homes as Sentinel teams secured the perimeter of the target's house, effectively sealing it off from neighboring properties. The Scout team approached the front door, rang, then knocked. No response. The senior Scout signaled to a Sentinel attending his vehicle who removed a hand-held device, and powered it up. The Sentinel deployed the unit in its usual fashion and aimed it at the Talbot residence, scanning for life-forms inside as well as any signs of movement. He looked over at the senior Scout, and shook his head—empty.

Wrong again, the senior Scout engaged his secure COM-link, contacting the Detachment Commander for further instructions. The return directive was to sweep the area for Rose Talbot, and the unidentified male target. If found, they were to take them to the Command Center for interrogation. In addition, an immediate alert would be initiated for the individual named Tag, listing him as a potential threat, directing the team to deal with him accordingly. A final directive indicated that in the event the search for the other two individuals proved fruitless, the Scout team—accompanied by at least one Sentinel unit— was to again question Claire Booth.

Meanwhile, Tag was applying the finishing touches to his campsite—close to a stream, and under good cover. He chose the secondary location he and Rose discussed—more secluded, and not too far from his arrival spot. He spent a few minutes cataloguing the equipment and supplies the girls packed for him, and they did an excellent job considering they had little time. Tag had everything he needed to last him for the next week and, if he were lucky, he could supplement his supplies by snaring small game to add to the menu. There was only one difference between camping now, and in the past—then, it was for fun.

Now, it was for survival.

****

Monique Booth lifted the receiver of the ringing COM-link, waving to greet to her daughter coming through the door.

"Monique here." She noticed an unusual humming over the open line.

"Auntie? How are you?" The voice sounded slightly hollow, and it took a few moments to process and recognize the voice of her favorite nephew.

"Joshua! I'm fine! It's so nice to hear from you! I didn't recognize your voice at first—there's a strange interference on the line."

"There's nothing the matter with the line, Auntie— I'm using a jammer to make our conversation completely secure. There are some things happening here that you need to know about—they affect Claire!"

Claire waited as Monique answered the COM-link in the event the call was for her. As the conversation progressed, Monique looked at her daughter, and pointed to a chair. The suggestion was clear—sit! She remained absorbed in the one way conversation as Joshua disclosed all of the significant details of the SCF investigation, as well as its broadening search. It wasn't hard to figure out—without even being part of the conversation, Claire instinctively knew it had to do with the SCF's investigation.

****

Rose pulled over at a nice location screened by foliage and off the main road, featuring a good view of the surrounding hills. The heat of the day was waning and, as she opened the driver's side window, the gentle hint of a breeze stirred freshly against her face. No traffic. No people. No activity. Despite all that happened during the last several days, it took little time to achieve a tranquil state of mind. *Perhaps*, she thought, *my subconscious ordered a timeout.* She closed her eyes, allowing her thoughts to wander, dabbling in one area for a moment, then skittering to an unrelated subject. She filled her mind with calm, enjoying the feeling of being unencumbered. But, despite her efforts to resist, structured thoughts wormed their ways to the forefront of her mind, impossible to ignore. Hers wasn't an issue of self-doubt—rather, a critical analysis of the current situation. And, in order to understand it, she needed to analyze her response to Tag's unexpected arrival. She allowed her mind to relax, thinking about his dilemma— what was it that compelled her to stay involved? A simple question really, and the answer was obvious—*because it's the right thing to do*. The only reason the authorities were after Tag was because he was different. An interloper. And, because he was different, they couldn't control him—yet. *It's all about control*, she thought. *Why is it they have the right to control us—especially, on such a wide scale?* Anger surged as she focused on the issue of authoritative control. There was no justice in the situation—they allowed it to happen. Like lemmings, each surrendered freedom of choice, choosing not to resist.

They chose to accept the status quo.

On a personal level, Rose considered why she wanted to stay involved with Tag. She had to be honest—*it's because he's from another reality. A different world. He's like a brand-new, shiny, exotic toy . . .* but, that was only part of it. If she were to be completely honest with herself, she had to admit there was an element of danger, and she liked it. Tag was exciting, but with that excitement came a healthy dose of fear. He represented a new path for her—a path she could choose. That in itself was a different way of looking at life— she loved the idea of a new challenge, but she also realized she wouldn't go down such a dangerous path for anyone but Tag. Yes, the attraction was obvious—but there was something more. A magnetism she couldn't quite define—*on one level, it makes me want to work together, to join him. On another, I'm willing to follow his lead, wherever that may take me.*

It was a lot to think about.

****

There was no doubt about it—Claire Booth was on the hot seat in front of her parents. Monique and Wesley squared off in front of her, their matching dark green leather chairs positioned for optimum grilling. After the conversation with Joshua, Monique brought her husband up to speed regarding the SCF's interest in their daughter, and they still weren't clear about the whole thing.

"Well, we seem to have a situation . . ." Monique was always the master of understatement. "Perhaps you should tell us what's going on."

Claire eyed her parents, surprisingly relaxed—although, to be fair, it was her nature. Maybe it was genetics—or, her upbringing—but, she was always a practical, independent thinker whose nature was one of peaceful calm. Without hesitation, Claire accurately recounted the last several days—Rose, Tag, and the idea that Tag was from a different world. When she finished, her parents remained sitting in silence—not a stunned silence, rather a contemplative silence.

Claire watched her mom process what she just heard. Monique was an attractive, willowy, blonde with a strong rational mind—she knew her goals and dreams, and others drew strength and inspiration from her. Everyone loved Monique, and her clear mind and caring personality often resulted in others benefiting from her wise, common-sense approach to life. As Claire sat before her, it was easy to see where Claire got her logical mind.

Her dad was the opposite—slightly shorter than his wife, he was dark-haired and strongly built. His strong, positive ego balanced humanitarian concern for his fellow man and, as a Pisces, he possessed an overriding concern— an obligation—to help others with a will to act upon it. Those who knew him respected him, and he was well respected by many for his drive and perseverance. Again, traits easily recognizable in his daughter.

Both sat for several moments, finally acknowledging what Claire told them.

"I think we need to involve Nelson." Wesley shot an affectionate glance at his daughter, and Monique immediately agreed. "We know how to help in this situation."

Claire was stunned! Help? She hadn't considered such a thing! But, truth be told, they needed all the help they could get.

Even if it came from her parents.

CHAPTER FIFTEEN

Jackie's initial reaction was mixed and, the way she saw it, she had two choices—let go of his hands, and run away shrieking, or let go of his hands and hold him tighter! Then, it dawned on her she had a third option—he was pulling her leg, and she should simply go along with the joke. None of those choices, however, compared with her next thought—*maybe he had a mental breakdown because of Tag's disappearance.* She was speechless, and Kyle clearly recognized her disbelief.

"Please, look me in the eye and listen carefully," he pleaded, waiting until he had her full attention. "One, I'm serious. Two, I'm not crazy. Three, this is entirely a possibility."

She studied his face—he believed what he was saying. His were eyes clear, his gaze direct, and he was relatively calm. She couldn't see any reason to reject his theories—but only if she were prepared to ignore the fantastic, mind-blowing nature of his ideas.

A wormhole of all things!

"If this is really true, who would do such a thing?"

"Not us—we don't have the technology yet." On that he was clear.

"Then how could this happen?"

"It's a two-fold scenario, I think. Either, a more advanced civilization has the capacity to create and control a wormhole event, or it was naturally occurring. In any case, Tag—somehow—interacted with it, and he was transported to somewhere else."

"You really think that's possible?"

"Not really, but it still remains one of several possibilities—however, it does dovetail nicely with the physical evidence we saw at the scene of his disappearance. Or, at least, what we think was the scene of his disappearance—concentric rings of strangely flattened plants, and the disturbed soil were obviously affected by an energy source."

He paused briefly before continuing, "When we were at the site maybe you didn't notice, but I used a small measuring device which signaled residual energy and low-level radiation in the disturbed area. Both readings were above normal background levels in the areas surrounding the hotspot."

It was a lot to take in. Jackie thought for a couple of minutes before asking the question plaguing them. "If that actually happened to Tag, can we reach him? Or, contact him?"

And, there it was—the million dollar question. "Theoretically, yes. However, if he were transported, then where? We must consider possibilities—did he transport to another place, or to another time?"

"An issue that complicates things . . ."

"Yes—tremendously. If we can control the sequence of movement to the right spot—wherever that is—for which time slot do we aim? However, if he's in our time, it simplifies things considerably in an already insanely complex process."

Jackie wasn't sure what to think—all she knew was she had to believe the man whose hands she held. "To follow that analogy," Kyle continued, "it would require the exact atom at the very tip of the arrowhead to intersect with a specific atom at the very center of the target. Much easier if that occurs within the same timeframe."

"Seeing that the authorities are currently conducting a rather simple, old-school search of this area for Tag, I strongly suggest we refrain from mentioning our current theory of his whereabouts."

"No shit—that would send them around the bend!"

****

Claire quickly weighed the possibilities indicated in her mom's statement, ranging from 'we can get you out of this,' 'we can help your friends and you,' too, or, 'screw your friends—we're shipping you off to Uncle Nelson's.' Unsure, she looked at her father for clarification. He knew her wheels were turning as she struggled to understand their take on the situation, and Monique's nodding signaled her understanding that Claire needed additional explanation.

No time like the present. "There are some things," he began, "you need to know about our family, and I think you're mature enough to appreciate the sensitivity of what I'm about to tell you. This information is especially pertinent to the current situation involving you and your friends."

Emotion washed through Claire, a finely-balanced mixture of apprehension and excitement. Anticipating something profound she leaned forward in her chair, stealing a glance at her mother who encouraged her with a smile.

"We all know that, worldwide, our society is totally controlled and significantly repressed by the ultimate authority, the World Ruling Council—and, the Security Control Force backs them in the form of henchmen. My statement proves itself by the reality that no one dares to openly discuss opposing views." He paused, letting what he just said sink in. "Sure, on the surface, daily life appears to be good—the standard of living is relatively high, and we live on a level well past the level of basic human needs. However, behind all of that, we live in a state of underlying fear—not only from the actual criminals and other supposed bad guys, but mostly from the very authorities who purport to protect us from the undesirable element." Claire understood her father's comments for she, too, privately questioned their society.

"Until now and unknown to you, key elements of the Booth family have been covertly operating as best we can to counteract the unwelcome efforts of the authorities. And, we have been doing it for several generations now!"

What? What does that mean? Claire sank back in her chair as her mind grappled with her father's revelation. Clearly, there were ramifications. *Weird—this isn't the huge shock it should have been.* "I always wondered," Claire commented to her dad. "I was aware of something going on behind the scenes—I just didn't have any idea it was something of such magnitude. Well, it's good to hear we may be able to help Rose and Tag—I have a feeling I may need your help, too." In fact, Claire was certain she would need their help.

"It's a shame Tag is in such a situation—not only did he arrive here inadvertently, he also has the SCF thugs gunning for him. Moving him into the countryside is a good, temporary step—the main thing is we need to get him out of here. And, if Rose is also at risk by association, then she needs to be moving also." Monique obviously had a good handle on their situation.

Wesley agreed. "Tag, in a way, has advantages and disadvantages in this case. No access to our electronic credit system will hamper his movements because he won't be able to pay for things he needs. But, on the positive side, the authorities have absolutely no way to track him electronically—and, trust me, they have their ways. That makes him immune to their primary targeting resources."

Monique picked up on where her husband was heading. "Rose, on the other hand, will have to completely separate herself from anything that can track her electronically since she's already integrated into the system."

"Whatever we're going to do," Claire pointed out, "it has to be quick because as we heard from Cousin Joshua, the SCF is moving in a sweep to collect Tag and Rose!"

Taking everything into consideration, within fifteen minutes Claire and her parents established a game plan to evacuate Rose and Tag—where they'd go, and how they'd get there. Monique and Wesley long since planned for such a possibility, so it took little time to ramp up, putting their plan into effect.

After a quick hug as well as a few last second instructions, Claire was on the road driving an older family vehicle that was stored in a secondary garage at the rear of their property. She wasn't sure how, but, without her knowing it, the vehicle was carefully maintained, fully fueled, and stocked with sufficient provisions for several people. Most important, this vehicle had its GPS and backup systems carefully deactivated in such a way as to send false signals to the authorities—no one would know their true whereabouts. As soon as she felt safe, Claire pushed a button on her COM-link.

"I'm on my way . . ." Quickly, she disconnected.

No sense taking chances.

****

"Nothing! Absolutely nothing!" The Senior Scout's frustration ballooned as the three Sentinel teams completed a broad sweep of a twelve block radius from the Talbot residence.

"Let's move on to secondary targets. Maybe we'll get lucky and they'll lead us to the primaries." The Junior Scout Member had even less patience than his partner, and he was ready to nail them.

"Sounds good since we're getting diddley squat from this . . ." He checked his electronic handheld again which produced the address of Claire Booth, automatically kicking out a reference concerning another male individual associated with this investigation.

"We've got the guy who filed the original verbal complaint about the assault—he's the one who gave us Rose Talbot. Plus, the guy with the bum leg—he corroborated the informant's name. Better yet, there is the full COM-link interview with Floyd, the SCF Spotter—voice recognition identifies him as Leon Church." The Senior Scout looked up at his junior partner. "Leon Church's address is closer than Claire Booth's—let's do him first."

Following protocol, they advised their Commander that the ground teams were redirecting to apprehend individuals Leon Church, and Claire Booth—in that order.

****

Leon stewed over the situation ever since he made the COM-link call. *I have a bad feeling about all this—why in hell did I open my big mouth in the first place?* The more he thought about it, the more he realized he should have planned it better. But, as usual, the impulse to strike back won out, and now he might be in a big, fat mess.

His self-control was sadly lacking.

For a guy who thrived on panning the streets, the situation forced him to keep a low profile—until he couldn't stand it any longer. He knew the SCF had his name, and it probably wasn't going to be long before they came knocking. Nonetheless, Leon had to get out. He needed fresh air. He needed to clear his mind. As he stepped across the threshold of his front door, turning to lock it, a presence loomed behind him. A glance to both sides registered more figures moving toward him.

****

Fully alert by the second ring of her COM-link, Rose sat up straight in the driver's seat. "Yes . . ." she answered tentatively.

"Are you still there?" The voice transmitted had an unusual hollow sound to it, but she recognized Claire's voice. She responded with their agreed-upon code.

"I'm stopped, part of the way back."

"Stay put, I'm coming to you."

"Roger that. I'll wait for you here."

The realization hit Rose like a blow to the gut—she wasn't going home anytime soon.

CHAPTER SIXTEEN

All preparations complete, Tag put together a relatively comfortable outdoor experience. He always enjoyed camping, especially with his brother, and he could make do with few resources. He built a small campfire, cooked an early supper, and cleaned up before dark which left him the option of dousing the fire prior to full nightfall to lessen his chances of someone's detecting him. He appreciated being away from city life, and the closest thing to a rush-hour was birds flitting about, establishing territorial boundaries.

He allowed his thoughts to drift to his current situation—he knew from experience that allowing his mind to wander often resulted in his subconscious providing useful ideas and, right about then, he could use a few. He focused on the portal that transported him to Durango City in the first place wondering if it would reappear. If so, would he enter it—again? He also wondered if he had the opportunity to reenter the portal, would he end up in the same place—or, in a different world and time? All were serious questions, and Tag understood they required serious thought before acting upon any of them.

His thoughts rested on his two new friends. *If the portal appeared in front of me right now, would I enter it and abandon Rose and Claire?* The concept of abandoning them troubled him, and he realized his strong attachment to both of them. Strange, since it had only been a couple of days . . .

****

Claire drove at a steady pace, looking for Rose. Even though her father gave her a shielded and encrypted COM-link that would prevent decoding of a conversation by the SCF, she thought it prudent to keep electronic communications to a minimum. She scanned both sides of the road as she searched without a glimpse of her friend, cataloguing the recent sequence of events—her hurried, final conversation with her parents, and their developing the necessary steps to get Tag and Rose on their way out of this area.

Aha! There she is! Rose's vehicle was almost completely screened by foliage, and had Claire not noticed a glint of reflection from the sun on her windshield, she may have driven by. Moments later the girls were together, locked in a mutually comforting embrace, neither speaking. Then they drew apart, each examining the other, as if to memorize every detail of their friend in the event it may be their last opportunity to do so.

"In a way, it's hard to believe I have to leave here—who knows for how long. It's surreal." Rose's thoughts lingered on her family as the seriousness of their situation sank in. "I haven't even contacted my family, about all of this."

"Look, this may very well turn out to be a temporary situation. Somehow, it may get all sorted out . . ." Claire found it difficult to hold it together, yet she knew she had to be strong for her friend. However, her statement lacked confidence, despite her outward appearance of trying to reassure Rose. "Between my parents and me, we'll contact your family and let them know what's going on. My folks previously met yours and, while they weren't close buddies, they know each other well enough to rely on what will be said. Besides, I hang out at your place enough that your parents can consider me as suitable adoptive material."

Rose actually laughed at this last comment, and felt better for it. "Okay, what's the plan?"

"Well, my parents had quite the revelation for me! And, get this . . ." Claire recounted everything, allowing Rose to fill in the blanks. "So," she continued, "we'll go back to the parking area where you dropped off Tag, hike in to find him, and both of you can be on your way. You'll take the vehicle I drove here because it will be harder for the authorities to track. Meanwhile, I'll take your vehicle back, and park it at your house."

"Then what? What will happen from there?"

Claire smiled. "All in good time . . . why don't you wait for the rest of the story until we have Tag with us? Then, I can go through it with both of you."

"Works for me!" Rose trusted her friend, knowing she would always have her best interests in mind.

The girls drove their vehicles to the trailhead where Rose dropped off Tag, and prepared to connect with Tag. Claire's COM-link chirped, listening intently for several minutes before responding to the caller. "Okay—I'll call you back when I get there."

"What's wrong?" Rose noticed Claire's concerned expression.

"That was my Mom—she just heard from my cousin, Joshua, at the SCF office." She paused, considering her words. "Apparently, the Security Control Force is after me now."

"Claire, I am so sorry to involve you in all of this!" Rose couldn't think of anything else to say.

"Would you and Tag like some company on your road trip?"

****

For the first time in his life, Leon was truly frightened. The rumors, half-truths, and unknown created a demented dance in his mind as terrifying expectations layered one upon another. The Sentinels collected him rather effortlessly, cuffing and transporting him to Command Headquarters, then ushering him into the interrogation room in a sequence of well-rehearsed moves. When they swooped in on him, he was alone contemplating events. The Senior Member sat opposite of him while the Junior Partner stood to the right, slightly behind Leon.

"Full name and date of birth," the Senior Member commanded. Leon jerked in his seat, as though a thrown switch sent an electrical jolt through him. Recovering, he answered. The Senior Member then cut loose with a series of short questions, fired in a quick barrage, seeking to overwhelm his defenses. To his credit, Leon fielded them well—some he parried, to others he offered half-truths. His final tactic was to play stupid. After the initial onslaught of questioning, Leon felt surprisingly better than he did prior to the beginning of the interrogation.

A small window of hope opened.

The Senior Scout team member eased back in his chair, winnowing the chaff from the grain of Leon's answers. There was nothing, really—most of it was bullshit mixed in with deflection. Even so, somewhere in there were a few kernels of truth.

Time to up the ante. The Senior Scout leaned forward again, his voice soft, forcing Leon to also lean forward if he wanted to hear. "I understand you are playing a game with me, and you figure you've done pretty well so far. But, I know better—what's going to happen here if you don't start to immediately answer my questions correctly with all the information I require—is I'm going to make a COM-link call."

Who the hell is he going to call? Leon fixated on what was coming next.

There was a flicker of a haunting smile on the Senior Scout's face as he drew the moment out, letting the target's imagination do the real work for him. Finally, he whispered, "The call will be to the Keeper's office—they're right next to us, and they work with the Eliminator Division."

Leon sat back in his chair as if struck by a blow. The color drained from his face, a cold sweat bathing him as nausea forced him to gag, and he struggled to hold down the vomit.

"Shall we begin again?"

Leon panicked, at that moment feeling like a frightened animal. In that moment, he chose to spill his guts. Yes, he told the truth—but in his scramble to survive, he convincingly fabricated much of the information.

After all, Tag was his target.

By association, he knew this would reflect badly on Rose, and he felt a deep sense of regret for what he was likely doing to her. She was a casualty—but, he had to do whatever it took to deflect this problem from him.

The two Scout Team Members reviewed Leon's information—unconvinced his answers were true—they decided to play it safe, and act upon it. They upgraded the threat level concerning Tag and Rose and, as they inputted their report into the system, additional resources were already dedicated to locating and apprehending the targets. A separate Scout Team dispatched to locate and bring them in for questioning, including Claire Booth.

She was a loose end—maybe a loose cannon.

CHAPTER SEVENTEEN

Rose glanced at her friend, slightly envious of her steadfastness, confidence, and calm. But, like well-worn veneer, cracks and blemishes were apparent to those who knew where to look. Claire's usually relaxed manner was subtly charged with tension, especially evident with a marked tightness around the eyes.

"Of course, you can come with us! Where else would you go?" Rose focused on her friend, knowing now all of them were in danger.

"I knew you'd say that! Look, it's getting to be late afternoon—we shouldn't start a major trip this late in the day." Her comment made sense, and Rose concurred. "From what both of you told me, I presume it would take us an hour to hike to the rendezvous location with Tag."

"Probably less than an hour, unless he's not at either the primary or secondary spots we talked about."

"Well, we're likely going to have to overnight out there, and start the trip in the morning." Claire paused for a few moments. "Your car's GPS will paint a big arrow to our location—the SCF will follow."

"Well, we'll have enough light to find Tag—what direction did you plan for us to travel out of the area?"

"East . . ."

"Good—then let's take my car, travel west far enough to act as a suitable diversion, and then dump it. We can return in your car since it has the inactive GPS."

The girls agreed on the plan, and executed it to perfection, leaving Rose's vehicle past the junction heading west into the next state. After returning to the trailhead, they selected extra supplies from the ample stock contained in Claire's vehicle, and began the trudge up the trail to locate Tag.

Forty-five minutes later, Tag heard voices as he scouted the adjacent area next to his campsite. Since he was upwind from his small campfire, it was unlikely interlopers would detect it—or, him. Still, he had to be cautious. He found a suitable hiding spot with decent cover, and waited. As they approached, he distinguished two female voices he instantly recognized as Claire and Rose! As pleased as he was to see them, he couldn't resist—he let them pass his position, stepped out behind them. "Hello ladies, going my way?"

Their reactions were mixed—Claire's startled response involved body movements akin to a good-sized electrical jolt. Rose immediately spun around and crouched in a balanced stance allowing quick movement, looking intently for the source of the threat.

They didn't know whether to be pissed or relieved. "Damn it, Tag! You scared us to death!"

"You're right—it wasn't funny." He paused. "Well, it was kind of funny . . ."

After they recovered, the girls updated Tag on their situation—i.e., the Security Control Force's upgraded investigation and by the time they reached his campsite, he was up to speed on everything.

"I'm so sorry my coming here made this much trouble for you. I . . ."

"Look—everybody's sorry. No one wants to be in this position, so let's knock off the apologies and get on with things." Claire's way of taking charge.

Rose looked from Claire to Tag. "What she said!"

"Okay, you're right. So, where do we go from here?"

"We should head east to New York City—my Uncle Nelson lives there." Claire paused. "He is—wired—into this kind of situation. He thinks we should get lost in the clutter of a big city, thereby improving our chances of avoiding the SCF knuckledraggers."

"Makes sense—however, getting there could prove interesting." Tag appreciated the thought and care of their plan, but still had a few reservations.

Claire understood his concerns. "I know—the plan is for us to get to Wichita. I have a contact there who will provide assistance and, hopefully, give us directions for the next step." The trio approved the plan, agreeing to depart the following morning. Until then, they needed rest and food.

"I presume with all of your running around today, neither of you had anything to eat lately." The girls nodded. "Well, in that case, I welcome you to my world and your—'Chez Tag!'" He punctuated his statement with an exaggerated hand flourish. Taking each by the hand, he led them to a convenient rock, executing a commendable bow as they took their seats. "Please observe the well-orchestrated preparation of culinary delights captured totally in the wild." He made the most of his pregnant pause. "I'm a trained professional, on a closed course, and working without a net—therefore, don't try this at home!"

It worked—the girls broke into laughter, releasing pent-up nervous energy. Everyone relaxed, and Tag proceeded to make the best meal he could under the circumstances.

****

If he were to be completely honest, Leon had to admit there were things he did in the past that were of marginal legality, all without dire consequence. So, it seemed ironic his incarceration reflected a case of bad judgment regarding his social interactions with Rose—in other words, becoming a punching bag for Tag. Well, that and creating a few fabrications to deflect the authoritarian eye upon someone else. But, despite the current circumstance, he appreciated the gallows humor of his situation. *Next time, if there is one,* he thought, *keep your mouth shut!*

The longer he sat alone in the cell thinking, the more he experienced a fierce, internal debate about what to do next should the SCF call on him to continue the interrogation. *Did I say enough? Too much? Is my best option to clam up? Should I clam up?* Alternatively, he considered using an opposite strategy. *I already strung enough lines of crap, so I need to keep it going before it collapses back on me.*

For a smooth operator, Leon's indecision was particularly unsettling. Two things dominated his thoughts—one, he was the only occupant in this eight-cell section of the detention area. Two, down the left corridor running between cells was a closed, strongly reinforced steel door with a nameplate affixed for everyone to see.

Eliminator Division.

****

All things considered, Rose and Claire had to admit Tag's culinary expertise was pretty good—it must have been because they devoured everything on their plates! Cleanup was swift and, as the girls discussed the coming trip, Tag spent time expanding his shelter to accommodate his guests—the original design was meant only for one. There was just enough light remaining to complete one more recon of the area which, thankfully, turned up nothing of interest.

They surrounded the campfire, and conversation turned to supplies and itineraries for their travels, eventually lapsing into quiet introspection with no idea of what the future held. Rose wondered when she would see her family again—she couldn't imagine what they would think of her when they finally learned of her situation. But, more important, she wondered if the authorities would hold any of them accountable for their actions.

Of course, there were no answers.

Claire, too, was contemplative, but her thoughts traveled in a different direction. She knew she had her parents behind her, and she was looking forward to arriving in New York City as well as seeing Uncle Nelson. Arriving in NYC was an achievable goal pleasant to consider—wondering how they were going to pull it off, wasn't so great.

Tag, however, was thinking about something else. He missed his brother, and wondered how Kyle was handling his disappearance. *His oversized brain is no doubt operating at warp speed considering all of the possibilities, including what actually happened—he'll figure it out.* He also wondered if Kyle's new girlfriend were helping his brother deal with it—did she bail, or stick around? Surprisingly, he was most emotional when he thought of Lego. *Jeez, I miss that dog!*

Within the hour, darkness cloaked the woods, and Tag doused the fire to avoid detection, suggesting to the girls that everyone should get some sleep so they could get an early start in the morning. With Tag still outside, they laid out their sleeping bags within the tight confines of the shelter, considering who should sleep next to whom. Without speaking, they nodded their consent.

Tag had soft bookends to bump into if he chose to roll over!

CHAPTER EIGHTEEN

I t was getting close to ten o'clock in the evening by the time the Secondary Scout Team arrived at the Booth residence looking for Claire. Wesley anticipated their arrival, surprised it took them that long to get there. As it turned out, Monique was on the main floor—closer to the front of the house—when the doorbell chimed. She opened the door to a two-man Scout team. Without being obvious, she looked past the investigative team in front of her, observing several unmarked SCF vehicles parked on the street. *They brought backup*, she thought, instantly knowing they surrounded her home.

She refocused her attention. "Good evening. May I help you?" Monique maintained a controlled, relaxed, and innocent attitude with only a dash of apprehension. Precisely what they expected to see from an individual taken somewhat by surprise at their arrival.

"We need to speak with you—may we come in?" The lead Scout Member addressed her in a neutral tone. Since his superior told him the household contained only a secondary target wanted for follow-up questioning, he decided a heavy-handed approach wasn't required. He was pleased the attractive lady appeared cooperative.

"Certainly . . . " Monique stepped back from the door, allowing them to enter.

As they entered the living room, a solidly built man descended the stairs, nodding his acknowledgment of their presence. "Gentlemen . . ."

"Are you the parents of Claire Booth?"

"We are . . ."

"We need to speak to Claire."

"She's not here right now. What's this about?" Wesley wanted to know the exact reason for their visit.

"We're conducting an important investigation concerning another individual, as well as your daughter's contact with that person."

"Who's the other person?"

The agent wasn't interested in game playing. "Where can I find your daughter?"

Monique's turn. "Claire left with some school friends on a camping trip for a few days."

"That's rather sudden, isn't it?"

"Not at all—they planned their trip several weeks ago."

The Scout Leader wasn't buying it—before arriving, he studied background information about Claire. "She's in grade twelve—why would she leave if she still has final exams?"

"Claire's exam schedule doesn't start until the middle of next week, and they planned a break for a few days to relax before diving into the heavy-duty studying thing. Besides, she took a few books with her . . ."

The agent considered the plausibility of her answer. "Where is she now?"

"I'm not exactly sure—they were going to camp wherever as they went along."

"Which direction did they go?"

"Southwest, I think—toward the Grand Canyon area."

Time for a different approach. "Who's traveling with her?"

Monique paused for affect, sounding surprised, when she responded, "You know, she didn't specify who she was traveling with—Claire only said it was some school friends."

"Which of your vehicles did she take?"

"Neither—one of her friends was driving."

The Scout Leader realized GPS tracking wasn't possible since they didn't know the identity of the owner, nor which vehicle was involved, so he directed his attention at Wesley. "Do you have any knowledge of where your daughter is?"

"Not really—I know less than my wife. I've been busy at work, and really didn't speak to Claire about this trip." Wesley mustered up a disgusted look. "Hell, I didn't even find out about it until this morning!"

"Do either of you know your daughter's friend, Rose Talbot?"

"This is about Rose Talbot?" Wesley hoped his question would elicit something that would provide information.

"Just answer the question."

"Yeah, we've met her a few times—nothing special, and not too bright. In fact, she's kind of flaky—her mother and I have tried to discourage Claire from associating with her."

Accepting he arrived at a dead-end, the Scout Member left final instructions. "When your daughter returns, we'll have to speak to her. Please let me know when she gets home."

"Sure, that'll be fine." Monique escorted the two men to the front door.

After they left, Wesley plopped down on the softest chair in the room. "So, what do you think?"

"Well, we bought a couple of days, at best," Monique offered. "Let's hope they have a clean run eastward!"

****

Tag awakened at the first suggestion of dawn, enough light to promise a sunny day. Their trip would be long, starting with having to double back through Durango City—a formidable prospect. Surely, they would increase their exposure in the epicenter of the Security Control Force manhunt for them. However, if they could clear town before there were too many people around, they had a chance of a clean getaway.

He awakened the girls, and the three of them broke

camp and hiked out to the vehicle within the hour. The consensus was to get on the roadway and through Durango City before breakfast.

As it turned out, it proved anticlimactic—Tag and Rose scrunched down in their seats, making it seem Claire was the only occupant in the vehicle. She took a direct route at a reasonable speed, obeying all traffic regulations. Nobody paid attention to an older, nondescript vehicle, passing through . . .

By early afternoon, they reached the major junction with the interstate leading north to Denver, or south to Albuquerque, New Mexico. They switched drivers every two hours in order to keep everybody fresh, and there was some debate whether Tag should drive considering he wasn't licensed in that reality. It was finally Claire who pointed out if the authorities pulled them over and requested a driver's license and, even if one of the girls were driving, each of them would be flagged in the system by that time.

Tag paid close attention to road signs and place names along the way, estimating how many differed from his world. As near as he could figure, place names varied about sixty per cent of the time from his world to theirs— in a few cases, towns or villages he expected to see didn't exist in his new world. Conversely, the opposite was true. A roadmap indicated larger cities were situated where he expected them to be, tending to blossom in conjunction with available rivers and other convenient topographical features. Mountains, waterways, deserts, and other physical features were much the same.

As they traveled east, they needed to keep rest stops to a minimum—they took advantage of light traffic in certain areas and, when no one was around, they stopped to stretch their legs.

"We're doing okay so far—but, at this pace, we won't make Wichita until late evening. So, do we want to arrive there during the day, or well after dark?" Rose's question was a good one.

"Does Nelson or anyone in your family expect us to maintain a certain schedule?" Tag figured if they had to keep to a specific timeline, then it would dictate if they traveled during the day or at night.

"Last question first—there is no schedule. We simply show up, whenever. We have a long way to go before reaching New York City—presumably, we will arrive at various centers during daylight and nighttime, and I see no distinct advantage by choosing one over the other. We may have to leave the answer to that issue up to our contact person—so, I suggest we time our arrival close to the city for late afternoon, make contact, and follow directions from there." As usual, Claire was the voice of reason.

"Well, if we're going to time our arrival in Wichita for late afternoon tomorrow, we need to select a place to stay tonight."

"We're about an hour and a half away from La Junta," Tag commented as he studied the map. There's a river there that converges with two other rivers a short distance east of town. My guess? Camping is available . . ."

"Excellent! That way we'll keep a low profile, without having to pay for accommodations." Rose agreed with Tag, and Claire nodded her agreement.

"Sounds like a plan. However, I will expect tomorrow morning's wake-up call to be improved upon from the methodology used today." Claire tried not to smile as she chided her new friend.

"Hey, I could've banged pots and pans!"

****

Kyle studied Jackie as she sat next to him, thinking how lucky he was that she arranged time off work to help him through Tag's disappearance. He never experienced such selflessness, and he was more than grateful to have her at his side.

She felt his gaze. "Kyle, I know the search teams have come up empty—but, that doesn't mean anything bad happened to Tag. It just means they haven't found him yet." She attempted a tepid smile. "Besides, you can take comfort from that fact as support for your theory."

"Yeah, there's that . . ."

He remained quiet for a while, as though listening expectantly for a voice to be heard in the distance. "Somehow, I know he's okay, but I get the feeling he's on the move . . . but, wherever he is, I established a tenuous connection with Tag. I can sense certain things with him . . ." Suddenly he realized how crazy that sounded. "Am I being weird?"

"For you, my dear, not at all!"

****

It was a toss up as to whether time spent sleeping exceeded total time awake. Leon supposed it really didn't matter since any sleep would be chopped into small restless bits, interspersed with bad dreams and repetitive wake ups. He was tired to the point where it was difficult to keep his eyes focused—but, it was the steel door keeping him mesmerized, refusing to let go. Given his lowly circumstances, Leon appreciated his mother didn't know where he was, or what was happening. Two years ago, he was content to move out on his own and, since then, keeping in touch came in a distant second. Besides, she had her own problems in life. He never had to worry about what his father thought because Leon never knew who he was. Then, there was another aspect to consider—chances were good his job was gone since he didn't show up for work. *It probably doesn't matter, anyway* . . . such a thought served as little consolation.

He looked at the steel door with a sign indicating it was the entrance to what could only be compared to Hell. Eliminator Division. Leon knew without question if they hauled him off through that door, nothing else would matter. Ever.

Of course, he was afraid of dying.

But, what ran a close second was the fact that no one he knew would realize what had happened to him—or, if by some chance they did find out, they most likely wouldn't care.

****

Tag and the girls located a nice camping spot on the northern stream just before it joined a southern partner a few miles east of La Junta. It was off a seldom traveled gravel road with the area immediately around the water supporting enough foliage to provide good cover. Claire's parents' vehicle was well-stocked with items of logistical support for their trip including a tent for two—maybe three if there were no other alternative.

Dinner consisted of canned and vacuum-packed items suitable for heating, supplemented by dried fruits and nuts. A small fire allowed them to boil water to make tea they found in their provisions. The good thing was there wasn't much to clean up, and they made sure the rest of their campsite was organized before nightfall. Again, it seemed prudent to extinguish the campfire while it was still dusk to prevent attracting unwanted attention. Shortly after dark they turned in, each welcoming a good night's sleep.

Tag was awake at first light, well rested and ready to meet the challenges of the day. He arose quietly so he could scout the area—the girls were sleeping soundly, and he didn't have the heart to disturb them. With the journey they had in front of them, he figured they would need as much shuteye as they could get. He tiptoed from the tent, scanning the area for anything unusual. Nothing—birds chirped, and he could hear the slapping of the river on its banks. As far as he could tell, there wasn't too much difference between his world and theirs.

When he finally returned, he thought he might find Rose and Claire fixing tea. Nope—they were still dead to the world. *Time for a quick bath*, he thought as he grabbed soap and a change of clothes from the vehicle. After checking out a couple of areas, he settled on a private bend in the river, immediately implementing the 'quick plunge into cold water' method. Unpleasant as it initially was, he found it always worked best.

After a last plunge to rinse off, he turned toward shore

to see Rose and Claire standing just above the waterline, Claire holding his clothes in one hand and, with her bent forefinger of the other hand she motioned for him to come on out. Rose pretended not to look through splayed fingers.

Tag, standing 'au natural' in the river was faced with one of life's choices—a defining moment. He considered a bashful approach, standing chest deep in the water, hands blocking the family jewels from view. Or, he could take the James Bond approach, inviting the ladies in to join him, sans clothes. Then there was a third option—emerge from the watery deep in the face of danger, holding the remnants of his dignity together, genitalia exposed to the world.

The internal debate was short-lived, figuring there was little point in standing there like a prune, prolonging the moment. Usually a man of action, Tag adopted the 'once more into the breach' approach, striding forward, arms at his side, gradually emerging from his watery cover. Well, now he was committed! *Oh, what the hell,* he thought. *They can take a peek if they want to!* And, peek they did before Claire dropped his clothes by the shoreline. Both girls ran off, taking turns shrieking and laughing in mock outrage.

By the time he returned to the campsite, they regained a semblance of control, and were in the process of breaking down the tent and storing sleeping bags in the vehicle. Neither commented on his graceful exit from the frigid waters. Grateful for that blessing, Tag began breakfast preparations—de facto, they somehow elected him camp cook, which was fine with him.

As much as they would have enjoyed taking their time, truth was they needed to get on the road. They ate, and the girls cleaned up, packing everything in the vehicle in record time while Tag policed the area to be certain they were leaving no clues behind.

"Okay, Poseidon, if we're going to make Wichita before dark, stop flopping around on land and get in the car!" Claire smiled at him, and there was a loud snort from the front seat passenger. As he climbed into the back seat, Tag suspected it could be a painfully long road trip . . .

****

The initial Scout Team was designated the primary investigators on the case and, after meeting with the Secondary Team and hearing details of the Booth parents' interview, the Senior Scout Investigator was undecided as to what to do next. Search protocols were already upgraded once to include an area covering southern Colorado. Claire Booth was, purportedly, on some camping expedition with friends—a situation he wasn't at all sure was true. At least there was the prospect of her returning—Rose Talbot, their primary target, vanished.

What really stumped the Investigator was the fact they had Tag showing up on a remote security camera, but their facial recognition system—which was pretty damned good—completely failed to identify him. If that weren't enough, there were no records of his existence, as well as no records of inoculations or implantation of the GPS device. But, how could that be? Inoculations were mandatory worldwide, and had been for the past thirty years.

The Senior Scout considered his options. He could request a further upgrade for search protocols to include statewide, as well as interstate and regionally. In order for the search to go national or international, it required a decision made by someone with a considerably higher pay grade than his. Yes, there were things he could do locally such as direct a broadened contact list to include schoolmates and friends of Rose Talbot and Claire Booth to see what they know, if anything. He could also extend the investigation of the Talbot family. Currently, the parents and siblings of Rose Talbot were electronically identified as being in the San Diego area. Maybe it was time to direct a local Scout Team to contact them for a little chat about their darling daughter. When he thought about it, the latter seemed the best option. *By extension*, he thought, *we could do a more thorough background investigation of the Booth family, too.* But, as he chewed on it, he decided the time wasn't right. There was no point in stretching their resources for a group appearing to be only peripherally involved—Claire was simply off with other friends apart from Rose.

What he did have were the three guys who were in a fight with the mystery man. If he sent somebody to speak with the two who were injured, those discussions may reveal something more. And, he could try to squeeze more out of Leon—since he was still in custody, at least he would be easy to find.

The Senior Scout tapped his hand-held. "Call Keeper Division." He ordered the device to remind him of his task in thirty minutes as he again reviewed the electronic surveillance files. *I'll get you*, he promised.

I'll get you . . .

****

As they made their way eastward through a number of small towns, the trip was uneventful. Even larger city centers such as Garden City and Dodge created no problems and, traveling further into the heartland, Tag noted the Federated State of Kansas was just as flat there as it was in his reality. They discussed the historical Old West significance of Dodge compared to his world's Dodge City, and its colorful background with Boot Hill and outlaws from the past. He was glad to hear most of those people and events did play a part in this area's history, including the Dalton Gang's hideout located not too far away.

Traffic thickened as they approached the western side of Wichita around six o'clock that evening. Rose was driving, and when they were thirty miles out she pulled into a rest stop. For the first test of the network, they were going to rely on assistance in getting them safely to New York City.

Claire plucked her COM-link device from a bag and prepared to call the contact number. Her parents gave her a device specially modified by her cousin to provide a secure transmission, free of the omnipresent ears of the SCF—however, despite its technical wizardry, she was to keep conversations short and vague, and without mention of anyone's real names. Suddenly, pangs of nervousness stabbed at her stomach.

"Would you like me to make the call?" Tag noticed her hesitation, something he thought unusual for his new friend.

"I don't mind, either," added Rose.

All Claire needed was a little support. "No, it's okay— I've got it." She entered the number, initiating the call. After several rings, a husky male voice answered, "Who's, calling?"

Using the code word her parents provided, Claire responded, "It's Traveler—I'm with two others, close by."

"Good, I've been expecting you. Here's what I'd like you to do . . ."

CHAPTER NINETEEN

Evening traffic was remarkably light and, following provided directions, they managed to pass through central Wichita without notice or fanfare. In his normal reality, Tag never visited Wichita so he didn't know what to expect. In his current reality, he wasn't wild about the downtown building structures—a different construction and layout than he expected in a typical large city. What he found extraordinary was the total absence of a dingy sky marking the normal pall associated with big-city pollution. *At least that's one thing they got right here*, he noted as they made their way east.

Soon, they were on the eastern edge of where city and country life meet. A right turn onto a secondary road, and a ten minute drive brought them to a T intersection where they bore left onto a gravel road leading to a solitary house standing sentinel in a vast, flat area. Single storied, the house was a sprawling design including elements seemingly added on at the whim of the owner. Landscaping was sparse with only a couple of ancient trees providing minimal shade for residents.

Rose pulled the vehicle to a stop in a circular driveway, cutting the engine. They sat quietly for a few moments, expectations building in preparation for the upcoming encounter. Turns out they didn't have long to wait—the front door opened, and a man approached with a shambling gait. He stopped, taking his time, studying them carefully. *He's exactly as I pictured him*, Claire thought as she watched every move he made. *That's a plus . . .*

"Claire, I presume?" He directed his attention to the smallest member of their group.

"I am." It was her turn to study him. He was huge, close to seven feet, with a bear-like physique. He had an unruly look—dark-hair, and a shaggy beard. But, for all of his formidable attributes, he exuded unexpected warmth and gentleness.

"This is Rose, and he's Tag . . ." Claire gestured to each of her friends as she introduced them.

"I'm Seth. I've prepared something to eat . . ." As the man shook their hands, he placed his left hand on the shoulder of the other, imparting a deep feeling of welcome. He then turned toward the house, leaving it up to them as to whether they followed. *A man of few words, I see . . .* Claire shot a look to her friends as they trailed after their benefactor, and into his home. As they crossed the threshold, a creature with four legs propelled toward them, its tail creating a sideways, less forward motion. It gravitated to Tag first, obviously sensing the dog owner in him. About thirty pounds, it was a wiry haired, tan coated bundle of exuberance!

"That's Chico—not exactly what you picture as guard dog of the month! C'mon in—get settled."

Seth disappeared around the corner, leaving them to contend with the excited dog who was pole bending between their legs as fast as he could!

"Hey, Chico . . ." Tag knelt, extending his hand for the dog to sniff, his tone calm and soothing. Chico responded instantly by calming down, choosing not to leave Tag's side as they headed down the hallway toward the kitchen located at the back of the house.

Seth was busy filling plates from various pots still simmering on the stove, placing them on the kitchen table two at a time—it seemed Seth wasn't into formalities, so each took a seat in front of a plate of steaming food. After their rations of the last days anything would have tasted good, but Seth's meal was incredible! They limited dinner conversation to the occasional, "Please pass the salt," as they helped themselves to seconds—Seth grunted his acknowledgment.

The three of them insisted on doing after dinner cleanup while Seth wandered off, opening and closing doors somewhere within the rambling house. It felt good to relax and, after cleaning the last dish, they joined their host and parked themselves in surprisingly comfortable wooden chairs on the east section of the wrap-around veranda. Seth sat silently, staring at the darkening horizon—if they listened carefully, each could detect the faint sounds of city life. Facing a peaceful view of pastoral countryside, they were contemplative and relaxed, sipping full-bodied coffee provided by their host—cowboy coffee, he called it.

"I know your father from before." Seth's statement startled them from their own thoughts. "Wesley and I were in college together and when we finished our basic ranks, he went into the workforce. I continued to putter around with other courses interspersed with trips abroad—that's when we grew apart simply from a lack of contact."

Claire struggled to remember him. "I never knew that—did you meet up again?"

A small grin flickered, then vanished. "Once—years later in Denver. That's when I met your mother . . ." Seth paused as if lost in a warm memory. "A fine woman, Monique."

Claire smiled. "I won't argue that!"

The soft moment quickly dissipated into reality. "Okay—what do you need to continue on your way?" He scanned each of their faces although the question appeared to be directed to all of them.

Rose answered immediately. "We're getting low in the fuel cell—replenishing it requires using credits."

"I'll take your vehicle to a place where I have an understanding with the owner—I'll top it off without leaving a record of your being here."

"Won't that result in an electronic trail directed at you?"

"No, not really. He and I aren't big on record-keeping— I'm sure there will be something I can do for him soon enough."

"Rose left before she could gather more clothes," Claire added. "My folks stocked our vehicle with extra sets for me . . ."

Seth eyeballed Rose before answering. "I'll see what I can come up with—don't expect a lot of fashion sense, though."

Rose smiled at the caution.

"We could use a bit more canned or dried food to keep our supplies in good shape in case we need to camp along the way." It made sense for Tag to know exactly what rations they had available since they dubbed him head chef at the beginning of their trip.

"I have a good selection in my storeroom—help yourself."

"Thanks—we appreciate it."

"We appreciate everything you're doing for us, but I have to wonder—why? Why are you risking yourself to help us?" Leave it to Claire to ask the question for which everyone needed an answer.

Seth shrugged. "You're not the first people to come through here—I've traveled extensively in my time, and I know how widespread our system of total control is . . ." His expression softened as he met the eyes of each of them. "I believe people weren't meant to be subservient to others, especially a small controlling group. Everyone should have the opportunity to unfold and develop according to their intrinsic needs—suppression of this, in any way, limits our ability to grow as a society." Seth chuckled at their blank expressions. "Yeah, I can get a little philosophical at times."

Claire leaned forward in her chair, placing her hand on his. "You're preaching to the choir here! What you are doing to help shows you not only care, you're trying to make a difference—to change things." She looked over her shoulder at Tag. He also leaned forward in his chair, elbows on his knees.

It was time.

"I have a few things to share with you—you'll be pleased to know there are places where individual freedoms still account for something—getting there, however, is the trick!"

****

The Talbot's holiday was proceeding nicely, and they rented a beach house south of Oceanside in the San Diego area. The parents found if the kids burned off enough energy on the beach and in the water, they could actually enjoy themselves. Neither voiced concern for Rose's staying home alone—she was responsible, and an independent young lady. So, when a dark colored vehicle pulled up to the curb close to the side of the house, Lori Talbot didn't think for a second it had anything to do with her. Even though it was unmarked, she immediately recognized it as a vehicle favored by the Security Control Force.

"Nathan! Nathan!" Lori inched toward the sliding glass door, calling to her husband who was inside preparing lunch for the family. As he approached, Lori signaled with a subtle head nod, directing his attention to the two men exiting the vehicle, moving toward them. Nathan stepped outside and joined his wife as the SCF Scouts approached. They stopped a few feet away, surveyed the kids on the beach, and then focused on the two adults standing on the deck.

"You're the Talbot family, correct?" The lead Scout looked at them expectantly.

"Yes—what's this about?"

"Your daughter, Rose."

Lori's hand found its way to Nathan's.

****

The Commander of the SCF Federated State of Colorado Headquarters located in Denver paused over the report by the Technical Division indicating a series of shielded communications intercepted in Durango. By rights, the only secret communications allowed were those internal to the SCF—any private individuals moving into this arena were viewed as potential security threats. The report jogged her memory of another report she reviewed recently and, after a few minutes of sifting through computer archives, she found it—records of similar occurrences in the Wichita, Kansas area. A coincidence? Perhaps, but she doubted it. She immediately dispatched agents in the Technical Division to investigate, directing them to coordinate their efforts with their counterparts in the SCF Kansas region.

****

Leon finally caught up on much needed rest. Physically inactive, he was surprised at how much anxiety could drain and fatigue someone, and it wasn't until he heard approaching footsteps that he jerked back to the here and now. Wide awake and aware of his circumstances, he once again felt the crushing weight of fear as he lay still, expecting the two guards from the Keeper Division to stop at his door. They did. He studied them, trying to glean something from their neutral expressions—any hint of what was to happen to him was better than nothing. He also stole a glance at the steel door with the Eliminator Division nameplate announcing certain doom for anyone who entered.

The guard on Leon's right pushed a series of numbers, signaling the door to open. It glided silently across the breadth of the cell, disappearing into the solid frame of the cell wall.

"Step forward."

As he stood, Leon willed they would have him turn to the right to face whatever was there—a left turn through the doorway of death spelled his demise. His legs refused to move.

"I said, 'step forward.'"

He complied, waiting for what seemed like the longest few moments of his life.

"Turn right."

Leon nearly crumpled, crying with relief.

CHAPTER TWENTY

The next morning Tag awakened early after spending the night in his sleeping bag on a comfortable cot tucked away in a corner of the veranda. Sleeping outside always agreed with him, and doing so usually left him feeling well rested. Seth had only one spare bedroom, so it made sense for the girls to share it while he roughed it under the stars. In the cool of the morning, Tag reviewed his conversation with Seth the previous evening—it turned out disclosing Tag's situation was the right thing to do. Seth asked innumerable questions regarding Tag's world, making comparisons between the two, sometimes brutally criticizing his own.

Tag liked Seth—for all of his rough and gruff, he was an intellectual with curiosity about things. Straightforward. Tag learned Seth shunned city life in favor of a more natural setting and, according to some of his stories, Seth was well-traveled, as well as eager to learn about others and their situations. If Tag had to pigeonhole his new conspirator, phrases such as 'perpetual student' and 'spiritual person' seemed appropriate.

As much as he would have enjoyed hanging out on the veranda, they needed to get an early start on the day. He folded the sleeping bag, cinching it tightly, and threw it in the back of the vehicle before heading inside for a bite to eat. As it turned out, Seth got up early, too, and while the girls were struggling to plant their feet on the floor, he took their vehicle to renew the fuel cell. On the kitchen table there were substantial packages for Rose—Seth did the best he could when it came to choosing her clothes, and when she appeared in the kitchen, she was delighted by his fashion sense. He had a good eye for size, too—everything fit comfortably.

Tag organized a breakfast of eggs and sausage for everyone, and they enjoyed a spirited discussion about a range of topics. It felt good to joke and laugh as they pushed their predicament to the backs of their minds, if only for moments. Each knew they must leave and, finally, they packed and headed to the car. Even though they met Seth mere hours before, it felt as if they knew him for years, and their being there was simply a renewal of that friendship. Seth, too, felt a kinship—he warmed to the girls, and Tag's circumstances piqued his curiosity. Rose and Claire turned to Seth to say goodbye and, before words were spoken, with a huge arm he swept each of them into a group hug. Feeling his arms around them, they felt a renewed confidence as he wished them well.

"I certainly appreciate our discussions, and your choosing to share your experiences with me. However, I suggest you be very selective with whom you disclose the facts regarding how you got here!"

Tag accepted his friend's sage advice. "I'll certainly keep that in mind—thanks for all you've done for us!"

Seth smiled. "You would do the same. Okay—off you

go, and good luck!" Chico wagged his tail as if bidding them farewell. Tag slipped behind the wheel and, as he glanced in the rear view mirror, he caught the last sight of their host standing side by side on the veranda with his furry companion.

****

Lori and Nathan Talbot sat in wooden chairs on their beach house deck watching their kids enjoy the summer sand. Neither spoke, but each knew the other was dissecting the concluded interview with the Security Control Force Agents. Shocked at their allegations, they couldn't imagine how Rose—a bright, law-abiding teenager—could transcend to what the Agents were now labeling her. A fugitive.

True to her nature, Lori was the first to break the silence. "If any of this is true," she speculated, "there has to be a powerful motivating factor for Rose to go down that road . . ."

Nathan nodded. "I agree. Chances are the version laid out by the SCF people in San Diego—getting it from the Durango City office, I mean—is skewed. The truth is we don't know the reality of the situation."

"Good point. They did mention Claire Booth—so my immediate reaction is to contact Claire and her family to see what they know."

Her husband considered the idea, then shook his head. "We don't want to initiate any electronic communication with anyone until we learn the details firsthand, and in person. The last thing we need is the SCF intercepting our calls and recording our discussions. We can't run the risk of someone saying something that may place us, or others, in danger.

"You're right—we have to be careful." She paused, then continued. "Who in the hell is Tag?" Lori glanced at her husband, then the children playing on the beach, each parent knowing what the other was thinking.

"We need to get home—now!"

****

On the way back to headquarters, the Junior Scout Team Member called in to ensure the Technical Group was isolating and recording COM-link communications by the Talbots. Such surveillance was a testament to the nature of their society in that the Security Control Force neither sought nor required permission or decree allowing such a thing to occur against its own citizens. If they needed to know something, they implemented the means to acquire the intended knowledge.

"All we need is for one of them to slip up . . ." he muttered as he disconnected. "It won't be long."

****

Traveling north toward Kansas City, the day was shaping into a hot one, straining the outdated vehicle's climate control system. Rose was at the helm, obeying all traffic rules and regs, when she noticed a dark vehicle, emergency lights activated, rapidly overtaking them.

"I sure as hell hope they're not after us!" Claire and Tag were dozing in the heat and monotony of travel, but instantly awakened at the sound of alarm in Rose's voice. In a matter of moments, a passive, relaxed trip turned into one of heightened tension—negative circumstances were slipping out of their control. Rose's fight or flight reflex kicked in on the high side, encouraging her to subconsciously accelerate.

"Whoa! Slow down! If they're not for us, we don't want to attract attention!" Claire, of course, was right. Rose looked at her and after several moments, her friend's warning registered and she eased off the accelerator. Tag monitored the progress of the fast-approaching vehicle, desperately hoping for it to pass without notice. When the vehicle was parallel to their car, he turned his head to the right in the event they might get a good look. Claire pretended to laugh as if she and Rose were enjoying a private joke. Nothing seemed out of the ordinary as the SCF vehicle sped by without either of the two occupants glancing in their direction.

They were safe—for now.

"I'm not exactly sure what we can do, but I think we need to develop some sort of plan should we be stopped and questioned." Tag's suggestion seemed obvious, and Claire twisted around in her seat to look at him.

"As far as we know, they're aware of Rose and me, and they have little knowledge about you—however, we do know they're looking for all three of us. I'm not sure what, if anything, we can do to improve our situation."

"You could say I kidnapped you, and forced you to

drive me wherever."

Rose looked at him in the rear view mirror. "Yeah, like that's going to work!"

"Well, at least it's better than saying I just landed on your planet, take me to your leader." His joke broke the tension and, for the next leg of their trip, they spent time hashing out a plan.

****

In the few minutes it took to arrive at the interrogation room, Leon somehow managed to gain control of his emotions. He shuffled down the hall accompanied by a guard, his partner stopping to open a door, motioning for him to enter. Once inside, he faced the original Scout Team Investigators and, again, the Senior Member was seated on the other side of a worn, chipped, medium-sized table. His partner stood to the side, slapped up against the wall. The door closed behind him.

"Leon! It's good of you to come! Please—sit down." The Agent's face radiated a smile which, under other circumstances, could be described as friendly. "I thought we could continue our chat about matters of interest to us. Since you have had time to reflect on our last encounter, I assume we can dispense with the previous unpleasantness, and move on in a more amicable fashion."

Cut the buddies crap, Leon thought as he assessed his situation. His street smarts told him he was being invited to have drinks with a cobra and, no matter how nice it started, the guy was still a snake . . .

The Agent continued. "We've had other agents speak to your friends who were involved in this street incident—apparently, one of these fellows still walks with a cane. The other was just discharged from the hospital with multiple fractures to his right arm." He smiled. "I understand you experienced only a temporary loss of the use of your arm—of course, there must be residual soreness and bruising. Everything considered, it appears as though you came out of this encounter the lucky one."

Leon listened as the Agent leaned forward, resting his elbow on the table. "Except, of course, this fellow . . . Tag. Did anything happen to him?"

Leon's first reaction was to present an aura of bravado—macho bullshit—even if it were false. However, recalling his first encounter with these SCF goons, he answered truthfully. "Unfortunately, I don't think any of us really touched this guy—he moved like a cat, and in ways I've never seen before. It was over in seconds . . ."

The Senior Agent considered his answer. "Thanks for the honesty about that—we can get into the specifics later. I understand your buddies said you knew the girl involved in this—is that correct?"

Leon nodded. "Yeah, I've seen her around."

"Come on, Leon! They said you have a thing going for her. Tell me about that . . ."

"Well, she's hot and everything, but I didn't get too far on the social side of things, if you get what I mean."

The Agent couldn't control a smirk. "Well, that sometimes happens even to the best of us." Enough of the pleasantries—it was time to get down to business. "What I need from you, Leon, are more details about Rose Talbot.

You are going to help me find her."

Leon sat back in his chair. *I really don't want to do anything to hurt her. How am I going to get around this?*

****

The medium height, slimly built man moved with a distinct grace from his seat across the room to answer the activated COM-link call chirping away on the finely crafted wooden table.

"Traveler here. My companions and I are outside the city limits, just west of you."

"How many?"

"Three of us altogether—we're traveling in an older motor vehicle."

"That's fine. Here's how to get to me . . ."

Claire disconnected the COM-link and passed the information to Tag who was taking his turn at the wheel.

CHAPTER TWENTY-ONE

She was worried about him. He ate little, slept less, and seemed to work all the time—he was definitely getting rough around the edges. Jackie looked at Lego sprawled on the floor, figuring he was all she had for company for the time being. "I guess it's just you and me, kid!" But, like Kyle, the dog wasn't the same since Tag took a powder.

For Kyle, his two most important questions regarded Tag's disappearance—did the portal occur naturally, or was it artificially created? In his mind, the difference between the two led to a divergence in his calculations at a certain point. *Maybe I should sleep on it*, he thought as he rubbed his tired eyes. *Sleep—there's an interesting concept. Maybe, I should get some of that.* Kyle pushed away from his desk, placed his head between his legs to stretch his back, and held that position for several seconds. If he hadn't heard chaos in the kitchen, it was a good bet he would tackle the problem at hand again without taking any sort of break, let alone a nap. But, since he had no clue about what was happening outside of his study, he figured he should check on the noise to be on the safe side.

He ambled down the hallway and stood at the entrance to the kitchen, watching Jackie fend off Lego's mock attacks. She sat on the floor, arms outstretched, Lego, running circles around her—both were happily involved in playtime. Realizing Kyle was watching they suddenly stopped, and Lego, still wired from his playtime, bounded over to his owner, nearly knocking him off his feet. It was just what Kyle needed—he spent a few minutes roughhousing with the dog, and he could feel his tension relax. He laid by Lego on the kitchen floor, and looked at Jackie.

"Sorry if I were putting you on ignore—I get a little involved with things, sometimes."

"Seriously, I didn't notice—I actually came over to see Lego!"

Kyle smiled, got up, and pulled her into an embrace. Delighted at the attention, she pulled back and looked him in the eye. "Hmmm—what else can I do to distract you?"

"I'm not sure, but maybe a little experimentation is in order . . ."

****

The SCF Technical Division Communications Team National Headquarters was in Chicago, and one of its primary functions was to facilitate and coordinate SCF communications—in every and all formats—nationally and internationally. Another was to monitor all private calls—a tremendous endeavor made possible by the dedication of a massive amount of computer power as well as a significant human presence. An offshoot of the organization was a small group tasked with the objective of intercepting unauthorized private communications, tracing their origins, and directing investigators to apprehend the individuals responsible.

One of the members of this group was tracking COM-link calls originating in the Midwestern region. He could identify recent calls within the Durango City area, from there to Wichita, and in the Kansas City region—but they were shielded, which prevented a direct intercept so he could eavesdrop. The best he could do was identify a private call was being made, the duration of the call, and its general location—most of which he concluded within a few seconds. There was an anomaly, though—a much longer call occurred within the last forty-eight hours, from Durango City to New York City. Since he had little else to go on, he decided to follow that trail to see if the pattern of calls continued moving eastward. *Maybe there's someone moving in that direction who shouldn't be—this could be entertaining to find out!*

****

Trying to locate their new contact in Kansas City was a tad more complicated than their last experience. Driving in from the west, they had to pass through Wichita to the eastern outskirts to easily locate Seth's home—in Kansas City, they had to locate a building in the center of the city, south of the confluence of the Kansas and Missouri rivers. Their target location was four stories high, constructed with a stonework material, and topped with a combination of gardens and solar energy equipment—obviously a multi-tenant structure. It resembled condominiums in Tag's world, but there were slight, subtle differences.

Tag expertly parallel parked their vehicle under a tree at the corner instead of right in front of the building. It would offer some cover, as well as keep the internal temperature of the car at acceptable levels. He checked the directions as they approached the building—their contact was in Suite 422. Rose activated the appropriate call button and, within moments, a male face appeared on a small security screen embedded in the wall at eye level.

The individual studied them carefully. "Traveling eastward, I presume?"

Claire smiled. "That seems to be the most desirable way to go, at the moment."

"I agree. Please, come in." The buzzer sounded on the security door, unlocking it.

The elevator was dynamic, modern, and silent. *Faster, too,* Tag thought as they exited on the fourth floor.

"Suite 422 . . . this way." Rose turned left from the elevator, past a vending machine illuminated in soft, blue light. One more turn, and they stood in front of their next benefactor's door. Tag knocked, and a forty something male with sandy colored, thinning hair and stylish glasses answered the door immediately. As he stepped aside allowing them to enter, Tag and Rose noticed the man had to look up to make eye contact.

As they proceeded into the main room of the suite, they marveled at the style and ambiance of the space. Fine woods blended together, contrasting beautifully with selected metals set upon a colorful, etched concrete-like floor. Incredible pieces of art adorned the walls without being gaudy, and effective overhead lighting highlighted the room's features. Cool air refreshed the room without a trace of a breeze. Together, they created an aura of unexpected tranquility.

"This is very nice!" Claire looked at the ceiling as if trying to locate the source of the cleansing air.

"Thank you—I find it comfortable." He moved toward them, extending his hand. "I'm Bennett, by the way."

They finished the round of introductions, and he led them into the kitchen that was stylishly outfitted and in keeping with the main living space.

"I assume young people would be famished at this hour—or, properly stated, at any hour." They laughed, agreeing with his supposition.

"Good—let's get to work to see what we can come up with!" Bennett doled out culinary tasks which resulted in one of the finest meals any of the Travelers encountered in quite some time.

After making sure everything was clean and in its place after dinner, the Travelers and their host settled in the main room, each claiming a comfortable chair. During dinner prep, they learned Bennett was a multi-talented, energetic, and task-driven individual. Combine that with an obvious high intellectual capacity and a lively social streak, and the result was a unique personality.

"Obviously, I know all of you need to head further east without our wonderful authoritative trolls knowing about it." He caught the eye of each in turn, and continued. "What we need to ensure is your arriving at your next destination safely."

Tag nodded. "So far, we've encountered no real problems in our travels all of the way from . . ."

Bennett held up his hand, halting him. "Stop, cease, and desist! It's best if I don't know your place of origin, or your ultimate destination. My part is to only know where your last stop was, and where your next one will be. In that way, if for any reason, I am compelled to disclose information about you, I will have a very limited ability to enlighten them about your quest."

"Makes sense," Claire agreed. "We appreciate all you're doing for us—and, the risks taken in doing so."

Bennett nodded his acknowledgment, retreating into what seemed to be distant thought. After a time, he looked up at each of them and, in a saddened tone, shared, "Not too long ago, a close relative of mine was taken by the SCF, never to be heard from again . . ." He paused for a few moments, then continued. "If I can help prevent something like that happening again, why would I not bend my will in that regard?"

The room fell silent as none of them needed to answer his rhetorical question.

"Do you have any other family living with you?" Rose asked.

"No—I live alone. I was married once, divorced, and no children. Besides, in my present state of affairs, I enjoy the company of an extensive association of ladies . . ."

Rose laughed, and added, "Good for you! Now I understand the motivation for your being such a sharp dresser."

Bennett grinned. "One does what one must."

Despite the pleasant conversation, he changed gears, pointing out, "We need to focus on getting you to your next destination tomorrow. Here's the plan . . ."

****

The interrogation lasted almost two and a half hours. The Senior Agent recycled the same questions, most of them inconsequential. The bottom line was Leon didn't produce any meaningful answers concerning Rose. The truth of it was he didn't have anything much to add to what they already knew. As he sat in front of the Agents, he thought of his so-called buddies coughing up information about him. *I'll have to visit those clowns, and have a talk with each of them when I get out of here,* he promised himself.

The SCF Agent seemed to be winding down on the questions. *Thank God,* Leon thought. *They have everything they need from me—that should be it.* The Senior Agent stopped talking, examining Leon as though he were analyzing some device, looking for flaws.

"I'm going to leave the room for a few minutes," he advised, producing a tight smile. "My associate will keep you company." Once clear of the interrogation room he strode down the corridor, activating a number on his COM-link, connecting with his immediate Superior.

"I just finished with this Leon Church character—I don't think there's anything left to get out of him."

"What do you think about his version of events concerning the assault situation?" The voice on the other end was calculating, and unemotional.

"Well, it's unlikely this Tag individual jumped these three stalwart members of society just for the hell of it."

"Do I recall correctly that you indicated Leon is a known bad actor?"

The Senior Agent paused to consider his response. "He hasn't been into anything serious before—but, we were aware of him, and did track some of his previous activities."

The voice paused. "What do you want me to do with him?"

"Do you think he has much to add to society?"

"Do what's appropriate . . ."

The Senior Agent ended the call. He went back to the interrogation room, accompanied by a guard of the Keeper Division. He looked briefly at Leon, who was relaxed in his chair by the table.

"Well Leon, it appears we're all done for now. This guard will take you back."

Thrilled he was done, Leon hopped up, and walked by the Senior Agent standing by the door to join up with the guard waiting in the corridor. As he passed his Interrogator, Leon felt it was odd the Senior Agent didn't attempt to make eye contact with him, but he didn't give it another thought.

Within minutes, they were back to familiar territory. Leon began to slow his walk, anticipating the guard's placing him in his usual cell. Just then, the heavy steel door at the end of the corridor labeled Eliminator Division, opened. Strong fingers gripped Leon's arm, propelling him forward toward the open door.

Stunned, Leon had no will to resist.

CHAPTER TWENTY-TWO

The door chime sounded, and Monique was up a second later, activating a security screen embedded in the wall beside the doorway—a man and a woman stood outside. She recognized them instantly, and called to her husband. "Wes—it's the Talbots!"

As Monique answered the door, Lori Talbot was the first to speak. "I'm sorry we came unannounced at this time of the evening . . ."

"Nonsense, please come in."

Monique showed them to the living room, inviting them to sit on the couch. "We expected you sooner or later . . ."

"We just arrived from a quick vacation to San Diego—as soon as the SCF paid us a visit, we knew we had to come home immediately."

Before Lori could continue, Wesley joined them. "We're glad you came . . ."

The Talbots and Booths met a number of times over the years, usually associated with school functions involving Rose and Claire. Occasionally, they bumped into one of them, but, given Durango City wasn't that large a place, it wasn't as often as one might think.

Lori continued. "We know they're investigating Rose and Claire, but they're also looking for someone named Tag. Who's he?"

Nathan picked up where his wife left off. "We stopped at home first, and Rose wasn't there—no note. No nothing."

Wesley Booth leaned forward in his chair. "Most important, Rose is all right—she's with Claire, and this fellow, Tag. Certain events occurred that required the three of them to leave Durango City—we know roughly where they are, and we know where they're going."

Lori and Nathan exchanged a troubled glance and turned back to the Booths, waiting for more information.

Monique smiled. "You'll understand the situation better if I start at the beginning, and explain how all of this developed. Apparently, Rose met Tag, and they were proceeding to . . ."

****

After leaving the Booth's, Lori and Nathan spent considerable time rehashing their daughter's circumstances—eventually, they tried to sleep, fitful as it was.

The kids woke them early the following morning. The

doorbell chimed as Lori was cleaning up after breakfast, while Nathan attempted to get his young offspring into suitable clothes for the day. Since they weren't expecting anyone to visit, he activated the security screen, observing two men standing on the doorstep.

"It's the SCF at the front door!"

"Shit! Don't these creeps have anything better to do?" Lori wished the whole thing would go away, and she would have her daughter home.

Nathan opened the door, and the Senior Agent started things off. "I presume you are Lori and Nathan Talbot?"

They nodded.

"We're here to discuss your daughter, Rose."

They stepped onto the front porch, both subconsciously barring the entrance to their family and home.

"Perhaps it's best if we discuss this inside?"

"It seems to be a pretty nice day out—we'll be fine talking to you out here," Wesley commented. He looked around the quiet neighborhood, then up at the sky as he answered the Agent's question that was really a statement. In the usual course of events, an SCF official made a suggestion and the normally placid civilian followed it. Not so with Wesley Talbot. The Senior Agent decided to let Talbot's insolence pass—however, since he sought information from them, engaging in verbal confrontation could be counterproductive.

"That's fine." The Agent glanced at the sky. "I agree— it's a delightful day." He lost no time launching his primary question. "Is your daughter Rose at home?"

"Actually, no she isn't." Her tone friendly, Lori was playing the game well.

"Where is she?"

"We haven't the foggiest."

"That's a little odd, don't you think?"

Nathan looked squarely at the Agents. "Not at all—Rose is an adult, and virtually comes and goes as she pleases."

Not to be dissuaded, the Senior Agent pointed out, "We are aware you cut your vacation short, and traveled back from San Diego yesterday."

Following her husband's lead, Lori looked him directly in the eye. "Yes we did—that was in response to your San Diego Agents suggesting she was missing! As responsible parents, we came back to find out what was going on!"

"Well, what did you find out?"

"We got here last night, and Rose wasn't here. She may be off with friends, but we're not sure."

"Speaking of friends—Rose has a friend named Claire Booth. Do you know where she is?"

Nathan gave them a surprised look. "No—why should we?"

"That's fair enough. Have you tried reaching Rose on her COM-link?"

"Of course, that's one of the first things we did. She didn't answer."

"Don't you think that strange?"

"Not at all—young people often get involved with whatever they're doing, and forget to turn it on."

Time to change topics. "Do either of you know a young man named Tag?"

"We never heard of that individual until your Agents in San Diego mentioned that name." It was the truth, and the Agent knew it.

"We're looking for this Tag fellow. As part of our investigation, we need to speak with Rose as well as Claire Booth—who is also missing."

"Is Claire missing? Or, is it a situation where you don't know where she is?" Lori's comment was barbed with condemnation.

The Agent studied her carefully. "We're not sure at this point—her parents said she's off camping with friends." Deciding it was possible they didn't know where their daughter was, he added, "If you find out where your daughter is, give us a call at this number." He handed them a standard card with the COM-link number of the SCF Detachment.

"Yes, we can do that," Nathan assured them.

They watched the Agents walk down to their vehicle. "I'd like to talk to the Booths again, Lori suggested. "Maybe they know how to get in touch with Rose and Claire."

Her husband agreed. "Let's walk—that way, those clowns can't track our vehicle."

****

Fifteen minutes later, when Wesley Booth opened the door he saw Lori and Nathan standing on his front porch. "I thought I'd see both of you today!" His greeting was warm and welcoming. "You probably have some loose ends to tie up." He shook hands with both as he gestured for them to enter the house.

Monique was in the middle of preparing brunch for herself and Wesley, and when she heard voices, she poked her head around the corner of the kitchen. As soon as Monique saw Lori standing next to Nathan, she went directly over to her, enfolding Rose's mom in a sustained, warm embrace. Caught off guard at first, Lori quickly relaxed and soon felt a virtual transference of energy and strength from this remarkable woman.

Tranquility began to overshadow anxiety.

The men stood back observing, Monique's warm hug seeming to draw the four of them closer together in their common cause. Monique placed a hand on Nathan's shoulder and said, "Why don't you come into the kitchen— I already fixed something to eat."

"We don't want to intrude if you're about to eat."

"Don't be absurd! What are you going to do? Stand on our doorstep until we finish eating?" She took Lori and Nathan by the arm, gently propelling them toward the kitchen. "C'mon—we have lots to eat, and more to talk about . . ."

****

Because the day's trip was shorter, the Travelers left

Kansas City by midmorning, hoping to arrive in St. Louis by midafternoon. Bennett insisted on preparing breakfast as an appropriate commemoration of their brief stay with him, a steppingstone to their ultimate destination. They shook hands as their farewell, but it was overlaid with Bennett's considerable emotion likely in remembrance of his missing relative who also was at odds with the authorities.

They parted with heartfelt thanks, and Claire climbed in behind the wheel as her private COM-link chirped. "Can you get that?" she asked Tag. She motioned to the unit on the vehicle's console.

He nodded. "Hello."

Lori Talbot gasped at hearing the young, deep, male voice answering her call.

Tag repeated his greeting. "Hello. Is anyone there?"

"Is this Tag?" Lori quickly recovered, figuring the man's voice was the mysterious friend of their daughter.

"Yes, this is Tag. Who's calling?"

"It's Lori Talbot—Rose's mom."

Her voice reminded him of his mother's, somehow sounding familiar, and he was immediately at ease talking with her. "It's nice to hear from you, Mrs. Talbot! I'm with Claire and Rose and, I assure you, everything is fine on our end."

As she listened, Lori knew the truth of the stranger's words—she could rely on them. "Thanks for that—it does ease my mind."

"Okay—I know you didn't call to talk to me, so I'll put Rose on."

"Thanks, Tag."

He reached into the rear left seat, handing the COM-link to Rose. "It's Mommy calling!" Lori smiled at the comment directed to her daughter, his affection apparent.

Rose grabbed the COM-link. "Hi Mom!"

Those words were all Lori needed.

****

The SCF Technician in the Chicago Detachment Intercept Team monitored a shielded call on a hand-held COM-link just outside of Kansas City, moving eastward. He couldn't understand words since he received only a static filled, garbled sound. On the upside, however, he could still estimate the approximate location in the Kansas City region by satellite triangulation without identifier chip involvement. The other end of the communication was based in Durango City.

It lasted twenty three minutes and fifty seven seconds.

Next time, he thought as he contemplated refinements to enable a successful intercept of a conversation the next time they used it. *Next time . . .*

****

Despite his poor upbringing—parental neglect, physical abuse, emotional detachments—he never felt as low as he did at that moment. Leon sat on a ruggedly constructed wooden chair, his head hanging low. His world collapsed to living in an eight foot square enclosure with a stone-like floor, block walls, and metal bars. No one spoke. Other detainees occupied surrounding cells and, periodically, guards walked the corridor. The atmosphere was like a weighted blanket trying its best to smother the occupants.

Hope was a concept that wasn't going to be on his itinerary.

His mind grappled with putting two coherent thoughts together in proper sequence—right then, the only cognitive function Leon could perform was to stare at the floor.

****

Although she was a strong-willed, independent young woman, Rose still felt a considerable sense of relief after talking to her mother. She was concerned, and felt guilty with the knowledge her parents were out of the loop regarding her whereabouts. Obviously, the Booths filled in the blanks as to their situation because Rose was careful not to leave written or electronic messages that could be intercepted by the authorities.

"It's so nice to be able to touch base with home to let them know I'm okay!" Moments after her words escaped her lips she noticed Tag wince, immediately regretting her thoughtlessness.

She leaned forward from the backseat, her hand on his shoulder. "Tag, I am so sorry—I blurted it out without thinking."

He turned in his seat to look at her—tears welled, and she struggled to hold them back.

He placed his hand on hers. "Hey—it's okay. I'm glad you could talk to your Mom. Just because I can't contact my brother right now, that doesn't mean you shouldn't talk to your family." She nodded understanding as more tears fell. She looked away, without saying anything, leaving her hand under his.

Eyes on the road, Claire kept driving.

****

The beautiful weather seemed to brighten as Lori walked with Monique from where she placed the call to Rose on the shielded, hand-held COM-link. Her preference was to have Rose standing before her available for a hug, but, knowing that wasn't possible, Lori drew comfort from talking to her daughter. Monique was with her so she, too, had an opportunity to speak briefly with her daughter. However, she couldn't escape a niggling thought. *The call was too long! Did we needlessly expose them to discovery simply to alleviate our worry?* She glanced at Lori, hoping she didn't see her apprehension.

****

The SCF Intercept Team Member in Chicago replayed the garbled transmission repeatedly, searching for a way to crack the security that was shielding the call. *Whoever designed the set up certainly knew what he was doing,* he

thought. *But, that's what makes this an interesting challenge
. . .* the fact he could zero in closer on the location of each
end of the call was encouraging, despite an attempt to
disguise the information. He knew if he could break that
part of the security, the rest would eventually follow.

A stickler for bureaucratic protocols, the Intercept
Team Member created a detailed report outlining his
recent findings, as well as his planned assault on the
security embedded in the transmissions. A segment of the
report was an estimate of the location for each participant
of the call—at one end, the caller was stationary within a
described six block radius in Durango City. At the other,
the participant was moving eastward on a major highway
between Kansas City and St. Louis.

He carefully reviewed his report, making several
modifications before deeming it satisfactory. Satisfied, he
entered the information into the system, sending a copy to
his immediate Superior.

****

Sitting in his office at the Durango City SCF
Detachment, Joshua wheeled over to his computer to take
a look—he rigged the alarm to go off when his computer
detected any record in the SCF system referring to the key
words 'Durango City' and 'intercept,' as well as 'shielded,' or
'encrypted' calls in any combination. Something triggered
the alarm and, as he read through the report of the Chicago
Intercept Team, his normally ruddy complexion paled
significantly. The report's description of the six-block
radius of the intercepted call in Durango City encompassed
the Booth residence.

Joshua initiated a call on his private COM-link, activating a special jamming device, and impatiently waited for someone to pick up the call on the other end. When the connection made a distinctive click, his voice was measured and urgent.

"Auntie, you have a problem . . ."

****

While their wives went off to place their call to the girls, Wesley and Nathan held down the fort at the Booth home. Because they didn't really know each other, initially they felt awkward as they each sat without their respective spouses. Both men were used to their wives as dynamic forces, initiating and carrying the conversation on whatever topic was at hand. Now, on their own, they discovered they were similar, and it didn't take long to immerse themselves in the conversation consisting mostly of their daughters' situation. Each silently acknowledged the benefit of a common cause uniting them as allies.

As their discussion unfolded, the men realized there was a definite advantage to their working together and, as soon as the women walked in the door, each husband felt the elevated tension in his wife.

"I just received a call from my contact in the SCF," Monique explained. For security reasons, she felt it prudent to protect her nephew's identity and position. "Apparently, the call we placed a few minutes ago to the girls was reported by an Intercept Team in the SCF system."

Both men edged forward in their chairs.

"The good news is the contents of the conversation as well as our identities remain unknown to them. The bad news, which really sucks by the way, is the SCF targeted a six-block radius, including here, for our end of the call. And, they know the general vicinity of the girls and Tag— they're a moving target."

"Are the girls safe?" Rose was Nathan's first priority.

"They should be okay for now. The SCF will likely know they're traveling by motor vehicle, and on which roadway. However, they wouldn't know which vehicle—it isn't registered in a name tied to our family."

Things were quiet for a few minutes as everyone thought it through. Finally, Lori asked, "If this whole assault thing happened because Tag was defending Rose, can't we straighten this out with the authorities as a simple self-defense situation?"

Monique looked at her husband for confirmation that it was time to fill in the last blank in the story. Wesley Booth understood the silent inquiry from his wife, nodding his consent to fill the Talbots in on everything.

"There is a complicating factor to this circumstance. Apparently, Tag isn't from here . . ." Monique and Wesley divulged everything about Tag. His hike. The portal. His journey.

"Are the girls safe with him?" Nathan asked.

Lori looked at her husband. "I talked to him briefly— he seemed responsible."

"But, we don't know anything about him—what he's like, or capable of . . ."

"Rose and I talked for a considerable time—she described what they were doing and how things were working out. Part of that discussion was about Tag."

"That may be true, but we don't know how they think and act, or what they consider normal behavior in his world."

Lori studied her husband for a few moments. "Nathan, she likes Tag—she trusts him!"

"Did she come out and say it in those words?"

"She didn't have to spell it out—I could tell by the way she talked about him."

"We talked to Claire at length about Tag before she left, and this situation," Monique added. "She's nobody's fool, and her opinion is that Tag is a solid and reliable person who needs our help."

"Given the information from our informant at the SCF that our communications are less secure, we must severely limit contact with the girls and our network." Wesley found the information about the SCF's intercepting their calls on the scrambled COM-link particularly disturbing.

"How will we know what's happening, and if they're okay?" Lori asked.

Nathan could hear the stress in his wife's voice. "We won't know until they reach the end of their journey . . ."

The parents sat quietly, each calculating various permutations of how their children's journey might unfold.

And, end.

CHAPTER TWENTY-THREE

The COM-link call ended, and he placed the receiver back in its cradle. The heads up by the New York City contact was moderately alarming, the conversation terse and one-sided.

Their shielded COM-link, so comforting and reliable in the past, was on the cusp of being breached by the SCF Intercept Team. Long-term, this was bad enough—the immediate problem facing Vernon was the previous call from Kansas City advising the Travelers were en route to him. His contact number was in their possession and they would be calling soon, but it was logical to assume—since he just learned moments ago about the COM-link security breach—the Travelers had no idea their pending call placed all of them in potential danger.

He paced back and forth, chewing on the obvious dilemma, finally realizing there wasn't a damn thing he could do to prevent their calling him. He certainly couldn't avoid the call, leaving them hanging—therefore, he needed to keep the conversation brief. Extremely brief. He had to hedge details regarding physical contact in vague terms based on the assumption others may be listening. The trick was to direct them toward a neutral meeting place, away from his residence, using obscure terminology. Nonetheless, he was confident in his skills, and he wished his adversaries luck—they'd need it as they sleuthed out his concoction of blended clues.

All he needed to do was plan . . .

****

Monique and Wesley sat together in the kitchen sharing a midafternoon snack. The Talbots left an hour earlier hoping the Booths didn't overstate the case when they assured Rose's parents everything would be all right. As soon as they left, Wesley grabbed his hand-held COM-link and bicycled for half an hour, placing distance from their residence before calling Nelson in New York City. He wasted no time, quickly describing their security problem. He biked back, hoping no one noticed his making the call.

"Have we done the right thing?" Monique was first to break the silence.

"You mean sending them eastward? I think so. Staying here wasn't an option, and where else would they go other than to Nelson?"

"I know—it's just they have so few choices. In effect, they're being herded toward an uncertain future." Monique did her best to manage a wan smile.

"Yup—unfortunately, that's the way it works."

****

It was Tag's turn to drive. Rose sat beside him, Claire in the back seat with the COM-link next to her when the call came in.

"Don't speak. When you make your next call, be ready to write down directions—the security of these COM-links is about to be breached!"

The call terminated.

Claire stared at the handset, processing the information she just received. Rose turned to look back at her friend, wondering why there was no conversation on their end of the call.

Claire stared at Rose. "I'm not sure who that was, but, we have a problem!"

Tag made eye contact with Claire in the rear view mirror. "Apparently, the COM-link shielding we're using is about to be penetrated."

Rose remained silent, trying to absorb the situation.

"The caller told us to be ready to write down directions when we call our next contact." Everyone in the vehicle was quiet, sorting through the ramifications of the new development which would undoubtedly affect the rest of their trip.

They pulled off at a rest stop by one of the tiny, one street hamlets dotted along the main highway between Kansas City and St. Louis. Tag killed the engine, Claire set the COM-link to speaker mode, and Rose sat poised with pen and paper—all acutely aware of the significance of this particular call.

Claire punched in the number Bennett gave them to contact the person at their next stop on their trek eastward.

"Yes."

"It's your guests who are about to arrive." She knew enough to keep things as vague as possible.

"Are you ready to receive directions?"

"Affirmative."

The well-modulated, male voice continued, "I will only say this once."

"Understood."

"Okay. I assume you came by the most swift, direct route from your last stopover?" Vernon needed to confirm the highway they were on in order to orient them properly, relay his planned sequence of directions, and get them to the destination he chose for them.

"That's correct."

As expected, they came on the main highway linking Kansas City and St. Louis. "Starting from the point where you will be over untroubled liquid, all directions flow from there." *If they don't figure that one out, they're screwed!*

Rose wrote furiously as Claire manned the COM-link. Tag looked at a detailed map of St. Louis he found in the well-stocked box in the trunk containing maps of most major cities in the country. His finger traced their route, extending along the highway into metropolitan St. Louis—over the Mississippi River, something clicked.

"Is a musical duo, Simon and Garfunkel, known here?" he whispered to Rose.

Rose nodded.

"He has to be referencing their song, "A Bridge Over Troubled Waters." He held up the map for the others to see, tapping his finger on the spot where their highway had a bridge crossing over the Mississippi River.

"Roger the starting point." Claire acknowledged.

Vernon mentally scored a point in their favor, then continued. "Excellent—now count backwards the number of intersections matching the number of people in your vehicle. Stay on the same roadway, and proceed in the opposite direction for the number of intersections equal to the letters contained in the name of the place you last slept." His contact advised him of how many there were, as well as their last location.

Tag traced back three intersections from the bridge, then eastward on the roadway for the distance of ten intersections—equal to the number of letters in Kansas City. He tapped the spot for Claire to see.

"Check."

"Great." After a few more turns, Vernon concluded. "That should put you at the top of the geometric figure, and I'll meet you there. I'll be attired to match one of your monikers! See you there."

The call terminated.

Tag pointed to the map, indicating a circular roadway contained within Forest Park in central St. Louis. "What's with the last comment?"

"Her moniker. Her name means red—that's the color this guy will be wearing . . ." Again, Claire knew exactly what to say.

****

In Chicago, the SCF Intercept Team Member had a choice of three different calls to work on—a shielded transmission from a hand held in Durango City to New York City. Again, he had the approximate location of the Durango City call, but, not a clue about the location in New York City. And, the content of that call remained a mystery. The most promising development consisted of two calls to a single hand-held COM-link located in St. Louis. The initial call recorded, although brief, its source remained elusive.

The second, longer call was developing nicely—he broke through parts of the conversation which seemed to be a series of directions from one of the participants to the other, their discussion relating to intersections and movement within that city. It sounded as if they were orchestrating a meeting, its whereabouts unknown due to the vagueness of the riddle-like conversation. Both parties were on a hand-held, one on the outskirts of the city, the other located deep within the metro. *If I can unravel the rest of that call, perhaps I can decipher the location of the meeting,* he thought. *The St. Louis, SCF Detachment needs a reaction team on standby . . .*

He composed a concise report directed to that office, eager to get back to the actual intercept puzzle. The last transmission was the least likely to bear fruit—this one, however, was different. It wasn't simply a shielded call—it was a jammed call, and no part of the call recorded. What made it interesting was its location was easier to source—a two block area within Durango City. *Someone,* he thought, *has a lot of balls, conducting these illegal transmissions right under the noses of the authorities.* He delegated that one to the back burner, making a mental note to report it to Detachment.

****

They parked the vehicle beside giant elm trees—people were on their own personal missions on foot and in vehicles, and it was critical the Travelers remain as inconspicuous as possible. By silent agreement, they watched the area for ten minutes, unwilling to leave the safety of their vehicle until they determined the area appeared safe.

Tag spotted him walking out of a thick stand of trees—initially, he appeared to be an individual out for a casual stroll, enjoying the warm day in a beautiful park-like setting. He wore stylish and well made clothes, the dress shirt unbuttoned at the top, and long sleeves partially rolled up the forearm. The garment's color almost matched the hue of Rose's long hair.

He appeared casual, yet Tag noticed a furtiveness about him. "This has to be our guy . . ."

They got out and walked toward the man, each surveying the perimeter, scanning for anyone paying more than casual attention to them. As they approached, a flicker of recognition crossed the man's face as to who they likely were.

In his mid-forties, he was of average height and build,

his brown hair nicely styled. Claire formed an immediate impression of a person with emotional conflict, strong beliefs, and a tendency to be a loner. Obviously, from his cryptic directions in their COM-link conversation, he was a careful, intelligent person. She did, however, sense a dichotomy between compassion and intolerance when dealing with others.

He stopped within a few feet, studied them briefly, then diverted his attention to the surroundings scoping out potential threats. "Using our COM-links has suddenly become a liability," he warned. "I suggest turning yours off from this point on." Satisfied no one was surveilling them, he focused his attention directly on the Travelers. "Introductions are in order—but don't shake hands or do anything to indicate to others that we are meeting for the first time." Each Traveler nodded in agreement.

"I'm Vernon. I think from the brief description received from my Kansas City counterpart, it's easy for me to determine which of you happens to be Rose, and the other Claire." He looked at each as he spoke their names, correctly identifying them. "I'm going to give you the address of my home which is close by—for security purposes, give me a five-minute head start before following."

He waited until each of them acknowledged before continuing. "Normally, I'm not too obsessive about this sort of thing—however, the recently obtained knowledge that our shielded COM-link communications may possibly be breached has me apprehensive."

He looked off in the distance for a few seconds, then continued. "It's a sad state of affairs when individuals in our society have to resort to these measures to hide from the same authorities that are in place to allegedly protect us!" He handed Tag a slip of paper with the address, and walked toward his vehicle.

Vernon went about ten feet when he stopped, turned, and asked a question as if an afterthought. "Your next destination is Indianapolis, correct?"

"Yes." Rose was the first to answer his question.

He thought for a moment. "Who has a good memory?"

Without hesitation, each of them acknowledged.

"Good—I want to give you the contact information for your next stop." He paused for a moment, and continued, "Just in case . . ." He provided the pertinent information, finally adding, "Don't write that down—we have to protect that person's identity as best we can." Vernon turned, and headed to his vehicle. The three of them watched as he pulled away before heading to their vehicle, allowing him the five-minute lead before striking out to their next destination.

Vernon's residence was close, and they elected to park their vehicle around the corner from his street. "Let's leave our gear in the vehicle, and check out his place first," Tag suggested. There was something bugging him, but he couldn't quite figure it out.

They walked down the west side of the residential block, alone on the street. Tag was in the lead and, when they rounded the corner, he stopped short. He immediately put his hand out, motioning for them to back up around the corner. They carefully retraced their steps, each of them stunned at the scene before them. The street in front of their contact's residence was filled with SCF vehicles, flashing emergency lights, reflecting off windows of each house on the block. SCF Scout and Sentinel teams dispersed around the entryway to his building, and Vernon stood between two Agents, arms bound, and in the process of being placed in one of their vehicles.

Once around the corner and out of view of disaster, each of them turned, searching for an avenue of escape back to their vehicle. Standing before them was an SCF Sentinel Agent completing a sweep around the block. After a moment, recognition dawned on the face of the Agent. Suddenly, violent movement, and the Agent reached for his weapon.

Tag was a blur moving toward him.

CHAPTER TWENTY-FOUR

As much as he hated to admit it, if Tag's disappearance were due to a natural occurrence, the likelihood of someone's surviving the transportation was a rather dismal proposition—yet, somehow, he knew his brother survived. Therefore, it was a natural conclusion that the occurrence had to be an artificially created event. *So, working from that hypothesis, how in the hell did they pull it off?* Kyle figured however they accomplished it, they had to be smart—and, advanced—to create such a thing. *So, what will stop me from doing the same thing?* It was an interesting thought, but he had to trade his idea for reasonable expectations. *Well, if I'm not likely able to develop it myself, at least I should be able to figure out how it works.*

With that fervent hope, he at last drifted off to sleep.

****

Young, over six feet tall and sturdily built, the Agent drew his weapon, raising it into a firing position. Tag closed the distance between them, planted his weight on his left foot, right leg rising in a crescent kick. Just as the weapon reached the apex relative to the firing position, Tag slapped it out of the hand of the Agent. Surprised, but undeterred, the young Agent continued to move forward, balling his right hand into a fist which was partially numb from the force of the kick dislodging his weapon.

That's when he ran into the real trouble.

Tag recovered his balance from the kick by planting his right foot behind him, and in one fluid movement immediately launched a front kick with his left foot, connecting with the sternum of the still-advancing Agent. His forward progress stopped, the Agent was focused on breathing—Tag's blow knocked the air out of him.

He never even saw the next strike coming.

Tag moved his left foot in an exaggerated step toward his opponent to shorten the distance between them, and from a Zenkutsu Dachi (forward stance), executed a knife-hand strike, the right hand snapping around just before impact. The contact of Tag's rigid hand, four fingers held together with the thumb tucked under, created a solid surface impacting the left temple area of the Agent's head—unfortunately for the Agent, his head absorbed the pent up kinetic energy of the strike. The Sentinel Agent was motionless for a moment before his eyes dimmed—he folded, crumpling to the ground.

Traditionally used as a killing strike, Tag took a little force off the blow at the time of delivery. He knelt next to the unconscious man, checking the jugular vein in his neck. *Good—a steady pulse.* Tag quickly surveyed the street and the windows facing it for evidence of someone's witnessing the event. Thankfully, they seemed unobserved.

He looked at the girls who still stood transfixed by the violent action. Only a few seconds had passed from the initial encounter, but they had to get moving!

"Let's get him out of the open before someone comes," Tag urged.

Both girls grabbed a leg while Tag lifted him by the arms. Awkwardly, they managed to maneuver his limp body into an alleyway, placing him behind a garbage bin. Tag returned to retrieve the weapon from the street, handling it carefully with a piece of cloth in order to not leave his finger prints, placing it on top of the prone Agent. Without a word, they headed for their vehicle located further up the same street.

Rose drove, Claire was shotgun navigating them out of the city, and Tag was in the back seat, decompressing from the sudden, intense action. Claire gave directions after consulting the city and area maps, and Rose followed them without comment. Soon, they were out of St. Louis heading eastward on the major highway leading to their next planned destination—Indianapolis.

Forty-five minutes later, Claire broke the silence. "There's a lake just south of here—maybe we should find a good camping spot for the night. . ." Dusk on the horizon, enough light remained to make camp, but that was about it.

"Sounds like a plan," Tag agreed.

Within a short time they reached the lake and found a delightful location close to the water, sheltered by a grove of mature trees. Tag raised the tent and prepared the sleeping gear, while the gals worked on a fire and dinner preparations. It was only after dinner they were ready to discuss and deal with the aftermath of the events in the city.

"Okay—we just made history, and we very much need to move on." Acknowledging nods. "This does put the icing on the cake when it comes to the SCF jokers wanting to get their hands on us."

She looked at Tag. "You left the unlucky Agent in a condition where he will wake up, didn't you?"

"Other than a major headache and some vertigo for a while, he should be fine."

"Well, it could have been worse . . ." Claire paused for a few moments, considering the events, and how things could have gone the other way. "Tag?"

He looked at her.

"Thanks for saving our collective asses back there!" Claire thought it a testament to his good nature that he actually looked embarrassed by her comment.

Rose piped up. "Okay, we're nice and safe for now—however, where and how do we go from here?"

"We should carry on with the ultimate plan of getting to Claire's uncle in New York City. But, can we trust various contacts—from here on in—aren't compromised, as well?" To Tag, it made sense that if one contact knew about them—well, so did others.

"How do we contact him or her without putting all of us in danger?"

Claire picked up on Rose's concern. "We can't call on

our COM-link, but Vernon did give us the next helper's address—maybe we can make the initial contact a personal meeting. You know—face to face."

"We'd have to do it in a way to not freak her out," Tag added. The girls looked at him oddly.

"Freaked out—it means to be scared, or startled." They seemed to understand.

"Let's sleep on it, and deal with the issue in the morning when we're fresh and, hopefully, full of more ideas," Claire suggested. Everyone agreed, and they went about cleaning up dinner as well as getting ready to bed down for the night.

Sleep didn't come easily.

****

Working late, Joshua decided to check for internal SCF reports of interest before heading home for the evening. There were two of particular concern—the first was a report from St. Louis via Chicago, outlining the successful COM-link interception as well as subsequent apprehension of a prominent individual using shielded communications. Apparently, he organized a clandestine meeting with other individuals who weren't found.

Interestingly, a Sentinel Agent was found unconscious in an alleyway directly around the corner from the residence of the arrested individual who wasn't thought to be the person responsible for the attack. The SCF Agent was conscious, and in the hospital for observation.

Joshua knew Claire and her companions were moving

eastward—however, he wasn't privy to their route. It wasn't a giant leap to presume chances were good her group may have been involved. If so, he was pleased they avoided capture. Nonetheless, taking out a Sentinel Agent would have the SCF St. Louis Detachment flooding the area in a major sweep with all available manpower looking for the perpetrators. If they were smart, whoever caused the mess would clear the area immediately—or, hunker down in a safe haven.

The second report he reviewed was considerably more personal. Purportedly, the Chicago Intercept Team took notice of his jammed transmissions to his Auntie Monique, and were within a two-block radius of locating him. If he were the one looking at this, the fact the SCF Detachment Headquarters for Durango City was in the middle of that zone would be highly suspicious. He'd start his investigation there, and work outward. He could no longer trust his jamming apparatus so, if he needed to contact Monique, it had to be face-to-face in a secure setting. As he powered down his computer, Joshua thought it would be advantageous to drop by his Auntie's house for a 'social visit' on his way home.

****

Sitting in her kitchen cradling a cup of tea before bedtime, Monique was within easy reach of the shielded hand-held COM-link when it activated.

"Yes," she responded.

"They're still moving—there was a hiccup on the way, but everything's apparently good now." The male voice at the other end of the call was strong and deep.

"That's good."

"Don't use this line again, unless I call you!"

"Roger that."

The call terminated.

It was Nelson in New York City, calling her with an update. The news was mixed—the Travelers were still en route—which was good—but something clearly went wrong. It didn't help matters their safe COM-link no longer was breach-proof.

She poured the rest of her tea in the sink, and headed for bed. Hopefully, her husband was already nodding off— the new information would keep him awake.

CHAPTER TWENTY-FIVE

Vernon knew things he shouldn't divulge to the authorities. He was part of a network of individuals who chose to place themselves at the forefront of undermining and opposing the regime, despite the vast resources of their society created to suppress and control personal freedoms. Their numbers were limited—but, they were growing as more talented people reached a point of intolerance.

The paramilitary entity known as the Security Control Force presided over the local population in every country in their world, thereby achieving mastery of the masses. Vernon was aware of some of the insurgent network's regional cells, as well as the leadership of their cause based in New York City. But, that was it—he had limited contact information concerning the person, and he didn't know his or her identity. Most important, he knew people working within the core system penetrated the SCF at multiple levels. They believed, as he did, they must replace the current regime which was based on domination. He knew the three Travelers were extremely important, and one of them experienced an extraordinary event—it was critical that anyone knowing of the event keep it from the authorities. Now, they had him. He knew the SCF's drones would implement their ways, and eventually he would crack. Hopefully, the three young Travelers avoided detection and were on the next leg of their journey—but, he would never know.

Despite his success in life—wealth, position, and influence—it meant nothing in his current circumstance. He was simply captured prey to be feasted upon by his captors. *But, I can negate the beast! There's a way for the quarry to deny the hunter!* Vernon delighted in the ultimate deceit—for all of their poking and prodding, body cavity and clothing searches, they didn't discover his ultimate line of defense. As a Regional Leader, his superior determined Vernon should equip himself with a fall-back device to protect information should the authorities apprehend him.

The two Scout Agents sitting across the table from him thought it odd their captive was so relaxed. Neither could see Vernon's hands—he pressed the nail of his right thumb sharply down on the small implant situated below the skin in the fleshy part of the back of his left hand, between the thumb and forefinger. The tiny vial fractured releasing a potent liquid which leached into the surrounding tissue, easily penetrating the thin walled surrounding veins. The process would take fifteen to twenty minutes depending on a variety of factors, including activity level at the time. Since the Agents cuffed him to his chair, Vernon figured the finish line would be more toward the twenty-minute limit.

****

Tag lay awake for a time, rewinding the previous day's events like a videotape on a continuous loop. Even though his actions were instinctive with no time for planning or thought, when he examined the situation, he realized he would have done the same thing if given the chance to repeat it. Knowing that, he couldn't come up with a reason to agonize over the choice he made.

The sky was clear and the air was warming nicely— from the position of the sun, he estimated it was close to seven o'clock, and only chirping birds broke through the early-morning silence. He managed to get out of the tent without disturbing the girls and, as he stretched the hard ground from his bones, he carefully scrutinized the surrounding area. No one in sight. The lake was calm and undisturbed, except for a few ducks feeding close to the shoreline.

It was a good time for a bath, and a leisurely swim.

Tag was several hundred yards offshore when he noticed the girls reviving the fire. Not to repeat his last lake-bathing experience, he swam back to shore, quickly toweled off and dressed, and headed toward their campsite.

"Why don't you take a turn in the lake, while I fix us some breakfast?" They did and, after eating, they sat on the lake shore coffee in hand.

"What do you think they're going to do with Vernon?" Rose finally voiced their concern.

Tag looked at each of the girls. "I didn't grow up in your environment, but, from what I've seen so far, nothing good will come of this."

"Although we only had a brief meeting with Vernon, he struck me as a man of importance. If that's true, it won't matter—once the SCF has their hands on him, he's cooked, especially if they know anything about his clandestine activities." Claire's insights were, most likely, accurate.

"Can we do anything for him?" Tag asked.

"Not without drawing undue attention—the last thing we want is to join him."

"What will happen to him?"

Claire hesitated to answer Tag's question. "They'll squeeze him for information in very unpleasant ways and, once there's nothing left, he'll be thrown away with the garbage."

Tag couldn't believe what he just heard! "Isn't there anything in your legal system allowing him a defense and fair trial?"

"There's no system to help someone in his situation. Here, lawyers help with real estate and a few other mundane things—if the SCF snatches you, they spew out very few."

"What happens to the people they keep?"

She looked down at the campfire. "That's the thing—they don't keep them for long. There's a group within the SCF regime called the Eliminator Division—as far as I know, the name means what it says."

"In my world, there are millions of people held in jails and prisons serving time for crimes committed," Tag advised. "Many are life sentences."

"Not here. Here, prisons don't exist, and jails are part of the local SCF Detachments. Short term only. If arrested, they either send you to a rehab center for a short visit to straighten you out, or they decide to get rid of you.

Permanently."

It was his turn to stare at the campfire. After a few moments, he announced, "This place can really suck!"

Rose didn't like thinking about their society, especially since they could soon be in the hands and mercy of the very people they were discussing. "Okay—let's talk about our next step, and how we go forward. I think we should . . . "

****

Monique waited until both of them showered, dressed and were seated at the breakfast table before telling Wesley about her cryptic conversation with Nelson. "Then, I was just about to head to bed when my nephew, Joshua, showed up on our doorstep!"

Knowing Joshua's sensitive position at the SCF Detachment, Wesley was immediately on guard. "Is there any danger?"

"Not directly at us, for now—apparently, he uses a jamming device for his private calls. They're aware of it, but they haven't narrowed it down to him quite yet. He suggested future contacts with him be face-to-face, and to keep a low profile."

"Can he still provide us with information we need to know? Will he?"

"Knowing Joshua, he'll keep going even when he shouldn't be!"

****

The Travelers were on the road to Indianapolis after talking everything out, and they were guardedly optimistic as they continued their journey. Reality dictated they had no choice other than to make their Indianapolis contact— their vehicle would be nearly empty by the time they arrived, and they needed help in getting it refueled. If they did it themselves, they'd be a giant blip on the SCF radar. All they had, however, was the first name of their contact, and their only option was to find the place, and hope for the best. There was an intense discussion about how the initial meeting would take place, and the girls felt strongly that all three of them should be present. Tag thought just the opposite—he was adamant he should meet their contact alone to minimize risk to the girls until he deemed it safe.

Neither side was willing to concede.

Eventually, they reached an agreement. Insofar as Tag would be the initial point man, Rose and Claire would be within visual range of the meeting—from their vantage point, they could join Tag or flee to safety.

****

Lori Talbot moved her grocery cart through the store in a daze. She was so preoccupied with her daughter that she bypassed several items she needed. Finally, she ended up stopping in the middle of an aisle, stocked shelves forming ramparts on either side of her. Alone, it gave her room to breathe. She closed her eyes for a second, then looked down at the floor.

"Well—are you just going to stand there?"

Lost in her thoughts, Lori didn't hear anyone approach.

"Monique! I'm sorry—I seem a bit slow today."

Monique smiled, enfolding her in a comforting hug, and there were tears as Lori let her tightly-held emotions slip. Claire's mom allowed her friend to gather herself, placing a comforting arm around her shoulders.

"I'm sorry about that—it just slipped out." Lori reached for a tissue in her purse.

"Nonsense! We both love our daughters—you're still adjusting to what happened to Rose. Believe me, I went through it when I learned about Claire. I've just had a little more time to adjust, that's all."

Lori wiped away a remaining tear. "You're very kind. It's different talking about this with you rather than my husband."

"I know—try as they might, it's not the same."

"Well, it's lucky we ran into each other in the store!" Lori mustered a weak smile.

"Actually, I came here looking for you—Nathan told me you were grocery shopping." Monique took a moment to phrase things correctly. "The girls are just fine."

Picking up the signals, Lori interjected. "There's a 'but' in there somewhere."

"Yes—there was an incident in St. Louis which likely involved the girls and Tag. We learned the SCF intercepted one of their contacts—an Agent was hurt, but he's recovering."

Lori processed the information, wanting to ask Monique how she knew the details, but she knew she couldn't. "The girls are fine?"

"There's no report of their being spotted in this incident."

"Do we know where they are? Can we call them?"

"Our COM-link security was breached." Monique paused for Lori to understand the full weight of her statement. "So, we can't contact them without escalating the risk of their being detected by the SCF."

"How will we know if they're okay?" Lori's voice was timid with fear for her daughter.

"We won't know anything for a while—eventually, the information we need will get to us, but in a different way."

They looked at one another to see if they really believed that.

****

She closed and locked the front door, placing the key in a small pocket in her running shorts. Part way down the walkway she stopped, spending a few minutes stretching to loosen up before her run. In her early forties, she sported short black hair, angular facial features, and naturally full, red lips. She was slightly taller than average, and athletically built with strong, muscular legs.

She opened the front gate, pivoting to close and latch it. When she turned back toward the roadway, a young man stood in front of her. He was tall and well-built, and his size could easily have been menacing. However, his relaxed manner and the calm expression told her otherwise.

She carefully looked him up and down, her interest piqued. "I didn't hear you."

A faint smile crossed his face, as he shrugged. "Yeah, I tend to get that a lot." His voice was deeper and richer than she expected. Matching his smile with one of her own, she inquired, "And, you are standing in front of me, why?"

The young man looked slightly uncomfortable. "Well, if you look over my left shoulder to the opposite street corner, you'll see two girls standing there trying desperately to look occupied with something."

The woman stood on her toes and looked over his shoulder, observing a tall, redheaded gal standing next to a shorter, wavy haired girl—both looked everywhere, except at them.

"They're with me." Tag looked directly at her. "And, we're here to see you."

Instantly, she recognized the situation. "Travelers are you? Do you need help?"

Relieved, Tag replied, "If you're Dina, then yes we are, and absolutely we do!"

"Well, you certainly found the right lady! You better tell the girls to come on over before they hurt themselves trying not to look this way . . ."

Tag motioned to Rose and Claire to join him, and introductions followed. "My run can wait—the three of you are much more important. Follow me . . ." Dina noticed the exchange of glances, and the Travelers' obvious relief.

When they were comfortably seated around the kitchen table, Dina grinned. "My now deceased husband, bless him, and I never had children—but, I do understand your need to eat! I'll put something together, and you can feed to your hearts' content while I finish my run." Dina grabbed vegetables, cheese, and a huge carton of milk from the fridge, spreading them out on the counter close to a cutting board.

"Thanks—that will be great! We're famished!"

"What else do you need?"

"Our vehicle is just about out of fuel." For this leg of the trip, it was Claire's responsibility to monitor their fuel situation.

Dina understood their predicament. "And, you can't fill it without attracting unwanted attention from you know who . . ."

"Exactly."

"Not a problem—I'll finish my run, then take your vehicle for fueling." Dina held out her hand for the keys. "Where is it?"

"Thanks—you're a lifesaver!" Rose provided the location of the vehicle.

"I'm just about done here with the food. Once I return, we can talk about St. Louis, as well as where and how you go from here." Five minutes later, Dina was out the door and the Travelers feasted on a garden fresh summer meal.

They showered at the suggestion of their hostess, and all three were sparkling clean when Dina arrived home about an hour later. While the girls were in the bathroom,

Tag poked around the main floor of the beautifully finished, older home located in a mature area of Indianapolis. The floors were a dark, planked hardwood buffed to a muted shine, every room containing a finely crafted area rug, setting the tone for the decor in each space.

The main living area contained a large stone-faced, wood-burning fireplace, and on its mantelpiece were several photographs in stand-alone frames—all were of Dina and a man, and Tag concluded it was her late husband. Even in the confines of the photographs, Tag recognized the deep emotional connection between them. Throughout the room, the decorating exhibited an interest in religion.

"Yes, I have a very spiritual temperament," a voice behind him offered.

He turned to see Dina standing in the middle of the room. "You're pretty sneaky yourself," he commented. "I didn't hear a thing!"

"I'm working on it. C'mon—I can hear the girls coming downstairs. It's time for a game plan . . ."

CHAPTER TWENTY-SIX

I t was pure enjoyment watching him run full out without a care in the world. *If only we were able to set everything aside and do the same, life would be a lot simpler,* Kyle thought as Lego turned in a wide arc, targeted their position, and closed the distance between them in a surprisingly short time. At fifty feet, he downshifted to an easy, loping stride with enough tongue hanging out to give Gene Simmons a run for his money.

Kyle was relishing the day for it was a welcomed break from the grind of attempting to solve the riddle of his brother's disappearance. Jackie was an unassailable juggernaut by making him stop working, get out of the house, and join her for much needed R & R. In such a short time together, she could read him as easily as a tattered, well-loved novel.

She looked at him, then shoved him backward, landing on top of him.

"Stop thinking! Enjoy! Enjoy!"

****

Before answering the front door, Monique checked the security monitor. "Joshua!" She threw open the door and gave him a hug, ushering him across the threshold.

"Thanks, Auntie—I can't stay long. You should know the St. Louis contact whom the SCF apprehended yesterday somehow committed suicide while in custody—before revealing pertinent information."

Monique couldn't help but think about Claire and her friends. "Did this involve them? Were they captured, too?"

"No—there aren't reports of their being seen, or involved." Joshua paused as he considered another possibility. "If they were there, they got away clean."

In shock, Monique buckled and sat quickly on the couch, her hand covering her mouth.

"They're probably just fine right now—I'll let you know as soon as I hear anything else." He placed an encouraging hand on her shoulder.

Monique looked at him, recognizing a male version of herself, the family resemblance so strong he could have been her son. "Thanks, Joshua—for everything! You're a savior . . ."

****

Dina stood in front of a massive fireplace, knowing there was no way to candy coat what she had to say. After careful consideration, she chose the direct approach. "I just learned Vernon is gone—he checked himself out without revealing anything about you three. Or anything else, for that matter . . ."

The Travelers sat, stunned at the newest development. Yes, their contact with him was brief, but the enormity of losing him was an ominous thing.

"I pray for his memory, and soul," she continued. "I knew Vernon well—he was the Regional Controller of our movement for this part of the country." She took a moment to look at each of them directly. "And, I am second in command. With Vernon gone, his duties fall on me."

"How widespread is your organization?" Tag asked.

"It's bigger than you may think. Think about this—I just gave you an important piece of information about myself. If captured, and you reveal that knowledge to the authorities, I must follow Vernon's example, if apprehended."

Tag considered her words before replying. "I believe I can speak for all of us by stating we won't share your information with anyone outside of this room!"

Rose and Claire agreed. "No way it gets out—ever!"

Dina studied each of them. "I believe you. Please don't take this as condescending, but there is an unusual amount of grit and resolve in your character for people so young."

Tag glanced briefly at the girls. "A previous contact advised us to be extremely careful when sharing certain personal information about our situation." He looked at each of the girls, in turn. "You leave no doubt in our minds that telling you is the correct thing to do . . ." Both girls nodded their agreement.

Dina listened attentively, without interruption, her active mind scrambling to comprehend and adjust her known reality with the incredible experience Tag described.

"Wow!" It was all she could say. "Well, I've certainly heard some whoppers in my day, but that beats all!" She paused for effect, then continued. "Seriously, that's an incredible account—I admit, I wondered why you're passing from point to point in our system. Typically, if we have to move someone because of security issues in their area, we usually care for them by keeping them in the nearest adjacent major center."

She stopped for a moment to let them digest that information. "Tag—with your astounding situation, there is absolutely no way we can let the authorities—with their perverse Machiavellian mindset—get their hands on you. They must never acquire knowledge of your incredible experience. Trust me—they will examine you, quite unpleasantly, like a bug pinned on a tray. Further, they will attempt to isolate and use the phenomenon for nefarious purposes."

Dina's gaze bore into Tag. "It gets worse—if they remotely think you're somehow directly linked, or you can control the phenomenon . . . well, then you become an obvious threat to them." She paused, lowering her voice. "Then, you become expendable."

The Travelers considered their possible fates if they weren't careful.

Dina softened as she added, "Do you understand what I'm telling you?"

Tag met her look. "Yeah—from what I've seen so far, it doesn't surprise me, at all." Then, he grinned. "Well, I guess

I'll just have to continue being Mr. Invisible, won't I?"

****

The mid-level authority figures in any large bureaucracy are often in a tenuous situation, possessing power over a multitude of rank and file, stroking egos, and expecting its minions to obey every order. The system was dictatorial with a firm, controlling grip on its populace. They were, however, high enough up the chain of command that any error on their part was a shining beacon seen by those who carry the real power.

The Sub-Commander of the Intercept Division, SCF Chicago Detachment, was acutely aware of the dichotomy as he faced a similar situation. Seemingly unrelated reports told of an attack on an SCF Sentinel Agent, the apparent suicide of a person of interest who was under interrogation, as well as sightings of a young male person unknown to their system. Perhaps most disconcerting was the communication jamming centered around the SCF Durango City Detachment .

The first two incidents occurred in St. Louis within close proximity to each other, suggesting potential connections. An addendum reported the attack on the Sentinel, including the version of events from the recovering Agent, thereby hinting at a Durango City connection. Apparently, the physical description of the young male involved in the St. Louis altercation matched nicely with that of the young man observed by security cameras in Durango City—a ghost in their system.

The Sub-Commander considered the possibilities. *Do*

I commit SCF resources on a national scale to the search, apprehending, and prosecution of the ghost individual? If he's the same man, obviously he traveled eastward without our ability to track his movement. Will he stay put in St. Louis? Or, did he already move on?

He again reviewed the Durango City and St. Louis reports, noticing the descriptions of two young females accompanying the unidentified man. According to the Durango City report, they knew who they were—however, considering the suddenness of the attack on the Sentinel Agent in St. Louis, he didn't have enough time to get a description.

It's decision time—this is a big country with a large population, and the SCF resources aren't limitless. If I order a national dragnet for this individual, and it comes up empty— I'm in the deep end chained to a big rock! In his gut, he knew everything tied together. A bit of gambler, the Sub-Commander decided there's little point in having power if its use is steeped in fear.

He pulled the trigger.

****

Dina had them fueled, watered, and fed—all they needed was an address, and directions for their next contact. She grew fond of them during their time together, and she regretted their having to leave. "Columbus is a relatively short drive from here, so you should arrive in good time—your next link in the chain of travel is Adrienne." She handed Tag a small piece of paper, adding, "This is her address. Memorize it, and give it back to me—we don't want certain written information to get into the wrong hands."

Tag handed the information to Rose who glanced at it, and passed it on to Claire. "Will you be giving Adrienne a call to let her know we're coming?"

"That won't be necessary."

"Why?"

"Oh, she'll know you're arriving . . . Adrienne is an Intuitive. She will undoubtedly already know things about each of you without being told."

"That's just downright spooky!" Rose looked at Claire for confirmation of her comment.

Claire picked up the ball. "But, we're hours away from her in travel time—how does she know from that distance?"

"Pretty neat trick, don't you think!" Dina smiled, noticing their reactions.

Neat trick, maybe, but Tag was concerned about something else. "How do we protect our personal information from her?"

"You can't—however, once you meet her and learn a bit more about her nature, you won't feel as if you have to ask that question again!"

Tag knew enough about Dina to trust her judgment. "Well, this will undoubtedly prove interesting—I guess we'll be on our way. Thanks for all you've done for us!"

Dina brushed his outstretched hand aside, enfolding him in a farewell hug. Amazingly, he suddenly felt a definitive increase in energy and confidence which seemed to flow from the incredible woman. As she stepped away, she gave him a knowing look, acknowledging what passed between them. The same for the girls.

She stood at her gate, watching them pull away from the curb, wishing them well. As they rounded the corner, Tag turned to Claire. "When she hugged you, did you feel anything unusual?"

"Yup."

"Ditto," Rose piped up from the back seat.

"So far, the ladies on this trip are definitely proving to be a source of wonder!"

Another comment from the peanut gallery in the back seat. "The universe unfolds as it should!"

***

They arrived at the outskirts of Columbus by early afternoon, their library of maps continuing to be a treasure trove of information for finding their contacts' locations. Claire, riding shotgun, acted as navigator as they entered the depths of the city, the detailed map revealing four waterways running north and south within the city limits. Before crossing the westernmost river, she directed Tag to turn north for several miles before turning east again toward their destination which was on the east side of the second river system. Once crossed, she guided him south into a district composed of small acreages lining the riverside. They wended their way along narrow roadways, flanked by large, deciduous trees on each side, reaching out to intertwine their branches high above them.

Tag pulled over into an entryway equipped with a closed metal gate that offered no evident means of opening, or contacting the residents. It was odd—no security cameras, but just as they were discussing how to deal with the situation, the gate silently opened. Exchanging curious glances, they proceeded up the winding driveway in search of the hidden residence. Finally, they entered a large courtyard with a decorative fountain in the center, and what a structure it was! Majestic, it was composed of a classical stone exterior reminiscent of an eighteenth century European villa in Tag's world. Artfully designed gardens graced the grounds with a variety of trees lending a natural backdrop.

Before they stopped their vehicle, the front door opened and a tall, big boned, almost hulking woman appeared on the steps to greet them. She had dark brown, shoulder length, wavy hair, and everything about her was large—her head, nose, jaw, and mouth. But it was the expressive gray eyes that were her most extraordinary feature—they felt like a warm embrace.

With the comfort of knowing she was their contact, they parked, got out, and approached her, observing her rough looking exterior belying the gentle soul within.

Stepping forward, she welcomed each of them in turn, correctly identifying them by their given names. "I'm sure Dina told you my name is Adrienne—you are most welcome here for as long as you need to stay." She paused for a few heartbeats, then continued. "Although, I see it will not be for the time you would like, and actually need." Without looking at one another, each of them felt a certain union of comfort, and wonder.

Tag went first. "I understand you're aware of certain things about us . . ."

"Aye," she confessed. "And, some things that will be. Although, part of it you may not wish to hear . . ." Adrienne shifted her attention to Rose and Claire. Her expression softened, and she added, "But, that's for later. Please— come in, relax, and let's get to know each other better." She turned, and headed for the massive door.

The three Travelers exchanged looks, echoing confused feelings about what was to come.

CHAPTER TWENTY-SEVEN

Kyle sat at his desk thinking about the portal—*are the limiting parameters governed by mass, shape, or weight? Maybe all of the above, some of the above, or none of the above . . .* He could draw inferences from what actually happened and, therefore, he should set the numbers slightly above what he already knew. *What does it take to move a flexible, cylindrical shaped object, two meters in length, and one hundred and ten kilos in weight out of his reality into another?* Despite his exhaustion he calculated multiple scenarios, none of which gave him the result he needed.

Back to the drawing board.

As much as he wanted to continue his work, Kyle knew he needed a break. He wasn't solving the riddle as quickly as he hoped—the problem was a sticky one, and solving it would take considerable time and effort. His greatest fear was his inability to solve the mystery—a fear he wasn't yet willing to admit. *What the hell*, he thought. *I need a rest*!

But, he refused to give up.

****

After a simple, exquisite dinner, Adrienne invited the three young Travelers to join her on the stone patio located at the rear of the house. It faced elaborate gardens surrounded by a small forest of densely packed trees, creating a lush, private environment. She asked Tag to start a blaze in the outdoor fireplace located in the center of the patio and, within minutes, it was perfect for roasting marshmallows.

Given the pressure of the last few days' events, the simple act of starting a fire provided Tag a measure of comfort—a kind of poultice for the infection of recent negative episodes. As he fanned its embers, it occurred to him Adrienne was aware of his outdoor experiences in his world and, somehow, she knew performing a familiar ritual would underline the similarities of his current situation in her world. *That's why she did it*, he thought as he sat back in his lounge chair, watching the billowing flame as the women chatted.

His thoughts drifted to shortly after their arrival—Adrienne showed them to their guest rooms, one for each, allowing plenty of time to shower and relax. They toured the house and grounds before dinner to make them more comfortable rather than to show off her impressive lifestyle. In addition to lavish grounds, Adrienne collected artifacts and memorabilia as she traveled her world.

He snapped back to reality as he realized conversation stopped, and the girls were focusing on him.

"Welcome back!" Adrienne teased before continuing. "I believe it's time to review your situation, including upcoming events—with your permission, of course." As she spoke her last words, Rose experienced an emotional tremor and a tactile experience, the hair on her arms and neck suddenly at attention. *Here comes the spooky part*, Rose thought as she waited for Adrienne to continue. Her peripheral vision caught Claire's small, visible shudder— Tag, however, appeared to accept Adrienne's comment without thought.

"Ladies, try to relax a smidgen—you're wound a bit tight . . ." The girls glanced at each other, both making a concerted effort to relax their bodies and minds.

"So far, you're doing well—many young people your age wouldn't make it out of Durango City in a similar circumstance. Worse, most of them wouldn't survive the unfortunate events in St. Louis." The Travelers squirmed at the thought of their close encounter with the Agent. "It was a pity about Vernon—but he always believed strongly in what we're doing, and he understood the consequences of capture."

Adrienne directed her attention to Tag. "You feel guilt, blaming yourself for this situation, especially involving the girls in everything." Without comment he nodded subtly, confirming the truth of her comment. "Tag, you can't carry this load on your own. I know you come from another place—not of this world—and you arrived without any idea of what would happen."

She glanced at Rose, and continued. "And, your defense of this young lady led to a sequence of events which brings you to my door. Now, could you have handled that particular situation in a more diplomatic manner? Possibly. However, injury was likely for you and Rose."

"I hear what you're saying," Tag responded. "But, it's hard to shake the stigma that all of our problems originate with me. The buck stops here . . ."

Claire shot him a quizzical look. "The buck?"

Tag chuckled at yet another aspect of his world that was foreign to them. "A former hat salesman," he explained, "arguably transformed into the most powerful man in my world, had a sign with that phrase sitting on his desk. A 'buck' usually refers to a monetary unit—however, this usage means to not dodge responsibility!"

Adrienne liked Claire's question's taking the edge off of Tag's guilt trip, especially since that was the intent. Clearly, the young lady was blessed with a considerable pool of abilities.

"As you probably figured out, I have the capability to read people and foresee events—the people part is easier for me, and past occurrences are hit and miss. Future happenings are the most difficult to perceive." She paused, allowing them to absorb the information. "I know this kind of thing can be spooky . . ." She smiled, focusing on Rose. " . . . but, understand this—my abilities are not magic nor witchcraft. I came into this world with them, similar to someone's being gifted intellectually, or physically.

"Without sounding like a smart ass," Tag pointed out, "I never thought you would howl at the moon—or, worse!"

"I could do that, if you think it fits the part appropriately!"

"Maybe a group dance around the fire . . ." Claire offered.

Rose joined in the fun with mock seriousness. "Yeah,

but I'm leaving my clothes on!"

"Damn! What's the point then?" Tag winked at Rose, a brief blush shading her face.

After the laughter died down, Adrienne continued, her tone taking a serious edge. "I see certain things in the near future concerning all of you—but the details aren't as clear as they could be. I know your ultimate, planned destination is to arrive in New York City in order to seek help from those who can provide it. However, you may experience a few bumps in the road . . ." She scanned their faces. "After you arrive, things become murky—there will be help for you, sometimes, when you need it. At other times, you will be completely on your own. The real crunch of it is this— each of you, in your own way, will face a fundamental life choice of great importance. I cannot help you with the details—all I can do is alert you. Each of you will make a life-changing choice."

The Travelers stared at her, completely transfixed.

"And, *that* is a lot for you to chew on . . ."

****

Everything synthesized to the moment. Even so, Leon's thoughts were jumbled and disconnected, external stimuli barely registering an impression upon him. When the Eliminators finally came for him, he innately realized their objective was to end his life. Yet, he didn't think of it as an objectionable event. *I'm not sure I'm really unhappy about this!*

It was his final thought.

****

The terse directive on his desk left no doubt as to its intent—find and apprehend the three Travelers by whatever means necessary. Reports attached. The Divisional Commander presided over Scout and Sentinel Teams nationally, and the orders he just received from the Intercept Department in Chicago fell directly within his authority.

After reviewing the materials several times, he recognized a pattern of the Targets moving eastward. He jotted down a note for his Analysis Team to work on a projection anticipating the next location of their Targets, as well as their ultimate destination. He found it odd the SCF Durango City Detachment failed to apprehend and interrogate the immediate family of the female Targets—after all, they knew the identities of their Targets as well as the whereabouts of their families. The male Target, however, was a different animal—he was a ghost to the system, presenting an excuse for the lack of family involvement. The Commander scratched another note as a reminder to look into the failure of the Detachment Representatives.

Next, a directive to initiate a national active sweep for the whereabouts of the Targets, noting a previous initiative to be on the lookout for them yielded little. Last, he ordered the apprehension and interrogation of the immediate families of the Booth and Talbot Targets. With sufficient SCF resources applied in the proper fashion, he was confident he would achieve his desired results.

****

By midafternoon, the SCF Durango City Detachment received the various directives concerning the Talbot and Booth families. As usual, they filtered through the IT office before dissemination to the Detachment, and it was only by sheer luck and chance that Joshua Ward was the first in his section to see them.

He sat up in his seat and gasped when he understood the full impact of the directives. He knew he couldn't stop all of the ordered actions—but he could, perhaps, delay the orders' reaching the various departments responsible for enforcing the initiatives. That, and two other things—one risky, one not. He altered several words in the Apprehension and Interrogation Order, from 'the immediate family' to 'the parents of' in an attempt to save the young siblings of Rose Talbot.

His cousin Claire Booth was an only child.

It was likely his amendment to the directive would be traced back to him, and he knew it—the easier task was to sneak away to warn his Aunt Monique of the danger coming her way.

No one noticed he left.

****

In their society, it was common to work from home. Monique was an independent interior designer, usually involved with commercial and public buildings. Wesley was a freelance business consultant, focusing on the retail marketing industry. So, it came as no surprise when Joshua found them home in the middle of the day. When his aunt opened the door, she knew instantly something was desperately wrong. She ushered him inside, and called for Wesley.

When both were in front of him, Joshua explained everything, stressing the necessity for them to evacuate the area.

"I delayed them a little, but the Order filtered through all departments a few minutes ago—Scout and Sentinel Teams will dispatch momentarily. You have to leave now!"

Monique put her hand to his face. "Joshua, you consistently put yourself at risk for us, and we are deeply grateful. We prepared for this eventuality, and we'll leave within the next few minutes. But, you . . ." Her voice caught as she realized his danger. "You must leave right now before they come looking for us. We'll be fine—we have a plan. Changing the SCF Order to protect the Talbot children will come back to haunt you soon—please consider leaving before they hunt you down."

He looked at her intently, memorizing all he could, knowing it would be the last time they would meet.

"I might be all right—I fudged things a bit with the electronic records to divert them away from me." Joshua hugged her quickly, extended a hand to Wesley, and he was gone.

Within two minutes, the Booth house was empty.

On their way out of town, they swung by the Talbots. It was too risky to warn them by a COM-link call, and, besides, they lived only a few minutes away. As they pulled onto the Talbots' street, SCF Scout and Sentinel Teams were exiting their vehicles, moving in a uniform manner to surround their home.

"Turn right—now!" Monique instructed her husband to turn into an alley running behind the houses on the opposite side of the street. He pulled forward, positioned the vehicle so they had a good view, and stopped in between several houses which provided cover. The SCF Teams positioned men at the front and back of the Talbot residence, preparing to block each exit. Monique and her husband exchanged a glance—there was nothing they could do.

They escaped in another nondescript vehicle registered under a fictitious name. Similar to the vehicle given to Claire and her friends, it was also stocked with necessities for Travelers needing to flee the authorities.

****

No civility. No respect. No concern for human rights. On signal, Team Members breached both doors to the Talbot residence, splintering wood with their initial impact. Lori Talbot was in the kitchen preparing a snack for her children, her husband seated in a small reading room engrossed in a book, as armed SCF Teams swarmed through the doors, commanding them to fall to the floor.

Lori ignored their orders and bolted toward the stairway leading to the children playing downstairs, only to be intercepted by two Sentinel Agents before she hit the top step. She fought like a mama bear, but one Agent overcame her resistance by inflicting a blow to the side of her head rendering her semiconscious, and lying on the floor.

Their Team Leader strode through the back door,

surveying the situation, arching his eyebrows when he saw the Agent cradling his damaged private areas—at least she got in one good blow.

"No one told me she was such a hellcat!" The Agent opted to stay in one place for a few moments.

Nathan's apprehension occurred without a hitch—two Sentinel Agents moved directly to his location, each training a drawn weapon upon him. Acquiescence seemed the best option, as other Agents dispersed throughout the residence looking for more occupants. They soon found the children downstairs, and unceremoniously ushered them upstairs to the main level.

As agents propelled Lori and Nathan toward the shattered front doorway, the SCF Team Leader reviewed his orders confirming the directive related only to the Talbot parents.

Lori resisted again, pleading with the Team Leader. "They're young children—you can't just leave them here alone!"

"Please," Nathan interjected. "We can arrange for neighbors to take care of them." Nathan couldn't bear to see the anguish on the faces of his wife and children.

The SCF Team Leader glanced at the parents, studied the three crying children for a few moments, then grunted, "They're old enough to start learning to do without you—especially where you're going."

He turned his attention to the Sentinel Team Members. "Get them out of here, and let's wrap this thing up."

The Team Members quickly forced Nathan and Lori Talbot through the open doorway, and into the waiting SCF vehicles.

Erin Talbot, age eleven, Sean Talbot, age eight, and Darius Talbot, age six, stood huddled together seeking comfort from one another.

They were alone.

CHAPTER TWENTY-EIGHT

Pittsburgh was their next stop and, given the short driving time, they didn't need an early start—that meant they could sleep in! Even so, Tag was the first to arise and, after the usual morning necessities, he dressed and went downstairs seeking their host.

Adrienne was outside in the gardens at the rear of the residence. She and an undersized black and white cat named Whimsical appeared to be examining the current state of botanical affairs. She smiled as he approached, signaling him to make himself comfortable in one of the patio chairs while she and her feline companion finished their rounds. Before long, she took a seat across from him, pulling her chair closer. Whimsical gracefully jumped in her lap, and she spent a few moments rubbing his belly before turning her attention to Tag.

"I'm glad you came down before the girls," she remarked.

"Why?"

She eyed him carefully before continuing. "Something happened regarding both of them . . ."

"Did you hear from someone?"

A flicker of a smile. "Not exactly—I just know certain things occurred concerning their families."

He hesitated, mulling over the implications of that statement. "Are they okay?"

"Yes, and no. The Booths are fine, for now—the Talbot parents are in trouble. The SCF arrested and detained them."

Tag considered the impact Adrienne's information would have on Rose, and it suddenly occurred to him she had younger siblings at home. "What about her sister and brothers?"

Adrienne looked past him for a time, her gaze far away. After several minutes, she returned her focus to him. "I sense they're fine, physically—but, I'm unclear where they are." Sensing Tag's empathy, she continued. "You know the girls are going to be upset by this news, especially Rose. I need you to be strong for them—they can't go back because doing so won't help matters at all. The three of you need to move forward on your own according to your plans."

She leaned forward in her chair, looking at him intently. "Do you understand?"

Tag held her gaze for a moment. "Got it. Rose's instincts, however, will push her to return to Durango City. It'll take a lot, but I'll get her to New York City—with us."

Adrienne examined him closely, satisfied with what she saw. "I know you will, and you'll do it well. Both girls will need an excellent friend right now." She looked off to her left as Rose and Claire stepped through the French doors of the kitchen to join them on the patio.

Whispering, she sighed, "Now comes the really hard part."

****

The Analysis Team Leader knocked gently on her superior's door. A muffled, grunting response seeped underneath the door which she chose to interpret as permission to enter. The Divisional Commander looked up as she stood at attention in front of his desk.

"Take a load off . . ." It was more of an invitation than an order.

She settled in her chair, thinking about why she liked working for him—no false ceremony, and he was only interested in getting the job done. When he was ready, she launched into her report. She paused for effect, then continued. "Although it's virtually impossible to predict where they are at any given moment—or, more important, where they will eventually go—we feel they will move east from St. Louis. As an aside, we feel strongly the male individual—accompanied by two females—who took out the Sentinel Agent there is the same person named Tag. He's possibly traveling with Rose Talbot and Claire Booth, both originating from the Durango City area."

"Any projections on where they'll turn up next?"

"Well, as I said, it's tough to predict—however, if I had to wager, I'll bet they turn up in Columbus, Pittsburgh, or

Philadelphia. Because they're hopping from major centers without substantial deviations to the north and south, we figure those three cities are the best candidates for where they'll land—and, we'll be waiting for them."

The SCF Divisional Commander considered his subordinate's information. He couldn't only consider the Analysis Team's conjecture—he had to take definitive and productive action. "Where do you think they'll end up?"

"New York City."

"You seem sure of that—why?"

"Because, that's where I'd go. It's large, sprawling, and you can dig in like a tick—plus, we know there's some level of organized opposition based in New York City. My guess is it's a control point for the region—maybe national. If they access this kind of help, it will make them harder to find."

He smiled at the thought. "Yeah—and, if we find them there, perhaps we can roll up their network." Both were silent, filtering through choices as well as their likelihood of success. Finally, his decision. "Okay—let's put it into effect. Notify the SCF Detachments in all four of those cities to increase their alert status." He paused, visualizing his strategy. "And," he continued, "dedicate Sweep Teams for the three Targets. We confirmed identities of the two females, as well as a first name and physical description of the male Target. Surely, they'll pop up somewhere . . ."

The Analysis Team Leader stood, nodding her confirmation. "I'm on it."

****

The three Targets traveled on the highway from Columbus toward Pittsburgh. After Adrienne related the litany of events in Durango City concerning their parents, Tag thought he would have to physically restrain Rose from heading back home to her family.

Claire's initial reaction was similar, but less intense—understandable, since it appeared her parents got away. But it was Adrienne's reasoned explanation of what should happen, as well as Claire's support in sticking to their plan that eventually swayed Rose to continue on to New York City with them. Tag drove, Claire rode shotgun as navigator, and she also kept an eye on Rose who was staring out the back seat window. Adrienne told them their next contact may have further information for them, but how they would obtain it was the question—perhaps as a report passed through their network, or through his own resources. Adam, their Pittsburgh contact, was also a gifted intuitive and, according to Adrienne, he was better at seeing future events than she.

Rose had to cling to that hope.

****

Feeling as if she were about to topple into a chasm of despair, she looked up from the map. "Garden City is just ahead—we should stop to feed the troops."

Without taking his eyes off the road, Wesley smiled. "Yeah, we can't have a mutiny on our hands."

Monique looked over her shoulder into the backseat, deciding to let them sleep for another fifteen minutes. Focusing again on the highway, her thoughts drifted back to the events of the previous day—after escaping the SCF's sweep on the Talbot's street, Monique and Wesley cleared the area to avoid any chance of being caught, giving it a solid thirty minutes before cruising back for another look. Although the immediate vicinity was clear of SCF Teams, they decided to park three houses away in the alley behind the Talbot residence.

A quick search of the home turned up the three children huddled downstairs, shattered by fear. Monique signaled for her husband to stay back as she approached them, watching them scoot further into the corner.

She crouched. "My name is Monique, and I'm a friend of your Mom and Dad. The man behind me is my husband, Wesley." The children stared at her. *Probably in shock*, she thought. *I need a different approach.* "Do you remember your big sister Rose's good friend, Claire?"

"Yes—I know Claire. She's nice, and really smart." The voice sounded small and timid.

Monique heard her own relieved sigh. "I'm Claire's Mom." Their bodies shifted, exhibiting interest in what she was saying. "Your Mom and Dad are gone—for now—and I'm here to look after you." She moved slightly forward, opening her arms.

The children rushed into her embrace.

They spent a few minutes gathering necessary clothing and personal possessions of the children before evacuating the house. They had to be careful on the off chance the SCF may return. From there, they traveled east all night, and into the late morning with few breaks. Monique felt slightly better after passing into the Federated State of Kansas shortly after dawn. The consensus between adults had been to put as much distance as possible between them and Durango City. Later, if they learned of the Talbots' release, they could easily return the children. If not, the children had no one, and Monique was adamant about looking after them for as long as it took.

Luckily, her husband was of the same mind.

****

Durango City's SCF Detachment's Interrogation Team questioned Nathan Talbot for over two hours with little to show for its efforts. Apart from his several requests concerning his children and their whereabouts, Nathan provided limited responses—single words, grunts, or silence depending upon the question. The Senior Agent signaled his subordinate to leave the interrogation room and, once in the hallway with the room door closed, they discussed their insignificant progress.

"I think we should check with the Interrogation Team designated for Lori Talbot to compare results," the Senior Agent commented.

"Agreed. If we still get nothing, we may need to bring in an Agent from the Eliminator Division. You know— physical encouragement." The Junior Agent spoke as if he expected that to be the case. A quick COM-link call brought the other Team into the corridor to join them.

"Anything?" the Senior Agent on the Nathan team asked.

"Not a hell of a lot . . ."

"Yeah—our guy's a clam."

"I wish! I'm getting a nice menu of verbal abuse, threats of physical rearrangement of my anatomy, and repeated demands concerning the whereabouts and safety of her children."

"Speaking of which—where are they? If they're here, we can leverage them against their parents, especially the mother. She'd open up nicely for us if we dangled their well-being in front of her."

"Well, I checked the Apprehension Order when the parents were first brought in—it named them only. Nothing about the kids . . ."

"What kind of boneheaded decision was that?"

"I hear you—look, I'll see the Detachment Commander, and maybe we can add the kids into the mix. He could authorize a team to go back to look for them."

"That's if they're still at home—but, let's give it a shot."

****

They approached the city from the main highway on the southwest side and headed north, crossing over an island as well as the Ohio River. Then it was east into the residential districts of northern Pittsburgh. After a few missteps, they finally located the correct address which was situated in an upscale neighborhood—one with widely spaced lots, and well-treed streets.

This time, Claire volunteered to be the icebreaker with their new contact—however, there was no answer at the residence, and she returned to the vehicle disappointed and deflated.

"Now what do we do?" she asked as she climbed back in the car.

"Maybe we should wait for a couple of minutes to see if he shows up." Rose knew waiting carried with it inherent risk, but she was eager to learn of news concerning her family.

"Too risky. Let's just go . . ."

Before they had a chance to pull away from the curb a vehicle approached, turning into the driveway of their contact's residence. A young man in his late twenties got out, and walked directly across the street to their parked vehicle. Medium height and slender build, he was well-dressed in tailored dress slacks, a light blue shirt, and a beige sports coat. Tag rolled down his window as he approached, and the man leaned over, eye level with him.

"Hi guys. I'm sorry I wasn't here when you first arrived—I was running a little late, and traffic was a bit snarled." He glanced at each of the occupants.

"Did Adrienne call to let you know we were coming?" Tag asked.

"No, that wasn't really necessary." He grinned, and Tag felt a slight shudder push through him. In the backseat, he heard Rose softly murmur, "Spooky . . ."

"Absolutely!" the young man teased. "I'm Adam, as you probably suspected. Why don't you grab your stuff and come on inside . . ."

****

Access to the house required little effort—broken locks, splintered door frames, and the rear door's hanging from only one of its three hinges made entry a whole lot easier. The SCF Detachment Commander ordered four Sentinels—two Teams—to apprehend the Talbot children. To the Agents, it was overkill to secure three young children—however, the Commander pointed out they may not be the only ones remaining in the residence. A sweep of the house proved it unoccupied, and there was no evidence of the children's whereabouts.

On the way back to Detachment Headquarters, the Agents speculated as to whose butt was going to be in a sling over the initial failure to include the kids when the parents were apprehended.

****

Joshua painstakingly crafted the official encrypted report update on behalf of the Durango City Headquarters. It was to be disseminated to all other Detachments nationwide and, normally, he could perform the task simply and efficiently. However, buried in the official jargon was a private message—a one-time code available to only one party capable of successfully decrypting the information.

The communication stated the facts—*Lori and Nathan Talbot were apprehended, currently undergoing interrogation. The SCF Sweep Teams missed Monique and Wesley Booth, and the Talbots' three children are traveling east with them.* He added the last fact based on the news from his aunt in a brief, coded call she made from a public convenience COM-link. Satisfied with the official and private messages, he initiated the send feature on his computer. With that out of the way, he had to refocus on the problem of the missing Talbot children, tinkering with the official Order, and the current ruckus the situation was causing in his Detachment. He was a battleground for an intense, internal conflict between the fervent hope his earlier electronic cover-up would hold, versus the absolute dread should the SCF discover his duplicity.

****

Adam's home wasn't exactly sparse in its furnishings, but each room's decor blended well with minimalistic, finely-crafted pieces. Claire noted its utilitarian yet comfortable surroundings. *Not bad for a bachelor*, she thought as she scanned the room. Adam gave them a quick tour to familiarize them with the layout before excusing himself to prepare dinner. They showered, and did a bit of laundry as they discussed their current situation until Adam called them for dinner—a meal comparable to that of a good restaurant. Afterward, everyone pitched in to clean up and, within twenty minutes, Adam invited them to relax in the main living area. His interior design was an open concept with little definition from one area to another, the flow pleasing.

Tag started off by thanking their host for the fine meal and accommodations, the girls seconding his gesture.

"Thanks—but, what you really want to talk about are the events in Durango City," Adam suggested.

"Have you heard anything about what's going on?" Rose leaned forward in her chair, ready to hang on his every word. Claire gently took her hand as a best-friend gesture of support.

"Rose, your parents are still detained and being questioned. Other than that, I am unaware of their status."

"What about my brothers and sister?"

"Ah! That's the good news! They're safe, and under the care of responsible individuals."

Claire gave Rose's hand a squeeze. "See? That's just great!"

Adam focused on Claire with a slight smirk, waiting.

"What?" she asked.

He waited a few moments before answering. "Here's the coolest part—the kids are traveling east escorted by none other than your parents!"

Claire's relief was tinged with guilt that her parents, not Rose's, were safe and free.

****

They drove down a back road, turning into the driveway leading to the rambling home standing alone in the wide-open countryside. As their vehicle rolled to a stop, a brown, furry object streaked directly at the children, chaos reigning as Chico and the kids engaged in a greeting ritual which was enough to disturb all wildlife within earshot. A hulking individual stepped across the threshold of the front door, walked a few steps, then stopped with hands on his hips, watching the disorder occurring in front of him. As Monique and Wesley approached, he grunted, "The reason I moved out here was to get away from the uproar—now look at what you've done!"

"I see what you mean," Wesley agreed as he turned to observe the commotion—it was good to see the children enjoying themselves.

"Seth, we really need your help," Monique pleaded.

Seth said nothing as he encased her slim figure in a warm embrace. After a few moments, without letting her go, he extended a hand to his old friend Wesley. With his arm still around Monique's shoulder, he mumbled, "Come on you two—into the house. We'll leave the noisy rabble outside, for now . . ."

CHAPTER TWENTY-NINE

"Sir, there's a problem within the Durango City Detachment." The Divisional Commander sat at his desk, myriad reports on his computer requiring his attention. He looked up at the Team Leader standing in the doorway. "What's happened?"

The subordinate stepped into his superior's office, closed the door behind him, and briefly stood at attention before being pointed to a chair. "Apparently, someone unofficially altered your Order of Apprehension."

"Explain."

"Your original Order was sent from here and received by the SCF Durango City Detachment—someone in that office modified your Order before the Detachment Commander reviewed it."

"How do you know?"

"We received a preliminary report from that office, indicating the apprehension of the Talbot parents—

but, their children were left behind. The Detachment Commander questioned why the children were left out of the original Apprehension Order, thinking they could use the kids as leverage on the parents." Pausing for a moment, the Team Leader studied his boss, before continuing. "So, we checked the original Order—it stated clearly to apprehend the Talbot family, yet the Detachment Commander received an Order to apprehend the Talbot parents. Therefore, there wasn't a thing about the kids. The on-scene Sentinel Team didn't take the initiative to include the kids. Finally, however, someone woke up, sending a Team back for the children. But, by then, they were gone."

The Divisional Commander remained silent, thinking about the botched sweep. "Too bad about missing the kids—however, they're not my main concern. Find out who modified that Order—get our people here to do an electronic trace. And, send a team from the Denver Regional Office with full authority to investigate and apprehend whoever the hell messed with my Order. Maybe there's more than one—I don't care what their rank is in that Detachment! Find them, and squeeze them!"

The Team Leader bolted from his chair. "I'm on it!"

The Divisional Commander's work load just doubled.

****

They convened, coffee in hand, to comfortable chairs on the broad veranda. It was early, the morning sun still low in the clear sky, the air already enjoyably warm.

Monique smiled as she watched the Talbot children and Chico running amok, glancing occasionally at her silent companions.

Wesley finally broke the silence. "I want to do two things—first, determine the current status of Lori and Nathan Talbot and, second, contact Rose to discuss her siblings."

"The first one," Seth replied, "shouldn't be too hard because we can check via a back channel source still in place, using a one-time code covered by an official communication. The second request may be a bit trickier— I'm not sure where Rose is in the pipeline. And, even if I knew, our normal shielded communications are now compromised."

Joshua! Monique thought. "Any information," Monique commented, "on Lori and Nathan would be great. We know where Claire, Rose, and Tag are headed, so is there any way to find out if Nelson—our contact in New York City—can check on their progress to let us know where they are? If not, maybe once they get there we can set up some sort of communication link."

Seth shrugged. "Well, I'll certainly give that a try— where are you going to be in the next few days?"

"Not sure—Wesley and I still have to discuss it. Our primary focus was to get the kids to safety."

"Rightly so. You're certainly welcome to stay for as long as you need—since we're not sure about Lori and Nathan, I presume you may not want to venture too far in case the SCF releases them."

"Do you think that's likely?" Monique asked, looking at him intently.

Seth took a while to respond. "Not bloody likely!"

****

As Adam entered the kitchen, the Travelers could tell he had news of some kind.

"What did you hear?" Tag asked. He was the only one who wasn't in mid-chew.

Their host quickly poured himself a coffee, and took a seat at the end of the vintage, solid oak kitchen table. "Well," he began, "it appears Lori and Nathan are still in custody at the SCF Durango City Detachment." He softened the description for Rose's benefit. "They're still undergoing some questioning . . ." There was little point in telling her it was more like a full-blown interrogation. He watched her carefully as she absorbed this information, only her subtle nod indicating acknowledgment.

With the gloomy stuff out of the way, he was delighted to try to boost her spirits. "I also heard Monique, Wesley, and the Talbot kids arrived to stay with the Bear." Adam sat quietly with an amused expression while each of them worked through it.

Claire, of course, was first to suggest a solution. "They're in Wichita—with Seth!"

"Exactly—you win first prize."

"The Bear?" Tag was curious why Seth had such a moniker.

"It's a nickname fondly used by those of us who know him—but, not to his face. However, I wouldn't be surprised if he's heard the term."

"It fits . . ."

Rose brightened at the news about her younger siblings. "Do you know if they'll keep moving toward us?"

"As I understand it, they will stay put with Seth for a while until they hear something more about your parents."

She was quiet for a bit and then looked at each of them, confessing, "This is really hard, you know . . ."

Claire answered for all of them. "We do, and we're here for you."

****

As the troop of Agents marched into Detachment Headquarters, dispersing throughout the building, they met with mixed reactions. Some stood with mouths agape, while others sat at their desks in stunned silence. Several turned turtle by physically contracting into their spaces, seeking somewhere to hide. One poor soul initially stepped forward, bristling with indignation until two Sentinel Agents turned on him—he immediately thought better of his outrage.

Sent from the Regional SCF Office in Denver, and pursuant to the National Divisional Commander's directive, they were to root out any and all traitors, dissenters, and persons operating contrary to the SCF interests—all of whom may work out of the Durango City Headquarters.

The Leader of the force, accompanied by a squad of Sentinel Agents, marched directly toward the Headquarter's Commander's office and, without knocking, burst through the door, interrupting the meeting in progress between the Commander and several of his senior staff. Appalled by such treatment, the Detachment Commander snapped out an expletive targeting the Leader. Although inferior in rank to the local Detachment Commander, the Task Force Leader showed no reaction—he simply handed over a written copy of the one paragraph directive, giving him absolute authority in the situation.

Watching the color drain from the Detachment Commander's face, the Task Force Leader permitted himself a condescending smile. With balance of power now shifted to his favor, he looked at the other local members seated around the table. "All right, this is how it's going to go . . ."

When the Task Force Leader finished, the local SCF senior staff witnessed something they never thought would happen—the Detachment Commander's wilting before them.

One floor below, members of the Task Force ordered Joshua and three other computer techs to vacate their workstations as replacements from the Regional Office began the search process on their machines. The four of them were invited—a polite way of stating they were detained—to remain in a nearby staff lounge. Outside the doorway, two Sentinel Agents stood at guard while two of the four Technicians stared at the floor barely comprehending what was happening. Joshua and the fourth member, Hansen, analyzed the situation, exchanging glances every so often.

Finally, Hansen caught Joshua's attention, miming the question as to what he thought was going on. Neither were willing to verbalize anything significant with Sentinels stationed just outside the open doorway.

Joshua shrugged, his body language indicating, "Your guess is as good as mine." The fact was he didn't know Hansen well enough to trust him with the knowledge that

Joshua understood—they were there for him.

In the sub-basement two levels below, Nathan Talbot glowered at the SCF Interrogator sitting across the narrow, scarred, wooden table from him. The Agent's partner paced within the restricted confines of the interrogation room and, clearly, both were frustrated at the appalling lack of information Nathan provided. Stalling was his best course of action in addition to playing the role of an uninformed, dimwit individual. Hopefully, if they bought his routine, they wouldn't expect much from him, eventually concluding he didn't know anything. If not, the true danger lay in his considerable knowledge of the underground network opposed to the current authoritarian state, as well as its SCF enforcement apparatus.

There was some comfort in knowing Claire and her friends would end up at Nelson's place in New York City. Presumably, he would relocate them in a permanent situation somewhere in the bowels of the nation's largest city. If things turned ugly, however, Nathan feared they would do something to him, enabling them to surpass his defenses, and thereby forcing him to reveal what he shouldn't.

In the adjacent interrogation room, Lori Talbot continued working the theory that her best defense against the SCF goons was an active offense. Each time they attempted to elicit new information from her, she counterattacked with questions of her own regarding the whereabouts and safety of her children, what was happening with her husband, and why they were holding her. The best part was she managed to sprinkle in a few direct, personally derogatory remarks aimed at the Interrogators. She worked them up enough to disrupt their line of thought, carefully balancing that against enough anger to initiate physical action against her. Even so, Lori had to admit she was running out of new ideas to portray the part of the indignant, falsely-accused citizen. *If it comes down to it,* she thought, *they can do whatever they want to me, but, there is no way in hell I'm going to say anything that will endanger my babies!* Convincing herself yet again to hang in there, she wondered whether her children were okay—such uncertainty was worse than facing the SCF buffoons.

As she focused again on her Interrogators, she thought about Monique—*if she avoided capture,* Lori thought, *she may have gone for the children, if she had a chance.*

Her thought was the anchor giving her a renewed sense of purpose.

CHAPTER THIRTY

What started out as an aimless activity to prevent boredom, ended up in a free-for-all competition between the two of them. First, it was about who could climb the highest—then it switched into who could climb out the farthest on the largest branch. They raised the stakes, however, by tweaking the last activity into who could climb the farthest out on the slimmest branch without tumbling out of the tree.

He approached the end of a dangerously bent limb where brilliant sunlight wasn't diffused by the other branches, illuminating his bright red hair. From a distance, it looked like a colorful Christmas ornament against all of the greenery of the large coniferous tree.

"Darius Talbot, you get out of that tree this instant!" Eleven-year old Erin Talbot wasn't into mincing words.

Not entirely sure he could comply with her request, he clung to the branch which was more vertical than horizontal. Clearly, climbing up the tree was easier than inching out onto the narrow limb.

His older brother sat situated on a higher, larger branch, considering his brother's dilemma to be hilarious. That changed when she directed her focus to him, instructing him to rescue Darius—no choice. He was clearly aware to deny his younger brother help would be the precursor to unfavorable consequences. Several minutes later, Sean Talbot and his younger brother reached the ground without going airborne—they stood together, feet shuffling, eyes to the ground, waiting for the impending lecture.

Erin stood looking at them, allowing her anger at their stupidity to dissipate before launching into the strip-tearing exercise they both deserved. However, she quickly realized what manifested as anger was really her fear of one of them being seriously injured—or, worse. So, instead of her lecturing them, she crossed her arms, and dished out 'the look.' "Idiots!" she admonished, although stated with less venom than originally intended. The truth was if anyone asked, she would have to admit it was difficult to stay mad at her younger brothers— especially Darius.

"Okay, both of you—into the house right now before I really get mad." She sounded just like her mother.

The chastised duo walked slowly toward the house until they reached a distance to safely reignite the ongoing competition by racing each other to the veranda.

Monique watched the whole tree climbing episode and the subsequent rebuke by the elder sister from a comfortable chair on the deck, enjoying the Talbot girl's preempting move. As it turned out, the boys suffered nothing more than a few scrapes and a reprimand, and Monique sat back and enjoyed the show. It was fascinating to watch the interplay of personalities between the Talbot children.

There was a strong family resemblance, but, that's where it ended—there were physical and character differences. As they sprinted towards the house, she focused on the boys, Sean the current leader. Already tall for his age, at age eight he inherited his father's dark hair and rangy body type. He could be quiet and contemplative just like his father, but he also possessed a playful streak most often directed at his younger brother.

In their travels with him so far, she noticed how close he was with his siblings. Considering his age, Sean displayed remarkable sensitivity when dealing with others, as well as glimpses of sound judgment when handling various circumstances. Except with his youngest brother—at least that dynamic kept him from becoming easily bored.

Darius, conversely, favored Lori with his flaming red hair. However, she had a petite trim figure and his was robust and sturdy. Several times, Monique witnessed exhibitions of unusual strength for such a young boy. But, what was really striking about him was the spontaneous and dynamic nature he used to march through life. Darius was fun-loving and open with an unusually sunny disposition. Despite his somewhat tank-like exterior, she knew he possessed a quick wit and insightful mind as well as a strong sense of self. *When he's old enough*, Monique considered, *the ladies will swarm him like moths to a flame!*

As the boys mounted the stairs to the veranda and disappeared into the house, her attention focused on Erin, slowly treading in their wake. She was strawberry blonde, slender, and almost as tall as her mother. She looked like Lori, yet her disposition was similar to her father and her sister, Rose—fine-featured, and attractive. She was social, but, perhaps, happiest when she was quiet and by herself. Previously, Lori described her youngest daughter as highly creative and artistic—but, given the dire circumstances of finding the children and fleeing Durango City, Monique had yet to see that side of her. *If we stay a while at Seth's place,* she thought, *maybe I should look into getting some art supplies so Erin has an outlet to take her mind off things. Yes, I'll ask Seth to look into that for me . . .*

By the time Erin hit the top stair leading to the veranda, she noticed Monique. She offered a shy smile which blossomed to a beam when the tall, beautiful woman motioned for her to join her. Monique hugged the young girl, whispering, "I'm impressed—I couldn't handle those young ruffians any better than you!" Erin clutched her tightly, feeling safe for the first time since her parents' apprehension.

****

At the Durango City Detachment Headquarters, the Regional SCF Team from Denver continued its prying and peering into corners—physically and electronically—acting with the presumption that subversives and traitors were in their midst. Their sole directive? To uncover the rot, and excise it before it had the opportunity to spread. So far, cooperation from local Agents ranged from unenthusiastic foot dragging to outright refusals, sparking incendiary friction between the local and regional SCF Agents. Everything was about to ignite as the SCF Team detained Joshua and three members of his Technical Team hours after their shifts ended. Regional techies painstakingly examined Detachment electronic records for inconsistencies and errors, hoping they would guide them to uncovering the alleged culprits in the office. For Joshua, it was a severe test of his nerves to maintain a façade of disinterest and boredom as he fully understood his complicity with others may be uncovered at any moment. On the flip side, he felt relatively good about camouflaging his tracks regarding his outside communications to his network—deep down, however, he knew his Achilles' heel would be his action in changing the Directive's wording in an effort to save the Talbot children. At least he had the satisfaction of learning they escaped with his Auntie Monique and Uncle Wesley.

****

Next—Philadelphia. Traffic was light, and Adam provided the necessary details so they could easily find their next contact. He also gave them directions for exiting northern Pittsburgh as they moved east. Rose was at the wheel, Tag rode shotgun, and Claire brought up the rear as they continued east, then turned northeast along the north side of the Allegheny River as it made a sweeping curve, changing direction. After crossing the bridge, they joined a major road connecting with the eastbound highway to Philadelphia. Estimated travel time—six hours.

The day was clear and shaping up to be a hot one, the Travelers assuming it should be a routine hop to their next destination.

****

Why is it I always end up with the most boring detail? The SCF Scout Agent was sitting in her vehicle for the last six hours. She was sore, stiff and hungry, and the need for a bathroom break was on the rise. Her assigned position was a mile south of the main eastern bridge over the Allegheny River, and she stationed her vehicle just off the main highway stretching northwest to southeast. She was merely a cog in a network of Scout and Sentinel Agents dispersed throughout the City of Pittsburgh with the sole purpose of apprehending their Targets.

The plan was to create a web of strategically placed Agents to ensnare three young persons of interest, potentially traveling through their location. They were advised no vehicle identification information was available for electronic tracking nor physical eyesight recognition. Additional Agents surveilled public transportation systems, as well. They hoped the Targets would pass close enough to an Agent to activate a monitoring device, tracking them by their implanted personalized identifier chips. The word was that only two of the three Targets had such chips.

It was a helpful system, but only if the Target were close to the monitoring device. The problem was it had a short maximum range—one mile or less—amidst buildings. It couldn't determine the Target's direction, and it worked best if the Target were stationary. Then, a minimum of three monitoring devices would triangulate the location.

I feel like a hunter sitting in a blind waiting for the prey to conveniently saunter by, the Agent thought, chuckling. *Good luck with that!* The urges became more demanding, prompting a report to her Supervisor to request a convenience break. But before she could initiate the call, her monitoring device chirped an alarm, warning the two Targets' personal identifier codes previously inputted into the device indicated they were within range of her location. The Scout stared in disbelief. *They're here! Somewhere close by!*

The device indicated the Targets were moving within

a 360° sweep of her location, and she quickly forgot about her request as she focused on what to do next. *Okay,* she thought. *The Targets could be moving on any road in any direction within my range.* She made an assumption. *They're probably on the main highway in front of me—I need to move before they get out of range. Are they heading northwest, or southeast?* The Scout started her vehicle and entered the ramp onto the highway leading northwest, accelerating her speed, and praying she got it right. But, by not having a physical description of the Targets' vehicle, the Scout unwittingly passed it as it headed southeast on the same highway—it took less than a minute for the Target vehicle to disappear from the monitoring device in the Scout vehicle.

"Damn it!" The Scout Agent slammed her hands on the steering wheel in frustration. It was several miles before she could exit the highway, and negotiate the interchange to get back on the highway traveling in the opposite direction.

Too late. The Targets turned off of the highway onto another, heading east and out of the city blissfully unaware they appeared on the SCF radar, escaping the dragnet.

After calling in the sighting, the Scout Agent drove the roads throughout her assigned area without result. She knew she had a fifty-fifty chance of picking the right direction, and, she chose incorrectly. Certainly, there would be a face-to-face with her Commander—something she dreaded.

＊＊＊＊

"Come in ..." The SCF Divisional Commander, National

Office, looked up as a Team Leader strode through the door, announcing, "We had a sighting of the three Targets we're tracking from Durango City—they were in eastern Pittsburgh. Unfortunately, the Scout lost them—but, her best guess was they were moving east out of the city."

The Commander sat back, locking his hands behind his head. "Well, it fits your earlier assumption of possible destinations for them—where do you think they'll turn up next?"

"It's a guess, of course, but if they keep moving eastward, I'm thinking Philadelphia, Baltimore, New York City, Washington, or Boston."

The Divisional Commander considered the choices. "Covering each of those cities requires resources—it'll bog us down if we try to cover each of those cities." He toyed with what to do, finally making a decision. "Pick your top three cities, and establish a net. Maybe we'll get lucky."

The Team Leader nodded. "I'll get on that immediately, Sir."

"And, make sure you pick the correct three cities." The Commander looked directly at the Team Leader, conveying the urgency of his message with a targeted stare.

As the Team Leader closed the door on his way out, he wondered if the Commander's last comment were a threat.

Probably.

CHAPTER THIRTY-ONE

Things were quiet for a while, each immersed in their private world, sequentially working through past, present, and future events. Twenty five miles west of the Metropolitan Philadelphia area, the Travelers pulled off the highway just outside the small town of Carlisle in the Federated State of Pennsylvania. Adam packed a lunch for them so they didn't have to buy it somewhere, thereby leaving an electronic footprint.

As they ate, Tag recalled his understanding of the geography of the area in his world. "Is there a Gettysburg here?" he asked.

"There is," Claire responded. "It was the focal point of a civil war here." She went on to further explain a number of American historical events of the 1800s did coincide with time and outcome—the same in each reality. They continued to compare the individual histories, determining there was a parallel track until the advent of World War I. At the end of that tragedy, the realities diverged as each chose its own course. The ramifications of their discussion stayed with Tag for a good portion of the remaining trip as he tried balancing the difference between their worlds, each having its own version of good and bad.

After lunch, the Travelers rotated positions in the vehicle—Claire at the wheel, Rose beside her, and Tag made himself comfortable in the back seat. Rose couldn't get her mind off her parents—but, no matter how she tried to banish the thoughts, imagined negative outcomes crept into her awareness. *Will they be released, but financially ruined? If they're still in custody, are they being interrogated? Tortured?* It was more than Rose could bear. Then she considered the worst. *Or, I may never hear from them again* . . . She stared out the passenger's side window, her eyes welling with tears.

She walked close to the edge of breaking down.

As she thought of her siblings, she silently thanked Monique for taking care of them. Soon, the tears dried, her spirits lifted, and she stuffed the horrible thoughts to a recessed corner somewhere in the back of her mind.

For now.

****

The sweep at the Durango City Detachment yielded speedy results—one local SCF Agent was arrested and removed to the cell block area. There was little doubt Durango City Detachment personnel were chafing under the thumb of the SCF Regional Force who was currently in control of their Headquarters. The Agent detainee decked his regional counterpart who chose unwisely to rub the situation into the local's nose—the 'deckee' was still undergoing medical treatment.

So far, the interlopers uncovered evidence of expected inefficiencies, common error, and sloth as they pertained to the incompleteness of required duties. Nothing surprising there. More worrisome were the hints of surreptitious, unofficial actions they may construe as sedition. There was nothing yet to indicate whether the individual were working alone, or whether there were a widespread conspiracy.

Downstairs, four members of Joshua's Technical Team were still kept in their relaxation area to remain available for consultation with the Regional Agents, if needed. Or, so they said—de facto, they were unofficially, yet effectively, detained. Again, no surprise.

They rounded up and detained the other shift of the local Technical Team which was usually at work when Joshua's team was off. Now, there were a total of eight highly-skilled techies jammed into a relaxation area which was designed for half their number. At least that shift had an opportunity to sleep, shower, and change within the last twenty four hours. Not so with Joshua's Team—they were cooped up for the past thirty-two hours, eating trashy food, and dozing if they were lucky. Plus, they were beginning to smell a little ripe.

Joshua brushed a few rogue strands of dark brown hair away from his face, struggling to keep negativity at bay. *I need a haircut as soon as I get out of here*, he thought. *That's if I get out of here . . .*

The Regional SCF Technical Team had been at it for almost a day and a half, painstakingly combing through all electronic information in the Detachment's network. *I could show you right now what you're looking for*, Joshua thought as he waited with his colleagues. *Please— anything to get this over with . . .* His nervous tension was building to an almost unbearable level. So far, his electronic tracks were still covered—but, for how long? They knew something was hinky without recognizing where the discrepancies lay.

Although his exterior showed nothing other than an unruffled and bored individual, on the inside were waves of tumultuous anxiety. He glanced at the others, earmarking two individuals who might try to rabbit out of there. One of them was the youngest on his Team who looked as if he just climbed out of the swimming pool, clothes and all. The other had enough nervous energy to boost the energy grid.

Joshua managed to catch the eye of the Number Two in authority on his Team. Throughout, Hansen managed to exude the same combination of calm and bored attitude. Joshua gave him a head motion indicating their Nervous Nelly. The 'Sweater.' Hansen understood. He moved over to the youngest member, leaned over, speaking quietly in his ear. Both moved to the corner of the room for a little chat.

As he glanced to his right he noticed Barton, the other Team Leader, studying him, raising an eyebrow when he had Joshua's attention. Joshua barely nodded acknowledgment, and glanced meaningfully at his Nervous Nelly. Barton caught on, and moved over to have his own wee chat.

Joshua leaned back in his chair, determined to banish the incessant negative thought processes clamoring for his attention. He looked at the SCF Regional Technician occupying his workstation. *Either find something, or get the hell off of my machine!*

****

Claire took an exit at the next interchange, putting

them on a smaller highway heading northeast on the west side of Valley Forge.

After consulting the map with regional roads included, Tag's idea was to circumvent the west side of Metro Philadelphia by traveling north of it, then enter the city on the northeast corner.

"Why the diversion?" Claire asked.

He didn't have a solid answer for her question. "I have a really strong feeling about this . . ."

They ended up on multiple secondary roads, heading primarily north or east depending on how the roads intersected. There was a litany of towns—Collegeville, Worcester, Montgomeryville, and Doylestown—and it wasn't until Buckingham that they turned south into the main metropolitan area onto a highway leading back into Philadelphia. Once they arrived close to their north-central destination—the address of their contact—they parked several houses away. Both girls turned to look at Tag in the back seat.

"What?"

****

With their primary grid and the SCF's sniffing around, their arena of communication safety was critically important. The young gentleman, comfortably seated poolside in a lounge chair, considered the prospect of ever-tightening security. *If disseminating our information becomes tighter, we'll be going retro—back to dead drops, and hand signals.* Word reached him earlier in the day that three 'hot potatoes' would be arriving shortly, requiring assistance before moving on. Since then, his workday was a flurry of activity to complete required tasks quickly, allowing him an earlier than normal departure from work. *Typical,* he thought. *Hurry up, then wait . . .* He got home several hours previous, anticipating the arrival of his guests. As the hours clicked by concern mounted, and he reviewed what could have happened to them between Pittsburgh and his location. Just as he considered the worst, the remote door security unit chimed.

He activated the view screen which illuminated a broad view of his front porch. *Finally!* he thought as he went to greet them. As he approached the front yard close to the entrance to his home, he stopped for a moment, observing the tall, attractive, redheaded young woman. Although he moved quietly, she turned to face him before he entered her line of sight. *Impressive—she's vigilant. Obviously, they're careful to not place all of them at risk at the point of contact.*

They stood looking at each other for a while before he smiled. "I trust you have two compatriots somewhere close by?"

She matched his smile, responding with a tip of her head toward the street. "Absolutely—in the car, down the road."

He approached, hand extended in greeting. "I'm Brent—let's round them up, shall we?"

****

His secure SCF COM-link sounded a warning of an incoming call. "I'm here—report."

"Sir, we canvased all of the Agent Teams and, so far,

nothing. Nada."

The Commander of the Philadelphia Action Team Group considered the response—it wasn't what he wanted to hear. They had all of the west side roads entering the city laced up tightly, and there was no way the Targets could slip through the deployment without SCF internal implants sounding an alarm.

He looked at his watch, noting the late evening hour. "If they left Pittsburgh early this morning, they should have arrived here by mid afternoon . . ." The Commander wrestled with it for a few moments, concluding, "They must be heading to one of the other cities." He paused, deciding what to do next. "Contact all Agent Teams and advise them to stay on station until six in the morning. If the Targets are a no-show, we'll shut it down . . ."

"Yes sir. I'm on it."

CHAPTER THIRTY-TWO

Sitting in a patio chair, long legs stretched to their fullest extent and ankles crossed, he still managed to radiate extraordinary levels of power and intelligence. While he focused on Rose, who was describing some aspects of their trip, it provided Claire the opportunity to study him.

Brent was tall—several inches taller than Tag—and in good physical condition. Thick, wavy blonde hair topped an interesting face sporting a slightly misaligned, previously broken nose. His jaw was strong, decorated with several faded scars, and deep set, piercing blue eyes gave him a rather hawkish look. She estimated him to be in his late twenties or early thirties and he was, she decided, a pleasing package. Suddenly, he looked directly at her, startling her with his intensity. But, Brent grinned, immediately putting her at ease.

Each of them related a portion of their tale from personal perspective. Brent was the closest in age to all of them, so the three Travelers easily shared their feelings and details of recent events.

When it came to the manner of Tag's arrival, Brent was incredibly curious—although he was a successful businessman in several ventures, his real love was historical and anthropological perspective. He and Tag talked well into the night, the girls earlier excusing themselves to retire for the evening.

At breakfast, the discussion turned to their immediate future. In between bites of eggs, ham, and fruit, Brent asked, "Have any of you been to New York City before?"

Three negative head shakes. "How about any other city that size?"

"Just the cities we briefly visited on the way here—in my world, I only ventured to Denver several times," Tag responded.

"My parents took us to Los Angeles about five years ago—but, being younger I didn't drive, of course. And, at that age, I didn't pay attention to how we got around while we were there." Rose recalled the adventure fondly as she thought of her siblings and parents.

"Like Tag, just Denver—our version," Claire added with a grin.

"Well," Brent continued, "driving in New York City is going to be completely different. It's huge, congested, and in parts—not exactly car friendly. Public transportation is the favored way to get around efficiently." He paused, thinking about what the Travelers had before them. "Once you get to the rendezvous point with Nelson, I suspect he will direct you to dump your vehicle, and move around by other means. Blending in with the masses is the obvious tactic to avoid unwanted attention."

"Will using public transportation pose any problems?"

Tag asked.

"Not after you are modified."

Modified? The Travelers looked at Brent with blank stares.

Brent paused a moment before clarifying. "Video surveillance cameras and facial recognition software are your two biggest challenges when avoiding detection." He paused again. "Each of you will undergo surgery to change your appearance."

Silence. "What's the other biggest challenge?" Tag finally asked.

Brent focused on the girls. "You're going to have to make a stop along the way."

"I'm not entirely sure about this . . ." Rose glanced at Claire, unsure about Brent's solution to their first major roadblock.

"It's something you both need to do." He left little room for contemplation.

"Yeah, well that's easy for you to say—you're not the one getting it done!"

****

His normally healthy, rugged looks transformed into a haggard version of his former self. The Interrogators were unrelenting in their demands for information, and they switched teams of Agents several times to keep their end of things fresh. He, on the other hand, received little in the way of respite from their demands. Finally, their frustrations turned to anger, leading Interrogators to convert methodical questioning into something more physical.

They called in an Agent from the Eliminator Division.

A Specialist well-acquainted with the discipline of mandated torture, she actually enjoyed her job, considering such an activity a perk of her employment. After several hours, Nathan doubted his ability to hold on much longer, and he intuitively understood the Specialist wasn't likely to frustrate easily.

****

Two rooms over, Lori had her own issues—the teams of Agent Interrogators were a collective pain in the ass, but she found she could handle them effectively. The Eliminator cretin, however, was a whole different matter—he raised things to an entirely new level as the pain approached those associated with the births of her four children. But, the good news was she drew comfort from the knowledge that escalating her interrogation experience meant they likely hadn't found Rose.

Normally energetic and vibrant, Lori was beaten—usually well-dressed and attractive, her red hair, wet and plastered to her skull, framed her unusually pale face. Her extremities spasmodically twitched as over stimulated nerve endings randomly fired.

They will not win! she thought as the Eliminator Agent ramped up the pain level with a new technique. Before she started screaming again, Lori overheard one of the initial

Interrogators comment to the other, "Too bad we never found the kids—if we could have used them as leverage against her, she wouldn't have to go through this shit!"

That's the kindest thing you've done for me since I've been here, she thought, preparing for the worst.

The Agent's words empowered her for what was to come.

****

"Does anyone see the sign?"

"I'm still looking . . ."

"There it is!"

Tag pulled into the small parking lot on the west side of the building, parked, and killed the engine. He looked at Claire beside him, then Rose in the back seat. "Okay—are you ready for this?"

Rose nodded.

"Yeah—let's do it." Claire still didn't sound convinced.

According to instructions from Nelson—passed to them by Brent—they turned off the freeway leading into Newark to find the address located in Linden, Federated State of New Jersey.

The buildings in Linden were a mixture of commercial business offices, light industrial operations, and a sprinkling of retail shops. The one-story structure they were about to enter housed a medical supply store on one side, and a single practitioner medical office on the other.

It was the doctor whom they were there to see.

A door chime sounded as they entered the small, empty reception area, and a middle-aged woman came out of a back office. "May I help you?"

"Trafalgar," Claire responded. She couldn't help smiling as she said it, reflecting on the choice of code word selected by her Uncle Nelson.

The woman's demeanor changed immediately. "It's good to see you got here alright! Come into the back—we're ready for you." She ushered them into a small operating theatre. "Please wait here."

Ten minutes later, the woman—who was actually the nurse—returned with the doctor, both scrubbed for the procedure. The doctor, a thirty-something, diminutive woman, nodded a greeting and indicated to the table in the middle of the room. "Who's first?"

Rose stepped forward. "I trust you'll be gentle with me."

The doctor looked up, her hazel eyes twinkling with humor. "You won't even know I've been in there."

****

Rose sat next to Tag as Claire took her turn. He leaned over, pointing to the small bandage on her upper arm. "Does it hurt much?"

"Piece of cake!" she muttered without looking at him.

Inside of an hour, all of them climbed back into their vehicle. Both girls had their identifier implants successfully removed—neither of them previously knew they were carrying the locater devices since their inoculations when they were five years old.

As they were pulling out of the parking lot to head back to the freeway, it occurred to Tag that in all of the time spent in the doctor's office, no one's name was mentioned, or, destination.

"You're good to go," were the parting words of the doctor.

****

"We missed them—shut it down." The Philadelphia Action Team Commander looked at his Subordinate, waiting for acknowledgment he understood his order. "Contact the National Command Office, and advise them it's likely the Targets are headed toward Washington or New York City." He was disgusted his Teams couldn't bring in the Targets, and it showed as he muttered, "Maybe they'll intensify the grid, and finally nail these guys."

****

One of Barton's crew bolted—even after his chat with the Team Leader, his agitation built up to the point where stress overcame external attempts at restraint. Before any of the Techs from either crew could react, the runner was out of his seat, through the exit, and starting down the adjacent stairway, blowing by the guard posted outside the doorway. The startled Agent drew his weapon as he moved to the stairwell in pursuit.

Moments later, a shot, ending the chase.

The remaining group of Technical Operatives looked at each other, stunned.

This could really boil over into something dangerous, between the local and regional SCF forces, Joshua thought, trying to keep his cool.

****

Before long, they were back on an intersecting freeway heading east. They crossed over a bridge, transited the north end of Staten Island, and crossed over a second bridge entering into the City of Brooklyn, Federated State of New York. Even at midday traffic was horrendous, and none of them ever encountered a city of such magnitude. Equipped with a detailed map and explicit instructions, they eventually made their way to the rendezvous point in the heart of Brooklyn, circling several blocks until someone pulled out so Tag could park. With the vehicle turned off, they stayed in their seats quietly soaking in the environment.

Rose thought back to their departure that morning— Brent was cheerful and optimistic when explaining the steps they needed to take that day. He seemed sympathetic and understanding of the prices they paid with lives uprooted to get to this point—the culmination of their journey. *All of this for something we didn't do—we did nothing wrong!* Nonetheless, they arrived safely and, for the most part,

Rose was upbeat.

Brent's second-to-last comment to them was a warning that their network learned the SCF was setting up a substantial screen of Agent Teams in Washington and New York City—an attempt to capture them as they entered either metropolitan area. Fortunately, he directed his final comment to how they would defeat the SCF plan—starting with the stop for the surgical removal of their identifier implants.

Their countermove worked.

****

She watched them play a board game on the wide veranda floor without the usual debate as to whose turn it was, or how to play correctly. *They seem subdued,* she observed. *Maybe they're tired from playing outside.* Certainly their sidekick, Chico, was done in as he lay curled up beside them.

It was clear Erin Talbot missed her Mom—her dad, too. She recognized the likelihood of seeing her parents again was dismal, yet she hoped for the best. But, she knew . . . maybe they would meet up with Rose someday, and doing so would take some of the sting out of missing her parents.

Sean Talbot considered their current situation to be tolerable. He looked at his sister sitting in the chair watching them, lost in thought. She seemed to live to ride his butt about everything, but the truth was he couldn't imagine being there without her. Being so close in age, they had a strong bond, and she helped make up for the raw nerve of their parents' absence. He wasn't entirely sure of what was going on, but he knew it wasn't good. He was old enough to realize they could've ended up in a much worse situation.

As for Darius? He loved being at Seth's. He enjoyed the countryside with Sean and Chico as playmates, and he got to spend more time outside exploring. He was certain he'd see his parents and Rose later . . . but, in the meantime, there was stuff to do.

To Darius, Seth was a bear—large, and appearing to be surly, but he didn't fool Darius for a minute. As often is the case, younger children see clearly to the core of a person for who and what they truly are—Darius knew the Bear was warm-hearted, gentle, and caring.

Sometimes, Wesley joined them, creating more neat stuff to do, but Darius thought Monique—with her tall, regal bearing—should be some sort of queen. Yet, when she held him, which was often enough, it was just like his Mom was there.

Seth stepped onto the veranda and, in a booming, deep voice, announced, "Everyone inside—we have food to eat!"

Darius walked over to the Bear, placing his small hand in his large paw. "Can I sit next to you this time?"

"Well, as long as you don't crowd me . . ."

CHAPTER THIRTY-THREE

"Fill me in . . ." The New York City Action Team Commander waited for her two Deputy Commanders to decide who would report first. "Come on—get to it before the bad guys blow past us!"

"Right—since this morning, we positioned Agent Teams on our side of every bridge, tunnel, and ferry terminal leading into Long Island, Manhattan, and Staten Island. To the north, we have Teams on every major thoroughfare entering metro New York City, and we equipped everyone with personal identifier reading devices, and the range is up to one mile."

The Commander nodded acknowledgment. "What happens if these devices don't pick up the Targets?"

"Well, Commander, we uploaded pictures of the three Targets into our system. The two females were already in our database, the male Target unknown—however, we captured him on a security video in Durango City, and his image is now in the system. We had our Techies configure facial recognition software to automatically issue an alert in the system if any of our security video cams capture their images."

"Okay—what's your backup if they ping in the system?"

"We have ten, two Agent Teams, strategically placed and standing by to react to any alert of a sighting. We will also call on regular SCF forces to deploy upon command—theoretically, Agents should be at a location within fifteen minutes of the Targets' being spotted."

She looked at each of her Deputies. "I don't give a damn about theoretical—make the response time ten minutes. Tops!"

"Yes, Commander."

What in the hell did the Targets do to warrant so much attention? she wondered as she heard her Deputies walk down the hall.

****

Disappointed by the news, Kyle was with Jackie at her place when the police called him on his cell. Even though it would have disproven his theories about how Tag disappeared, their sweep of the backcountry area yielded nothing—same for the state and nationwide missing person searches. He patched the call through the speaker so Jackie could listen and, after hanging up, Kyle stood lost in thought. Jackie had to take the phone from his hand to thank the officer before terminating the call.

She knew how badly he was hurting, but all she could

do was be there for him. She took him in her arms, the close personal contact coaxing him back to the present. Soon, his mouth found hers in a lingering kiss which seemed to relieve much of his pent up tension.

"Thanks for that . . ." he whispered.

"It's the least I could do—there's more where that came from."

"Is there now? Perhaps I should test that theory . . ."

****

They sat in their vehicle for almost half an hour, waiting for the appointed two o'clock meeting time. The area of Brooklyn was a welter of four and five-story walk-ups, small businesses, restaurants, and cafés. Sprinkled in the mix were a few small warehouses—their target location.

"It's time," Claire announced. She tried to recall everything she could about her Uncle Nelson. Claire met him once when she was nine years old when he visited Monique, his half-sister. She remembered him as a large man, confident, and easy going. Although he spent the majority of his visit with Claire's parents, he carved out valuable niches of time to spend solely with her. They did the expected visit to the park, going for ice cream, and other kid stuff—but, what she remembered well was the time he spent talking to her, learning what she was thinking and doing.

He listened to her.

She wondered if her girlhood memories would track

with the real man she was about to meet again, wondering if she changed as much as he. *Well, I'm about to find out,* she thought as she opened the car door.

The trio approached the front of the small, one-story warehouse building with a large overhead door capable of allowing passage for a good-sized truck and, to the side, was an entrance. Inside, the space was partially filled with a variety of stored items and, at the rear, a small office. No one was in sight.

Tag called out, his voice echoing off the back wall. They heard someone stirring in the office, and a few moments later, a casually dressed, gray-haired man stepped out and walked toward them. He stopped several feet away, surveying the trio.

"Good for you, getting here in one piece!" Nelson stepped forward and enveloped Claire in a tight embrace. After a few moments, he looked down at his much shorter niece and announced to the top of her head, "You can't imagine how much I've been looking forward to this moment . . ." Claire tightened her grip on him, as emotion rushed through her. He looked at Tag and Rose, nodding a silent greeting to them.

Rose's hand sought and found Tag's as she teared up for her best friend.

****

Physically, she was comfortable—emotionally, not so much. The news from New York City was good—Claire and her friends made it, contacting Nelson at the appointed time, and Monique was confident her half-brother would do all he could for them. The plan was to alter their looks and identities to keep them off grid, and avoid unwanted attention from the authorities. Doing so was good and bad—it would offer the best form of protection for them, but their going underground in a network safe house meant Monique likely wouldn't see her daughter for quite some time. And, word reached them from Durango City that the local SCF Headquarters was under investigation by the Regional Authority—that meant Joshua was at greater risk of exposure for his efforts on their behalf. From her chair on the veranda, Monique watched the youngest Talbots running rampant in the yard with their now inseparable buddy, Chico. Erin sat quietly on a swing attached to a substantial limb of the largest tree in Seth's yard.

After dinner the previous evening when the kids were in bed, the adults' conversation centered around the options for the well-being of the children. Obviously, if the SCF freed Lori and Nathan, the Talbots would have to be reunited in a manner not to expose Monique and Wesley to the authorities. Until then, it was a no brainer that they would keep the children in the event their parents were detained for a while. The real issue—one they hesitated to discuss—was what would happen if Lori and Nathan didn't come back. Ever. As far as Monique and her husband were concerned, their keeping the kids with them was their first choice. However, it wasn't about them—it was about what was best for the children. Perhaps they should live with their nearest relative . . . the problem with that was the authorities would track those relationships. If the SCF were on the lookout for the kids, the obvious place to start looking would be extended family. Since they weren't part of the network passively resisting the authorities, their relatives wouldn't be equipped to effectively shield the whereabouts of the children. But, maybe, they wouldn't want the problem—Monique hated that thought.

In any event, Monique was determined the SCF troglodytes wouldn't get their hands on the younger Talbots. Still, she worried. She already privately confessed the profound attachment she formed in her short time with them, and she knew innately the kids weren't going anywhere other than back to their parents if that situation played out. Her husband agreed—but, if not with them, then where? Despite his dramatic grunts and grumblings, Seth made it known all of them were welcome to stay for as long as they wanted, or, needed. Monique was aware of his strong attachment to Darius, and if Chico had a vote—well, he and the kids would be friends forever!

****

Nelson filled them in on the evening's plans—a team member would drop by to direct them to an address in Manhattan where they would begin their identity transition. In the meantime, they could relax in the Brooklyn safe house until dark.

****

"Then, there is an ongoing situation developing in the eastern part of the country—actually, it started in Durango City."

"Explain."

The bright and well-organized Subordinate recounted the litany of events from west to east, summing up with the last confirmed sighting.

"You're telling me three teenagers can move across the country— virtually undetected and avoiding preset traps— and we come up with nothing?"

"Apparently so."

The SCF National Division Commander got up and stood in front of the window—moving always helped when considering a problem. "Obviously, these three aren't the worst fugitives on the current list of targets," he commented. He paced, lost in thought, oblivious to the Subordinate Officer. The current list of national fugitives wasn't long—it never was. He was in tune with the standing directives which were meant to be repressive, instilling an underlying fear in the general populace. Individuals deemed 'criminals' were dealt with immediately—harshly. The process never drew out, and individual rights didn't exist. If the average citizen kept his head down, he was alright. Behind-the-scenes controlled everything, and little happened in an overt fashion unless there were a need to remove the Target from the equation. Society was safeguarded, their population on a leash.

The three Targets presented an intriguing situation— three teenagers moving about the country with apparent ease. Unacceptable. The only thing they had was a confirmed blip in the system, indicating their moving through Pittsburgh, tagged by their personal identifiers. Plus, an SCF Scout injured in a confrontation on the street—now out of the hospital—described a young male matching the description of one of the Targets. Apparently, the event occurred so fast the Agent didn't have the chance to get more than a cursory look at the individual. He did know, however, the unknown young man was accompanied by two young females.

They could be the Targets.

They took appropriate measures to alert and heighten security status in the projected pathway of the Targets for the cities of Philadelphia, Washington, and New York City. Unless the quarry diverted or went underground, they should surface in one of the centers.

"So far, nothing." The National Commander stopped pacing, and acknowledged his Subordinate standing to the side, waiting. "Okay—this is what we're going to do to finally nail these Targets . . ."

The Subordinate flipped open his tiny, spiral pad to take notes.

****

Local Technicians from the two Durango shifts were aware of a sudden increase in activity among the SCF Regional Teams' probing through their workstations and computer network. From what they could see through the glass partition separating the break and works areas, several Regional Supervisors were summoned to examine their findings. Sentinel Agents from the Regional Team were called in as well, receiving orders from a Supervisor who pointed toward the locals.

After forty hours of detention, Joshua realized the worst was about to happen—they discovered his work. He wasn't surprised, yet he subconsciously rubbed the faint scar on the web area of his left hand between his thumb and forefinger. The finality of that reflex motion dawned on him—years ago, when he had the capsule implanted, he understood its meaning intellectually. Emotionally, he was detached, never imagining the day would come when he would need to use it. But, then, as the Sentinel Agents moved toward the confined local Technicians, weapons drawn, Joshua realized he would, indeed, need it. At least, it would save him from the unpleasantness of an Eliminator Agent prying secrets from him. More important, they wouldn't force him to disclose vital information concerning the network's operations. There was no option—he had to protect those who chose to resist.

The moment arrived. They entered the room as a feeling of serenity settled over him. He positioned his right thumb nail directly over the scar on the back of the webbed area of his left hand, readying himself to push hard in order to break the capsule embedded beneath, releasing its deadly toxin. The muscles in his right arm tensed, waiting for the signal from his brain to push hard.

But, that input never happened.

Stunned, he watched as the Sentinels focused on Hansen, his number two, demanding he stand up and go with them. Hansen glanced at Joshua and, with a tight smile bordering on a grimace, gave him an almost imperceptible nod. As Hansen stood up, still looking at Joshua, he shrugged his shoulders slightly and began rubbing his right thumb over the small scar on the back of the webbed portion between his thumb and forefinger of his left hand. The movement was subtle, only noticed by those who knew. Within moments, Hansen left with the Sentinels.

As the other local Team Members broke into several animated, concurrent conversations Joshua sat quietly— he was drained. He worked beside Hansen for years, but he never knew Hansen as anything other than a work teammate, and it was enough to make him wonder about the others.

CHAPTER THIRTY-FOUR

She's developed into a fine young woman—better than I'd hoped, he concluded as he sat back in what he considered his 'thinking chair.' When they met that afternoon, Nelson advised them their new reality was going to be permanent hiding—completely off grid, living out their days in anonymity. They learned of the support network that would assist them by creating new identities as well as placing them in suitable housing. Possibly, in the future and, once they settled in, opportunities may exist to work within the network, opposing the authoritarian regime—if they wished.

Then it was a good news, bad news scenario. He had to explain to Rose her parents were still vigorously detained and interrogated. Nelson considered withholding that information, but, once he met Rose, he understood she needed to know the truth. He also knew she could handle it.

Much better news for Rose and Claire was his updating them on the current status of Monique and Wesley, as well as the Talbot children. Apparently, everything was going well—what he didn't talk about with them was where he would place them. For security purposes, the best scenario was to keep them apart in separate areas of the city without revealing their new identities one to the other. Then, if one of them were apprehended by the authorities, they couldn't disclose anything they didn't know when under duress.

Nelson realized the implications—it would be a tough situation since they bonded closely throughout their ordeal. Add the fact that Rose and Claire grew up together as great friends—he imagined their resistance would be profound. Nonetheless, they needed to do what must be done. The first order of business was to get them into contact with his Manhattan source.

Then, they could break them apart.

****

The last of the SCF Regional Force was just pulling out on its way back to Denver, confident they purged the infection at the Durango City Headquarters. The Regional Force and the Local Detachment hierarchy debriefed the remaining technical team, and things returned to normal at the Headquarters building. Joshua was ready to go home, eat a decent meal, and get some sleep. Only one thing left to do . . .

He went down to the lower floor area, ostensibly on official business, to covertly check on the status of Lori and Nathan Talbot. Feigning the requirement of learning details for a fictitious report, he asked the Administrative Assistant at the desk for information.

"The detainee, Nathan Talbot moved from Interrogation to the Eliminator Division for processing." The admin gal didn't bat an eye when delivering the news.

"What about his wife?" Joshua tried to ignore the cold feeling in the pit of his stomach.

"I'm not sure of her status."

He muttered an offhanded thanks, turned to leave, then stopped. He knew from her picture in the files who was being led down the corridor toward him—obviously, Lori Talbot was put through the wringer during her interrogation. Her usually lovely, well-kept red hair was matted with several apparent bare spots—clearly, she was tortured. An Eliminator Agent was on each side, supporting her as she attempted to walk down the corridor. As she passed, Lori looked at him carefully as though she should recognize who he was. He knew why—although they never met, it was his close family resemblance to his Auntie Monique that had Lori guessing. But, she couldn't make the connection and, sadly, he turned and left.

His report to Nelson in New York City would be difficult.

****

It was nearly ten o'clock, and the Travelers were getting restless. Cooped up in the small warehouse waiting for it to get dark enough to travel safely into Manhattan, all they needed were directions to meet their next contact. A mixture of curiosity and concern over their future touched each of them, yet conversation about it was surprisingly brief.

Claire was the first one to see her Uncle Nelson enter their area from a side door—her initial joy quickly dissipated as she saw the expression on his face.

Something was definitely wrong.

As he approached, Nelson looked at Claire and glanced at Tag, but he avoided making eye contact with Rose.

It was then she knew.

Claire turned to her best friend, noticing her quizzical expression—as if she were trying to figure out something. Then, it abruptly transformed into a look of dread as it clicked Nelson had news for her—bad news. Dreadful news.

He stopped in front of Rose. "I have news about your parents—it's not good." Claire moved beside her friend and took her hand. Tag, on the other side, placed his arm around her shoulders.

She stood, stunned. Waiting.

"I'm very sorry, but I just received news via the SCF Headquarters in Durango City that they finished interrogating your parents—they won't be released."

Rose didn't want to ask the obvious question, but she had no choice. "What will they do with them?"

Nelson wished he could provide a different answer. "They took them to the Eliminator Division—once that happens, nobody comes back . . ." He paused briefly, looking directly at her. "Do you understand what I'm telling you?"

Rose crumbled.

Both friends encircled her in a mutual embrace, trying their best to console her. Nelson stood back, allowing them time to deal with the tragedy. Eventually, they came over to him with Rose between them—it was obvious she drew energy and strength from her friends.

He looked at all three. "I have much better news." No reaction. "I heard from Monique and Wesley, and they're still at Seth's, and they know about Lori and Nathan. Rose, if it's all right with you, Monique says they will be pleased to look after your siblings as if they are their own. Obviously, Monique formed a strong attachment to them."

Rose nodded her acknowledgment of the plan.

"We're not sure where they will ultimately end up—but, for now, they're comfortable and safe at Seth's." A brief smile. "Perhaps, when things die down, you can reunite at least for a while. But, for now, the three of you are actively targeted, and the last thing we want to do is draw attention to their whereabouts through the SCF's tracking you." He paused for a few moments. "Does that make sense?"

Rose studied him before replying. "Yes, it makes perfect sense—it's just hard to take."

"You know Mom like your own," Claire suggested. "I can't think of a better person to step in and help Erin, Sean, and Darius right now."

Rose hugged Claire tightly, whispering in her ear, "I know—they'll be all right."

Within half an hour, they were in their vehicle on their way to Manhattan equipped with directions and information regarding their next contact. They discussed the apparent end of their travels, as well as the pros and cons of the upcoming permanent solution—the identity change—and living off grid. As Nelson made his way home, he considered them three of the finest young people he ever met. Rose dealt with the news of her parents better than he expected—it was some of the most horrific news one could receive, and Claire and Tag were there for her all the way. They accepted, without question, his pronouncement that for security integrity he would not see them again for quite some time. He did, however, reassure them the network protecting them would filter back information concerning their welfare. He wanted to be current with their situation, so he could make any warranted and necessary adjustments. *Once settled*, he thought, *maybe they can actively participate in the network, fulfilling a useful role.* The truth was they could use it—the network was stable, but it needed to grow if they hoped to challenge the perverted, autocratic leadership. *It'll happen one day— maybe after I'm gone. But, we have to start somewhere . . .*

As he was about to enter his apartment building, he stopped to observe the street. *Maybe*, he thought, *with Tag and the girls as symbols—his network would create a buzz over their cause. If nothing else, they should give hope to others.*

And, as a bonus, enhance recruitment.

CHAPTER THIRTY-FIVE

"Honey, will you please call the kids in for dinner?" Monique asked as she placed the plates on the table. Wesley headed toward the kitchen door leading to the backyard.

He winked at Erin who was helping with the preparations. "Why is it I get all the tough missions?"

"Well, if it's something you can't handle, I'll back you up!" Seth grabbed his coffee mug and followed Wesley out the door.

Monique glanced at Erin, who was helping with dinner preparations and they exchanged a smile. She marveled at how well Seth and Wesley bonded with the young Talbot boys and Wesley, in particular, was extremely fond of them. *Maybe because he didn't have boys of his own*, she thought as they put dinner on the table. After Claire was born, Monique suffered a complication which prevented her from having more children, and she sometimes wondered how their lives would have played out if they had more than one child.

Seth—a definite confirmed bachelor—formed a
strong attachment to Darius, referring to his diminutive
companion as 'The Tank.' Earlier, she, Wesley, and Seth
discussed whether to advise the Talbot children of the
dire news regarding their parents, finally agreeing with
Seth's recommendation to wait for a final conclusion—
or, disposition, depending. In the meantime, the younger
Talbots appeared to be comfortable and adapting to their
present situation.

****

They transitioned from Brooklyn into Manhattan
without any difficulties and, according to their instructions,
Tag parked their vehicle on the street when a spot opened
up. Coming from a small urban area, they were surprised
at the number of people still out and about on the streets
so late in the evening.

"We'll need to keep our guard up," Claire suggested.
"Too many people . . ."

"If the directions are correct, we're only several blocks
away from our meeting point. Don't make eye contact with
anyone . . ." Tag, too, was concerned, but he was confident
they could reach their target destination without incident.

****

Each Technician on shift was responsible for ten
security monitors—a task that quickly turned to boredom.
Distracted, they often chatted among themselves when

their Supervisors weren't present—precisely what they were doing when the second to last monitor on the bottom row sounded an alarm. One of the Techs wheeled over to the station and tapped in a few prompts which staged a replay of the street video—three young people moving through a relatively crowded street.

The facial recognition software outlined the individual on the right—a sad looking young woman, tall, with long hair. She turned her head toward the security camera, when she was apparently responding to one of her companions. The Tech entered another command, receiving a display of her picture ID as well as a concise report of her background as a Target of national interest. He noted the apparent failure of her implanted identifier to light up the system, prompting him to place a call to his Supervisor who appeared almost immediately.

Once he reviewed the Target information, the Supervisor activated his COM-link to call the Coordinator of the Action Teams based in lower Manhattan. He updated the order to concentrate all SCF Teams within range of the sighting. That done, the Supervisor again reviewed footage from the street security camera, noting the sad expression on the young woman's face. *I wonder who peed in her cornflakes this morning?* he thought as he watched the trio make their way down the busy street.

****

It felt good to clean up, down a decent meal, and get some rest. But after only a few hours, Joshua reported back for his regular shift. By that time, the last of the Regional SCF Team left their Headquarters, and things were getting back to normal.

While digging through the backlog of work delayed because of the investigation, his preset computer alarm sounded, warning of information pertinent to his secret network activities. With a keyboard stroke, he viewed a real-time report of the Target spotted in lower Manhattan, including video footage. Joshua immediately prepared a secure cryptic message to his contact in New York City. Within minutes, Nelson received the warning, but he could do nothing. The situation would resolve in one of two ways—either the SCF would apprehend them, or they would make the set rendezvous successfully.

****

By his reckoning, they were getting close to the rendezvous point in lower Manhattan. The crowds thinned, and the Travelers didn't feel like fish swimming upstream as they headed toward their target location, Tag began to recognize a few landmarks which were similar to pictures he saw of New York City in his reality. To the south, a good-sized park, complete with playgrounds, statues, fountains, and a small reflecting pool. Everything well-lit, it was easy to see at that time of night—but, there was something about the location nagging him. As they approached the area, more landmarks became familiar and he felt as if he should know it. It wasn't until they entered the park, that it struck him.

"In my world, this exact spot once held twin office towers called the World Trade Center—they were one of the most prominent features in New York City." He turned slowly, looking at the park.

"What do you mean 'were' prominent?" Claire asked.

"Since September 11, 2001, they don't exist anymore."

"Why not?"

"Terrorist attacks—a bunch of fanatics commandeered several large airplanes, and flew two of them into the towers. They collapsed, and thousands were killed or injured."

Both girls stared at him in disbelief. "That's terrible! We haven't had that level of violence here in almost one hundred years!"

"Yeah, well—we get that sort of crap in all sorts of places in my world."

"We never had anything like the World Trade Center here, as far as, I know—it's always been some sort of park," Rose confirmed. "And, I don't hear of terrorists—we're too controlled to allow anything like that. Yes, we get the occasional individual crime cropping up every once in a while, but they deal with it immediately. That seems to dissuade most temptations to deviate from approved behavior."

"Perhaps we could use a little of that where I come from," Tag pointed out, checking his watch. He scanned the area for any sign of his contact, but nothing yet. "We're early . . ." He was beginning to feel distinctly uncomfortable, wishing they were closer to their vehicle for an easy escape if things went south. But, Nelson stressed they must comply with their instructions—park the car, and leave it.

They wouldn't need it anymore.

In the evening light, Tag picked out an individual

walking under a streetlight by the reflecting pool who fit the description of their contact—she was carrying the requisite white backpack over her left shoulder. As he turned to the girls to let them know their contact was in sight, he observed several dark vehicles pulling to an abrupt stop on the adjacent streets. He glanced at their contact—she saw the same thing, and waved him off as she diverted in another direction away from them. The impact of the situation struck him as SCF Agents exited their vehicles, fanning out into the park.

"We're in danger! We have to get out of here now—stay close and follow me!" he ordered. A quick survey of the deploying Agents determined the pathway they needed to take. Tag turned, not looking back to see if the girls followed.

By now, they knew when to move it.

****

They traversed north. The park wasn't as crowded, and Tag quietly advised the girls to ignore any impulse to look behind them. It was a delicate balance—moving out of the area as fast as possible without drawing specific attention to themselves as obviously fleeing suspects.

They almost reached the northern edge of the park when, in an area of shadow, Tag chanced a glance behind them. The SCF Teams were sweeping the southern and central areas of the park, and additional SCF vehicles were pulling into the streets bordering the park to the left and right of them. Unoccupied space was at a premium, and the only opening was northeast of their position—no options.

The Targets jogged in line across the street to the walkway on the far side. Unfortunately, the activity of pedestrians crossing in mid-street drew immediate attention from one of the Sweeper Team Members still in the park. His COM-link call diverted several Action Teams to an intercept course.

Across the road, the Travelers proceeded eastward, heads down to avoid capture of their images by the remote surveillance cameras strategically positioned along the street. Without glancing behind him, he could feel it—they were closing in. Suddenly, ahead of them, an SCF vehicle pulled sideways on the roadway, and stopped—four Agents spilled out, moving in their direction. Tag scanned to the rear—more Agents exiting the northern fringes of the park onto the roadway behind them.

"They're close, stay right with me!" he urged the girls. He stepped into an alleyway on his left. Once the girls followed and all of them were out of the line of sight of their pursuers, he ordered, "Run as fast as you can, and follow my lead!"

And, run they did—flat out.

It was a long alley, and as they reached the halfway point, a Team of Agents appeared ahead of them. The Travelers stopped, and Tag looked behind them—another Team appeared at the entrance of the alleyway.

They were trapped.

There were no street or security lights illuminating the alley—only ambient light from some of the buildings betrayed the deep shadows.

"What do we do?" Claire gasped, trying to get her breath.

He again looked ahead and behind them, not entirely sure there was anything they could do.

"Is that an opening, to our right?" Rose pointed to what she thought might be a way out. Sure enough! In the recessed shadows, Tag saw what looked like an opening to another alley perpendicular to theirs—a T intersection.

"Quick—come on!" Tag led as the girls followed, entering the new alleyway after a five-yard sprint to its opening. As they moved into its darkened heart, they were limited to running at three-quarter speed down the middle. The SCF Action Team following them made it to the T intersection first, the tail-end Member of that Team on his COM-link.

"We have them—they just entered a blind alley."

CHAPTER THIRTY-SIX

A t the same time, they realized the alley was a dead end. The rear façades of buildings faced them on three sides, ranging in height from five to twelve stories, none of which contained ladders extending to ground level—only a few heavy steel doors allowed access. As if by command, the three Travelers sprinted to a different entrance, seeking a way out.

Each door, locked.

They huddled together near the end of the alleyway, their eyesight adjusting to the dim light, allowing them to faintly recognize each other's features. Their faces reflected what each was feeling—desperation. But, Tag also observed a combination of determination and defiance in Rose and Claire—enough to buoy his spirits, and give him strength.

"No matter what happens, we're in this together. Both of you have been there for me since the beginning—now, it's my time to return the favor."

He let go of them, turned towards the open end of the

alley, walking back to its entrance.

"Tag, what, the hell are you doing!" Rose protested.

"Ending this . . ."

As he looked back at the faint outline of Rose and Claire standing close together, behind them he noticed the beginning of a light source quickly growing in strength—within seconds, the end of the alleyway and the rear of the adjacent buildings were illuminated. Tag couldn't see the actual source of the light as it emanated from behind a dumpster located near the end of the alleyway, but it was familiar—the condition of the air changed as charged particles emanated from it.

By then, the girls turned to look at what was unfolding behind them. He moved cautiously back to Rose and Claire—they exhibited no fear. Only curiosity.

At the open end of the alley, they heard the voices of their pursuers as the SCF Team spotted them outlined by the illuminating light source.

"Come on," Tag ordered. As he approached the dumpster, they followed. Tag slowly walked around to the rear, revealing the source of the glow. There, approximately eight feet away from the back wall of the adjacent building, a pulsing, illuminated archway hovered a few inches above the pavement. Each Traveler was compelled to look into the shifting light.

"This, is what brought me here!" Tag stood, riveted at the sight of the portal.

CHAPTER THIRTY-SEVEN

The initial SCF Action Team consisting of four Sentinel Agents rounded the corner, proceeding a mere five yards into the blind alley when the far end suddenly lit up. From their vantage point, a diffusing, pulsing light reflected off buildings on all three sides. The actual source of the light was blocked from their view by a large object. The Team Leader stopped, holding his arms out to either side of him, indicating to the rest of his Team to halt their forward progress. He carefully studied the situation—there appeared to be shadows of something—or, someone—moving, but he couldn't hear voices. Unclear as to what they faced, the Team Leader called his immediate Superior on the COM-link, explaining the situation and seeking instructions.

"We'll hold here, until the Section Commander arrives to take over," he ordered his Subordinates. He strained to see what was going on at the other end. "Besides, the Targets can't go anywhere."

At that moment, each Traveler faced a choice—stay,

and likely be captured, or try to enter the archway and get away. But, get away to what?

Rose was torn—if she were truthful with herself, she knew her parents were likely gone forever. Her siblings were safe and well-cared for, and she trusted Monique and Wesley just like her own parents. But, she still wanted to see and hold her sister and brothers. To leave felt like abandoning them—staying would likely lead to capture, resulting in her probably not seeing them anyway. To her, it seemed as if she had less to lose by entering the portal— at least for now. *Maybe there's a way back, later—after all, Tag got here!*

But, she knew he'd leave for sure. Could she stand being left behind?

Initially, he considered it a no-brainer. Staying in Rose's world meant capture—if they ever got their hands on him, he was toast. Not only that, the objective was to get home to his world, and what he knew. At least no one was chasing him there . . . however, if Rose stayed—Claire, too—could he simply disappear into the archway and leave them to be captured? He also had to fess up to himself that he had a deep emotional commitment to both of them, especially with Rose.

Maybe, he considered, *I should follow whatever she decides . . .*

Claire wanted nothing other than to stay there and link up with her parents—but, her world's authorities didn't want it that way. *They'll want to capture us, and dispose of us like Rose's parents*, she thought as she struggled with her decision. She was close to Rose—a sister, really. *If she leaves, can I stand it?* she wondered. Although it was a relatively short period of time, she bonded to Tag as she would a big brother. Her biggest question, though, was if she stayed, could she get out of their situation—she wasn't sure.

****

As he sat at his desk creating a solution, his colleague's question startled Joshua.

"Sorry, I didn't get that . . ."

"I asked what you thought about their arrest of Hanson."

"It certainly took me by surprise." Not a lie—it did take him by surprise in ways his co-worker would never know. "You'll have to excuse me with all this Regional bull going on—I have a bunch of reports to finish."

"Yeah, sure. I'll catch you later." Joshua's colleague retreated to his own desk, ready to dive into his own pile of work.

The interruption allowed Joshua's subconscious to finish his thought process—it was a long shot, but he may have stumbled upon a way to actually help get them out of their drastic situation. Again, it would be a substantial risk to him, but, Lori and Nathan Talbot deserved any chance he could give them.

CHAPTER THIRTY-EIGHT

Tag and Claire looked at each other, recognizing the dilemma the other faced. They had to do something, but their decisions had to be a conscious choice—to stay, or, go. Both risky. Their attention shifted to Rose, who seemed paralyzed—no surprise considering the horrible news about her parents, as well as the separation from her siblings.

At the open end of the alleyway, the Section Commander arrived, accompanied by two more Action Teams. He quickly surveyed the situation, and turned to the Team Leader of the original group that sealed off the only exit.

"If I understand the circumstances correctly, we have three teenagers—apparently unarmed—fleeing, and now they're trapped in a blind alleyway. And, you were afraid to move in on them because you saw a light? Is that correct?" The Commander laced his question with purposeful incredulity. "What's your name, Officer?"

"Grimes, Sir."

"Okay, Grimes, fill me in . . ."

"Sir, we don't know if they're unarmed. Look! That's one weird light source down there, and who knows what's going on? Check it out—it's pulsing! And, that's not all— the air has an odd feel to it." Grimes glanced at his Superior, unsure if he were babbling. He was. The disgusted look on the Commander's face confirmed his suspicion.

"I don't have time for this bullshit." The Commander turned his back to the young officer, motioning his agents to gather 'round. "Move toward the light, and form two offset lines extending the width of the alley. Anything larger than a mouse doesn't get through. Flashlights, on. Let's move!"

As the trained teams stretched the breadth of the alleyway, inching forward, a raised voice echoed toward the three young people huddled at the end. Chaotic footsteps. Then, a booming command.

"Move! I'll hold down the fort—I'm right behind you! Move! Now!"

There wasn't time to debate the issue. Rose grabbed her best friend in a fierce hug, fearing the worst, while Tag placed his arm on her shoulder, his other hand to the side of her face. No words. Simply a smile, and a nod of acknowledgment. Without looking back, their bodies fueled the pulsating archway as they vanished into its core, creating a surge of brilliant white light.

Good! Claire glanced around the corner of the overstuffed dumpster shielding her from the approaching agents, their flashlights sweeping the area as they speculated on what they just witnessed.

It was time.

She retreated to her position directly in front of the archway feeling the immense void of the light's source drawing her toward its opening, filling her with an almost physical compulsion to step inside.

The voices! Closer now!

With little time to think, her mind formed a picture of her mother looking back at her, smiling.

"Oh, what the hell!"

CHAPTER THIRTY-NINE

Incredible speed. Intense light. Powerful energy. But there was one primary, overriding thought. *Don't let go!* Although she couldn't see or hear him, Tag clutched her hand and it was enough. Questions regarding their destination and the future didn't mean squat at the moment—her dominant force was being with him.

The portal travel was familiar to Tag, yet slightly altered. Had things changed, or, were they simply his perceptions of them? Rose was with him—he felt her beside him, the tight grip of her hand. Perhaps her presence with him—a new variable—modified the experience. One thing was certain—he managed the onslaught of sensations better this time. It wasn't so overwhelming, and his perceptions of the event were more acute. It was like having more time to study a complicated work of art, rather than seeing only a brief glimpse before it was gone.

The light surrounding them was intense, but not blinding, thereby allowing the viewer to see. Encased in an elongated tube, thickened in the middle where they were situated, was what he could only describe as pure energy. Moving at an unfathomable speed along a filament which extended ahead of them, there was no end in sight. The experience was exhilarating without the underlying fear he felt before.

It was fascinating.

****

"What the hell?" The Section Commander immediately stopped, as did every other Agent surrounding him. Twenty-five yards from the end of the alley with a dumpster between them and the source of the illumination behind it, suddenly the light source flared with two brighter pulses reflecting off of the surrounding buildings. The air additionally charged as each pulse occurred. After a thirty-second lull, another flaring pulse illuminated the end of the alleyway, stretching to the tops of the buildings. Despite its source being positioned behind the dumpster, the flare was so bright it forced the Agents to close their eyes and look away until it dissipated. Then, a popping sound, and the light snapped off as though someone threw a switch.

A strange sensation lingered in the air.

The Section Commander ordered a Team forward, weapons drawn, to advance toward the dumpster, flanking it from each side. When in position, the Team Leader ordered the strike, all four members sweeping around to the darkened rear of the dumpster. As Team Members stood in a combat stance, weapons trained, flashlights illuminating the area, their body hairs arose—moments before, three individual Targets and an inexplicable light source existed.

Now? Nothing!

****

Tag helped Rose to a sitting position. Undergoing the aftermath affects of dizziness, disorientation and nausea, it took her a little longer to gain control of her mind and limbs. As he leaned over to help her, he noticed the aperture was still there, behind them, light pulsing in the same rhythmic fashion. *Odd*, he thought, as he focused his attention on Rose. Suddenly, behind him, the aperture flared brightly, the air particles perceptibly charged, an object hurtling through the opening, landing on the ground beside them. For a few moments, the object lay still—then it slowly rolled over.

"Son of a bitch, I made it!"

Claire!

Rose managed a sitting position, and as soon as she heard the object speak, she broke into a broad grin. Rose stood, and slowly made her way to her friend. The aperture made a final flare of intense light, then disappeared with a distinct popping sound—everything was as it should be.

Tag supported Claire's head in his hands as her over-stimulated senses began returning to normal. "That's one roller coaster ride I can do without for a while!"

"I'll second that notion!" Rose piped up.

"Actually, the second time's a breeze . . ."

Claire sat up, waiting for the dizziness to subside. Certain she was okay on her own for a minute, Tag got up and scanned the area. They were still in an alley behind tall buildings—the dumpster, however, was missing, and each end of the alley was open rather than one end's being closed. It was dark, yet there was more ambient light filtering into the alley, allowing him to survey his surroundings in greater detail. In the background, the noisy bustle of a big city at night.

No squads of SCF goons.

The alley was empty.

Finally, Claire was up and positioned between them— legs wobbly like an inebriated sailor. As they made their way to the alley opening, Tag noticed considerable debris strewn on the ground—they had to negotiate around several larger pieces, smaller trash they kicked away. As they rounded the corner onto the next alley, several pages of a newspaper gently tumbled along the ground prodded by a gentle breeze—Tag let go of Claire briefly to snatch one.

"Hey, it's good news! This is the New York City Times newspaper!" The girls exchanged excited glances. "Better yet, the day of the week and the date match exactly the time we just left!" In that moment, Tag realized he may be home in his own world—soon, he would get to see his brother. "Come on, let's go!" They negotiated their way down the last alley, and onto the adjacent street, Claire fully recovered and walking normally.

The evening was clear and warm. They passed several groups of people walking on both sides of the street, vehicles passing by. The Travelers were thrilled they escaped their pursuers, as well as survived the transit to their current location.

Tag enthusiastically described the benefits of his world to the girls, and how the highlight would be his reunion with his brother. "You'll love him . . ." he said as he looked around. Mid-sentence, he stopped abruptly and looked up, staring and speechless. Rose and Claire drew up beside him, concerned by his sudden, startled reaction.

"Tag, are you all right?" Claire asked.

"Oh, shit!" He stood, staring.

"What's wrong?" Rose didn't like the look on his face.

"It's the World Trade Center towers—they shouldn't be there!" He pointed, and the girls looked to follow his direction. Indeed, two tall, matching twin towers stood illuminated in the night.

"Wherever we are, it's not my world!"

CHAPTER FORTY

Even though it were the midsummer with daytime temperatures warm and comfortable, the evening cooled appreciably, due in part to elevation as well as the thunderstorm in progress. It was a perfect circumstance to be in front of the fireplace—there was something special about a wood burner.

He shut down his impressive computer set up, disconnecting it from the power source as a safety net against the storm. Yet, the secondary benefit was almost as important—he didn't have to fight the urge to go back to work, trying to unravel the colossal, two-part riddle— where did his brother end up, and, how did he get there? Right then, though, there was invaluable down time for him, offering a chance to relax and recharge his batteries.

Kyle sat on the floor, his torso leaning against an oversized leather chair. Jackie lay beside him, the back of her head gently nestled in his lap. Lego was sprawled on the floor on his back, all four paws splayed out in different directions. Wood sizzled as sap burned, occasionally shifting as their physical mass changed, flames doing their dance. He deeply appreciated the moment of tranquility, shared with the woman he now admitted to himself with whom he was very much in love.

Kyle reached for his glass of red wine, just about to take a sip when he suddenly stopped, wineglass perched at his lips. Although her eyes were closed, Jackie was awake, simply taking advantage of this serene time together with her man. She felt his body abruptly tense. "What is it?"

His wineglass still in hand, frozen in place and in the process of taking a drink, he didn't respond.

"Kyle, are you okay?"

He said nothing, and worry scratched its way to the forefront of her mind. Jackie placed her hands on either side of his face, her touch breaking the spell.

He lowered his glass, placing it on the floor.

"It's Tag," he stammered.

"What about him?"

"He was with others, in danger . . . but, somehow, they got away safely." He paused for a moment, then continued. "I have no idea how I know this—they're gone, however, from whatever place they were in before. But, to where?

When?"

EPILOGUE

THE FOUR CORNERS REGION, SOUTHWESTERN COLORADO, EARTH

Under the Julian calendar, the year was 1276 A.D.—although, the local indigenous population didn't know that, nor did they care. At the bottom of a gentle valley system beside a softly burbling stream, a hunting party of four made camp for the night. The day's hunt was successful, their testament hanging from a nearby tree. The hunt team sat around the fire, each taking a turn regaling their fellow hunters with tales of their expertise in the tracking and consummation of a clean kill. As they described the events, the campfire in front of them outlined their arms gesticulating for emphasis causing moving shadows in the background. In the distance a wolf howled, soon answered by another, the hunters pausing their storytelling to listen to their four-legged brothers.

During a lull in conversation, the leader of the hunting party looked over the shoulder of another, noticing a bright light suddenly blossom into being. It slowly grew to reach above the height of a man, oval in shape, hovering close to the ground. An opening began to pulsate light with varying colors which moved inside of it. The hunters rose, riveted, staring at the spectacle—for several minutes, no one moved.

The pulsing light maintained a steady rhythm as the air changed, creating a novel sensation on their skin—finally, the youngest hunter glanced at his older companions, then moved toward the apparition. He approached with cautious steps, ready to flee at the least hint of danger as the pulsating light continued to illuminate the area. Within arm's reach he stood before it, studying its shifting lights, reminding him of clouds swirling in a crosswind.

The leader called out, urging him to move away. No response. Despite calls from the other three hunters and without looking back, the youngest member stepped into the aperture, then disappeared.

The brilliant light blossomed for a few moments before they heard a popping noise, followed by a sensation of a slight overpressure in the air, ending with the light's extinguishing.

It left no trace of their young companion.

ACKNOWLEDGMENTS

Thank you to all of my test readers who gave their time, necessary feedback, and encouragement to carry on—glad you enjoyed the read.

A special thanks to Faith for kicking me in the butt to publish my books that are waiting in the wings, already written.

A huge thanks to Laurie O'Neil, Editor Extraordinaire, for her guidance, and for being my friend.

To Roxanne for holding the fort on my day job, allowing me the peace of mind to write.

To my family for the love, support, and warm atmosphere in which to live and write. It makes a difference.

Lastly, to my early morning canine buddies who keep me company while I write—Boomer, Oreo, and Milo.

Ready for the rest of the story?

On the Edge of Now: Book 1—The Departure

On the Edge of Now: Book 2—No Man's Land
                          Launching December 9, 2015

On the Edge of Now: Book 3—Redemption
                          Launching March 9, 2016

On the Edge of Now: Book 4—Fulcrum
                          Launching June 9, 2016

On the Edge of Now: Book 5—Jagged Edge
                          Launching September 9, 2016

On the Edge of Now: Book 6—Enlightenment
                          Launching December 9, 2016

On the Edge of Now: Book 7—Prequel
                          Launching March 9, 2017

Brian loves hearing from readers!

www.OnTheEdgeOfNow.com

facebook.com/BMcCulloughAuthor

twitter.com/THEBMcCullough

instagram.com/bmcculloughauthor/

PROFESSIONAL ACKNOWLEDGMENTS

CHRYSALIS PUBLISHING AUTHOR SERVICES
Editor—L.A. O'Neil
chrysalispub@gmail.com

JEN KRAMP STUDIOS
Cover Art
jenkramp@gmail.com

45197143R00212

Made in the USA
Charleston, SC
17 August 2015